## THE AUTHOR

**MORLEY CALLAGHAN** was born in Toronto, Ontario, in 1903. A graduate of the University of Toronto and Osgoode Law School, he was called to the bar in 1928, the same year that his first novel, *Strange Fugitive*, was published. Fiction commanded his attention, and he never practised law.

While in university, Callaghan took a summer position at the *Toronto Star* when Ernest Hemingway was a reporter there. In April 1929, he travelled with his wife to Paris, where their literary circle of friends included Hemingway, Fitzgerald, and Joyce. *That Summer in Paris* is his memoir of the time. The following autumn, Callaghan returned to Toronto.

Callaghan was among the first writers in Canada to earn his livelihood exclusively from writing. In a career that spanned more than six decades, he published sixteen novels and more than a hundred shorter works of fiction. Usually set in the modern city, his fiction captures the drama of ordinary lives as people struggle against a background of often hostile social forces.

Morley Callaghan died in Toronto, Ontario, in 1990.

# ANCIENT LINEAGE
# AND OTHER STORIES

# MORLEY CALLAGHAN

SELECTED AND WITH AN AFTERWORD BY
## WILLIAM KENNEDY

**Library and Archives Canada Cataloguing in Publication**

Callaghan, Morley, 1903-1990
Ancient lineage and other stories / Morley Callaghan.

(New Canadian library)
ISBN 978-0-7710-1818-3

I. Title. II. Series: New Canadian library

PS8505.A43A52 2012          C813'.52          C2012-905252-3

We acknowledge the financial support of the Government of Canada
through the Canada Book Fund and that of the Government of Ontario
through the Ontario Media Development Corporation's Ontario Book
Initiative. We further acknowledge the support of the Canada Council for
the Arts and the Ontario Arts Council for our publishing program.

Typeset in Adobe Garamond by M&S, Toronto
Printed and bound in the United States of America

This book was produced using paper with a minimum of 20% recycled
content (20% post-consumer waste).

McClelland & Stewart,
a division of Random House of Canada Limited
One Toronto Street
Toronto, Ontario
M5C 2V6
www.mcclelland.com/NCL

1 2 3 4 5      16 15 14 13 12

# CONTENTS

ANCIENT LINEAGE
AND OTHER STORIES

## A NOTE ON THE TEXT

The text for the stories in this collection is *Morley Callaghan: The Complete Stories* (Exile Editions, 2005). The original publication date of each story follows the text.

# A GIRL WITH AMBITION

After leaving school when she was sixteen, Mary Ross worked for two weeks with a cheap chorus line at the old La Plaza, quitting when her stepmother heard the girls were a lot of toughs. Mary was a neat, clean girl with short, fair curls and blue eyes, looking more than her age because she had very long legs, and knew it. She got another job as cashier in the shoe department of Eaton's, after a row with her father and a slap on the ear from her stepmother.

She was marking time in the store, of course, but it was good fun telling the girls about imaginary offers from big companies. The older salesgirls sniffed and said her hair was bleached. The salesmen liked fooling around her cage, telling jokes, but she refused to go out with them: she didn't believe in running around with fellows working in the same department. Mary paid her mother six dollars a week for board and always tried to keep fifty cents out. Mrs. Ross managed to get the fifty cents, insisting every time that Mary would come to a bad end.

Mary met Harry Brown when he was pushing a wagon on the second floor of the store, returning goods to the department. Every day he came over from the mail-order building, stopping longer than necessary in the shoe department, watching Mary in the cash cage out of the corner of his eye. Mary found out that he went to high school and worked in the store for the summer holidays. He hardly spoke to her, but once, when passing, he slipped a note written on wrapping paper under the cage wire. It was such a nice note that she wrote a long one the next morning and dropped it in his wagon when he passed. She liked him because he looked neat and had a serious face and wrote a fine letter with big words that were hard to read.

In the morning and early afternoons they exchanged wise glances that held a secret. She imagined herself talking earnestly, about getting on. It was good having someone to talk to like that because the neighbors on her street were always teasing her about going on the stage. If she went to the butcher to get a pound of round steak cut thin, he saucily asked how was the village queen and actorine. The lady next door, who had a loud voice and was on bad terms with Mrs. Ross, often called her a hussy, saying she should be spanked for staying out so late at night, waking decent people when she came in.

Mary liked to think that Harry Brown knew nothing of her home or street, for she looked up to him because he was going to be a lawyer. Harry admired her ambition but was shy. He thought she knew how to handle herself.

In the letters she said she was his sweetheart but never suggested they meet after work. Her manner implied it was unimportant that she was working at the store. Harry, impressed, liked to tell his friends about her, showing off the letters, wanting them to see that a girl who had a lot of experience was in love with him. "She's got some funny ways but I'll bet no one gets near her," he often said.

They were together the first time the night she asked him to meet her downtown at 10:30. He was waiting at the corner and didn't ask where she had been earlier in the evening. She was ten minutes late. Linking arms, they walked east along Queen Street. He was self-conscious. She was trying to be very practical, though pleased to have on her new blue suit with the short stylish coat.

Opposite the cathedral at the corner of Church Street, she said, "I don't want you to think I'm like the people you sometimes see me with, will you now?"

"I think you are way ahead of the girls you eat with at noon hour."

"And look, I know a lot of boys, but they don't mean nothing. See?"

"Of course, you don't need to fool around with tough guys, Mary. It won't get you anywhere," he said.

"I can't help knowing them, can I?"

"I guess not."

"But I want you to know that they haven't got anything on me," she said, squeezing his arm.

"Why do you bother with them?" he said, as if he knew the fellows she was talking about.

"I go to parties, Harry. You got to do that if you're going to get along. A girl needs a lot of experience."

They walked up Parliament Street and turned east, talking confidently as if many things had to be explained before they could be satisfied with each other. They came to a row of huge sewer pipes along the curb by the Don River bridge. The city was repairing the drainage. Red lights were about fifty feet apart on the pipes. Mary got up on a pipe and walked along, supporting herself with a hand on Harry's shoulder, while they talked in a silly way, laughing. A night

3

watchman came along and yelled at Mary, asking if she wanted to knock the lights over.

"Oh, have an apple," she yelled back at him.

"You better get down," said Harry, very dignified.

"Let him chase me," she said. "I'll bet he's got a wooden leg." But she jumped down and held onto his arm.

For a long time they stood on the bridge, looking beyond the row of short poplars lining the hill in the good district on the other side of the park. Mary asked Harry if he didn't live over there, wanting to know if they could see his house from the bridge. They watched the lights on a streetcar moving slowly up the hill. She felt that he was going to kiss her. He was looking down at the slow-moving water wondering if she would like it if he quoted some poetry.

"I think you are swell," he said finally.

"I'll let you walk home with me," she said.

They retraced their steps until a few blocks away from her home. They stood near the police station in the shadow of the fire hall. He coaxed so she let him walk just one more block. In the light from the corner butcher store they talked for a few minutes. He started to kiss her. "The butcher will see us," she said, but didn't care, for Harry was respectable-looking and she wanted to be kissed. Harry wondered why she wouldn't let him go to the door with her. She left him and walked ahead, turning to see if he was watching her. It was necessary she walk a hundred yards before Harry went away. She turned and walked home, one of a row of eight dirty frame houses jammed under one long caving roof.

She talked a while with her father, but was really liking the way Harry had kissed her, and talked to her, and the very respectable way he had treated her all evening. She hoped he wouldn't meet any boys who would say bad things about her.

She might have been happy if Harry had worked on in the store. It was the end of August and his summer holidays were over. The last time he pushed his wicker wagon over to her cash cage, she said he was to remember she would always be a sincere friend and would write often. They could have seen each other for he wasn't leaving the city, but they took it for granted they wouldn't.

Every week she wrote to him about offers and rehearsals that would have made a meeting awkward. She liked to think of him not because of being in love but because he seemed so respectable. Thinking of how he liked her made her feel a little better than the girls she knew.

When she quit work to spend a few weeks up at Georgian Bay with a girlfriend, Hilda Heustis, who managed to have a good time without working, she forgot about Harry. Hilda had a party in a cottage on the beach and they came home the night after. It was cold and it rained all night. One of Hilda's friends, a fat man with a limp, had chased her around the house and down to the beach, shouting and swearing, and into the bush, limping and groaning. She got back to the house all right. He was drunk. A man in pajamas from the cottage to the right came and thumped on the door, shouting that they were a pack of strumpets, hussies, and if they didn't clear out he would have to call the police. He was shivering and looked very wet. Hilda, a little scared, said they ought to clear out next day.

Mary returned to Toronto and her stepmother was waiting, very angry because Mary had quit her job. They had a big row. Mary left home, slamming the door. She went two blocks north to live with Hilda in a boarding house.

It was hard to get a job and the landlady was nasty. She tried to get work in a soldiers' company touring the province with a kind of musical comedy called *Mademoiselle from Courcelette*. But the manager, a nice young fellow with tired eyes, said she had the looks but he wanted a dancer. After that, every night Mary and Hilda practiced a step dance, waiting for the show to return.

Mary's father came over to the boarding house one night and coaxed her to come back home because she was really all he had in the world, and he didn't want her to turn out to be a good-for-nothing. He rubbed his face in her hair. She noticed for the first time he was getting old and was afraid he was going to cry. She promised to live at home if her step-mother would mind her own business.

Now and then she wrote to Harry, just to keep him thinking of her. His letters were sincere and free from slang. Often he wrote, "What is the use of trying to get on the stage?" She told herself he would be astonished if she were successful, and would look up to her. She would show him.

Winter came and she had many good times. The gang at the east-end roller rink knew her and she got in free. There she met Wilfred Barnes, the son of a grocer four blocks east of the fire hall, who had a good business. Wilfred had a nice manner but she never thought of him in the way she thought of Harry. He got fresh with little encouragement. Sunday afternoons she used to meet him at the rink in Riverdale Park. Several times she saw Harry and a boyfriend walking through the park, and leaving her crowd, she would talk to him for a few minutes. He was shy and she was a little ashamed of her crowd that whistled and yelled while she was talking. These chance meetings got to mean a good deal, helping her to think about Harry during the week.

In the early spring *Mademoiselle from Courcelette* returned to Toronto. Mary hurried to the man that had been nice to her and demonstrated the dance she had practiced all winter. He said she was a good kid and should do well, offering her a tryout at thirty dollars a week. Even her stepmother was pleased because it was a respectable company that a girl didn't need to be ashamed of. Mary celebrated by going to a party with Wilfred and playing strip poker until four a.m. She was getting to like being with Wilfred.

When it was clear she was going on the road with the company, she phoned Harry and asked him to meet her at the roller rink.

She was late. Harry was trying to roller skate with another fellow, fair-haired, long-legged, wearing large glasses. They had never roller skated before but were trying to appear unconcerned and dignified. They looked very funny because everyone else on the floor was free and easy, willing to start a fight. Mary got her skates on but the old music box stopped and the electric sign under it flashed "Reverse." The music started again. The skaters turned and went the opposite way. Harry and his friend skated off the floor. Mary followed them to a bench near the soft-drink stand.

"What's the hurry, Harry?" she yelled.

He turned quickly, his skates slipping, and would have fallen, but his friend held his arm.

"Look here, Mary, this is the damnedest place," he said.

His friend said roguishly, "Hello, I know you because Harry has told me a lot about you."

"Oh well, it's not much of a place but I know the gang," she said.

"I guess we don't have to stay here," Harry said.

"I'm not fussy, let's go for a walk, the three of us," she said.

Harry was glad his friend was noticing her blue coat with the wide sleeves and the light brown fur.

They left the rink and arm-in-arm the three walked up the street. Mary was eager to tell about *Mademoiselle from Courcelette*. The two boys were impressed and enthusiastic.

"In some ways I don't like to think of you being on the stage, but I'll bet a dollar you get ahead," Harry said.

"Oh, baby, I'll knock them dead in the hick towns."

"How do you think she'll do, Chuck?" said Harry.

The boy with the glasses could hardly say anything, he was so impressed.

Mary talked seriously. She had her hand in Harry's coat pocket and kept tapping her fingers. Harry gaily beat time as they walked. They felt that they should stay together after being away for a long time. When she said it would be foolish to think she would cut up like some girls in the business did, Harry left it to Chuck if a fellow couldn't tell a mile away that she was a real good kid.

The lighted clock in the tower of the fire hall could be seen when they turned the bend in the street. Then they could make out the hands on the clock. Mary, leaving them, said she had had a swell time, she didn't know just why. Harry jerked her into the shadow of the side door of the police station and kissed her, squeezing her tight. Chuck leaned back against the wall, wondering what to do. An automobile horn hooted. Mary, laughing happily, showed the boys her contract and they shook their heads earnestly. They heard footfalls around the corner. "Give Chuck a kiss," Harry said suddenly, generously. The boy with the glasses was so pleased he could hardly kiss her. A policeman appeared at the corner and said, "All right, Mary, your mother wants you. Beat it."

Mary said, "How's your father?" After promising to write Harry, she ran up the street.

The boys, pleased with themselves, walked home. "You want to hang on to her," Chuck said.

"I wonder why she is always nice to me just when she is going away," Harry said.

"Would you want her for your girl?"

"I don't know. Wouldn't she be a knockout at the school dance? The old ladies would throw a fit."

Mary didn't write to Harry and didn't see him for a long time. After two weeks she was fired from the company. She wasn't a good dancer.

Many people had a good laugh and Mary stopped talking about her ambitions for a while. Though usually careful, she slipped into easy careless ways with Wilfred Barnes. She never thought of him as she thought of Harry, but he became important to her. Harry was like something she used to pray for when a little girl and never really expected to get.

It was awkward when Wilfred got into trouble for tampering with the postal boxes that stood on street corners. He had discovered a way of getting all the money people put in the slots for stamps. The police found a big pile of coins hidden in his father's store. The judge sent him to jail for only two months because his parents were very respectable people. He promised to marry Mary when he came out.

One afternoon in the late summer they were married by a Presbyterian minister. Mrs. Barnes made it clear that she didn't think much of the bride. Mr. Barnes said Wilfred would have to go on working in the store. They took three rooms in a big boarding house on Berkley Street.

Mary cried a little when she wrote to tell Harry she was married. She had always been too independent to cry in that way. She would be his sincere friend and still intended to be successful on the stage, she said. Harry wrote that he was surprised that she had married a fellow just out of jail, even though he seemed to come from respectable people.

In the dance pavilion at Scarborough beach a month later, she saw Harry. The meeting was unexpected and she was with three frowsy girls from a circus that was in the east end for a week. Mary had on a long blue-knitted cape that the stores were selling cheaply. Harry turned up his nose at the three girls but talked cheerfully to Mary. They danced together. She said that her husband didn't mind her taking another try at the stage and he wondered if he should say that he had been to the circus. Giggling, and watching him closely, she said she was working for the week in the circus, for the experience. He gave her to understand that always she would do whatever pleased her, and shouldn't try for a thing that wasn't natural to her. He wasn't enthusiastic when she offered to phone him, just curious about what she might do.

Late in the fall a small part in a local company at the La Plaza for a week was offered to her. She took the job because she detested staying around the house. She wanted Harry to see her really on the stage so she phoned and asked if he would come to the La Plaza on Tuesday night. Good-humoredly he offered to take her dancing afterward. It was funny, he said laughing, that she should be starting all over again at the La Plaza.

But Harry, sitting solemnly in the theater, watching the ugly girls in tights on the stage, couldn't pick her out. He wondered what on earth was the matter when he waited at the stage door and she didn't appear. Disgusted, he went home and didn't bother about her because he had a nice girl of his own. She never wrote to tell him what was the matter.

But one warm afternoon in November, Mary took it into her head to sit on the front seat of the rig with Wilfred, delivering groceries. They went east through many streets until they were in the beach district. Wilfred was telling jokes and she was laughing out loud. Once he stopped his wagon, grabbed his basket and went running along a side entrance, yelling, "Grocer!" Mary sat on the wagon seat.

Three young fellows and a woman were sitting up on a veranda opposite the wagon. She saw Harry looking at her and vaguely wondered how he got there. She didn't want him to see that she was going to have a baby. Leaning on the veranda rail, he saw that her slimness had passed into the shapelessness of her pregnancy and he knew why she had been kept off the stage that night at the La Plaza. She sat erect and strangely dignified on the seat of the grocery wagon. They didn't speak. She made up her mind to be hard up for someone to talk to before she bothered him again, as if without going any further she wasn't as good as he was. She smiled sweetly at Wilfred when he came running out of the alley and jumped on the seat, shouting, "Giddup," to the horse. They drove on to a customer farther down the street.

1926

## A WEDDING DRESS

For fifteen years Miss Lena Schwartz had waited for Sam Hilton to get a good job so they could get married. She lived in a quiet boarding house on Wellesley Street, the only woman among seven men boarders. The landlady, Mrs. McNab, did not want women boarders; the house might get a bad reputation in the neighborhood, but Miss Schwartz had been with her a long time. Miss Schwartz was thirty-two, her hair was straight, her nose turned up a little and she was thin.

Sam got a good job in Windsor and she was going there to marry him. She was glad to think that Sam still wanted to marry her, because he was a Catholic and went to church every Sunday. Sam liked her so much he wrote a cramped homely letter four times a week.

When Miss Schwartz knew definitely that she was going to Windsor, she read part of a letter to Mrs. McNab. The men heard about the letter at the table and talked as if Lena were an old maid. "I guess it will really happen to her all right," they said, nudging one another. "The Lord knows she waited long enough."

Miss Schwartz quit work in the millinery shop one afternoon in the middle of February. She was to travel by night, arrive in Windsor early next morning and marry Sam as soon as possible.

That afternoon the downtown streets were slushy and the snow was thick alongside the curb. Miss Schwartz ate a little lunch at a soda fountain, not much because she was excited. She had to do some shopping, buy some flimsy under-clothes and a new dress. The dress was important. She wanted it charming enough to be married in and serviceable for wear on Sundays. Sitting on the counter stool she ate slowly and remembered how she had often thought marrying Sam would be a matter of course. His lovemaking had become casual and good-natured; she could grow old with him and be respected by other women. But now she had a funny aching feeling inside. Her arms and legs seemed almost strange to her.

Miss Schwartz crossed the road to one of the depart-ment stores and was glad she had on her heavy coat with the wide sleeves that made a warm muff. The snow was melting and the sidewalk steaming near the main entrance. She went lightheartedly through the store, buying a little material for a dress on the third floor, a chemise on the fourth floor and curling-tongs in the basement. She decided to take a look at the dresses.

She rode an elevator to the main floor and got on an escalator because she liked gliding up and looking over the squares of counters, the people in the aisles, and over the rows of white electric globes hanging from the ceiling. She intended to pay about twenty-five dollars for a dress. To the left of the escalators the dresses were displayed on circular racks in orderly rows. She walked on the carpeted floor to one of the racks and a salesgirl lagged on her heels. The girl was young and fair-headed and saucy looking; she made Miss Schwartz uncomfortable.

"I want a nice dress, blue or brown," she said, "about twenty-five dollars."

The salesgirl mechanically lifted a brown dress from the rack. "This is the right shade for you," she said. "Will you try it on?"

Miss Schwartz was disappointed. She had no idea such a plain dress would cost twenty-five dollars. She wanted something to startle Sam. She never paid so much for a dress, but Sam liked something fancy. "I don't think I like these," she said. "I wanted something special."

The salesgirl said sarcastically, "Maybe you were thinking of a French dress. Some on the rack in the French Room are marked down."

Miss Schwartz moved away, a tall commonplace woman in a dark coat and an oddly shaped purple hat. She went into the gray French Room. She stood on a blue pattern on the gray carpet and guardedly fingered a dress on the rack, a black canton crepe dress with a high collar that folded back, forming petals of burnt orange. From the hem to the collar was a row of buttons, the sleeves were long with a narrow orange trimming at the cuffs, and there was a wide corded silk girdle. It was marked seventy-five dollars. She liked the feeling it left in the tips of her fingers. She stood alone at the rack, toying with the material, her mind playing with thoughts she guiltily enjoyed. She imagined herself wantonly attractive in the dress, slyly watched by men with bold thoughts as she walked down the street with Sam, who would be nervously excited when he drew her into some corner and put his hands on her shoulders. Her heart began to beat heavily. She wanted to walk out of the room and over to the escalator but could not think clearly. Her fingers were carelessly drawing the dress into her wide coat sleeve, the dress disappearing steadily and finally slipping easily from the hanger, drawn into her wide sleeve.

She left the French Room with a guilty feeling of satisfied exhaustion. The escalator carried her down slowly to the main floor. She hugged the parcels and the sleeve containing the dress tight to her breast. On the streetcar she started to cry because Sam seemed to have become something remote, drifting away from her. She would have gone back with the dress but did not know how to go about it.

When she got to the boarding house she went straight upstairs and put on the dress as fast as she could, to feel that it belonged to her. The black dress with the burnt orange petals on the high collar was short and loose on her thin figure.

Then the landlady knocked at the door and said that a tall man downstairs wanted to see her about something important. Mrs. McNab waited for Miss Schwartz to come out of her room.

Miss Schwartz sat on the bed. She felt that if she did not move at once she would not be able to walk downstairs. She walked downstairs in the French dress, Mrs. McNab watching her closely. Miss Schwartz saw a man with a wide heavy face and his coat collar buttoned high on his neck complacently watching her. She felt that she might just as well be walking downstairs in her underclothes; the dress was like something wicked clinging to her legs and her body. "How do you do," she said.

"Put on your hat and coat," he said steadily.

Miss Schwartz, slightly bewildered, turned stupidly and went upstairs. She came down a minute later in her coat and hat and went out with the tall man. Mrs. McNab got red in the face when Miss Schwartz offered no word of explanation.

On the street he took her arm and said, "You got the dress on and it won't do any good to talk about it. We'll go over to the station."

"But I have to go to Windsor," she said, "I really have to. It will be all right. You see, I am to be married tomorrow. It's important to Sam."

He would not take her seriously. The streetlights made the slippery sidewalks glassy. It was hard to walk evenly.

At the station the sergeant said to the detective, "She might be a bad egg. She's an old maid and they get very foxy."

She tried to explain it clearly and was almost garrulous. The sergeant shrugged his shoulders and said the cells would not hurt her for a night. She started to cry. A policeman led her to a small cell with a plain cot.

Miss Schwartz could not think about being in the cell. Her head, heavy at first, got light and she could not consider the matter. The detective who had arrested her gruffly offered to send a wire to Sam.

The policeman on duty during the night thought she was a stupid silly woman because she kept saying over and over, "We were going to be married. Sam liked a body to look real nice. He always said so." The unsatisfied expression in her eyes puzzled the policeman, who said to the sergeant, "She's a bit of a fool, but I guess she was going to get married all right."

At half past nine in the morning they took her from the cell to the police car along with a small wiry man who had been quite drunk the night before, a colored woman who had been keeping a bawdy house, a dispirited fat man arrested for bigamy, and a Chinese man who had been keeping a betting house. She sat stiffly, primly, in a corner of the car and could not cry. Snow was falling heavily when the car turned into the city hall courtyard.

Miss Schwartz appeared in the Women's Court before a little olive-skinned magistrate. Her legs seemed to stiffen and fall away when she saw Sam's closely cropped head and his big lazy body at a long table before the magistrate. A young man was talking rapidly and confidently to him. The magistrate and the Crown attorney were trying to make a joke at each other's expense. The magistrate found the attorney amusing. A court clerk yelled a name, the policeman at the door repeated it and then loudly yelled the name along the hall. The colored woman who had been keeping the bawdy house appeared with her lawyer.

Sam moved over to Miss Schwartz. She found it hard not to cry. She knew that a Salvation Army man was talking to a slightly hard-looking woman about her, and she felt strong and resentful. Sam held her hand but said nothing.

The colored woman went to jail for two months rather than pay a fine of $200.

"Lena Schwartz," said the clerk. The policeman at the door shouted the name along the hall. The young lawyer who had been talking to Sam told her to stand up while the clerk read the charge. She was scared and her knees were stiff.

"Where is the dress?" asked the magistrate.

A store detective with a heavy moustache explained that she had it on and told how she had been followed and later on arrested. Everybody looked at her, the dress too short and hanging loosely on her thin body, the burnt orange petals creased and twisted.

"She was to be married today," began the young lawyer affably. "She was to be married in this dress," he said and good humoredly explained that yesterday when she stole it she had become temporarily a kleptomaniac. Mr. Hilton had come up from Windsor and was willing to pay for the dress. It was a case for clemency. "She waited a long time to be married and was not quite sure of herself," he said seriously.

He told Sam to stand up. Sam haltingly explained that she was a good woman, a very good woman. The Crown attorney seemed to find Miss Schwartz amusing.

The magistrate scratched away with his pen and then said he would remand Miss Schwartz for sentence if Sam still wanted to marry her and would pay for the dress. Sam could hardly say anything. "She will leave the city with you," said the magistrate, "and keep out of department stores for a year." He saw Miss Schwartz wrinkling her nose and blinking her eyes and added, "Now go out and have a quiet wedding." The magistrate was satisfied with himself.

Miss Schwartz, looking a little older than Sam, stood up in her dress that was to make men slyly watch her and straightened the corded silk girdle. It was to be her wedding dress. Sam gravely took her arm and they went out to be quietly married.

1927

# LAST SPRING THEY CAME OVER

Alfred Bowles came to Canada from England and got a job on a Toronto paper. He was a young fellow with clear, blue eyes and heavy pimples on the lower part of his face, the son of a Baptist minister whose family was too large for his salary. He got thirty dollars a week on the paper and said it was surprisingly good screw to start. For five dollars a week he got an attic room in a brick house painted brown on Mutual Street. He ate his meals in a quick-lunch near the office. He bought a cane and a light-gray fedora.

He wasn't a good reporter but was inoffensive and obliging. After he had been working two weeks the fellows took it for granted he would be fired in a little while and were nice to him, liking the way the most trifling occurrences surprised him. He was happy to carry his cane on his arm and wear the fedora at a jaunty angle, quite the reporter. He liked to explain that he was doing well. He wrote home about it.

When they put him doing night police he felt important, phoning the fire department, hospitals, and police stations, trying to be efficient. He was getting along all right. It was disappointing when after a week the assistant city editor, Mr. H.J. Brownson, warned him to phone his home if anything important happened, and he would have another man cover it. But Bowles got to like hearing the weary, irritable voice of the assistant city editor called from his bed at three o'clock in the morning. He liked to politely call Mr. Brownson as often and as late as possible, thinking it a bit of good fun.

Alfred wrote long letters to his brother and to his father, carefully tapping the keys, occasionally laughing to himself. In a month's time he had written six letters describing the long city room, the fat belly of the city editor, and the bad words the night editor used when speaking of the Orangemen.

The night editor took a fancy to him because of the astounding puerility of his political opinions. Alfred was always willing to talk pompously of the British Empire policing the world and about all Catholics being aliens, and the future of Ireland and Canada resting with the Orangemen. He flung his arms wide and talked in the hoarse voice of a bad actor, but no one would have thought of taking him seriously. He was merely having a dandy time. The night editor liked him because he was such a nice boy.

Then Alfred's brother came out from the Old Country, and got a job on the same paper. Some of the men started talking about cheap cockney laborers crowding the good guys out of the jobs, but Harry Bowles was frankly glad to get the thirty a week. It never occurred to him that he had a funny idea of good money. With his first pay he bought a derby hat, a pair of spats, and a cane, but even though his face was clear and had a good color he never looked as nice as his younger brother because his heavy nose curved up at the end. The landlady on Mutual Street moved a double bed into Alfred's room and Harry slept with his brother.

The days passed with many good times together. At first it was awkward that Alfred should be working nights and his brother the days, but Harry was pleased to come to the office each night at eleven and they went down the street to the hotel that didn't bother about Prohibition. They drank a few glasses of good beer. It became a kind of rite that had to be performed carefully. Harry would put his left foot and Alfred his right foot on the rail and leaning an elbow on the bar they would slowly survey the zigzag line of frothing glasses the length of the long bar. Men jostled them for a place at the foot-rail.

Alfred said: "Well, a bit of luck."

Harry, grinning and raising his glass, said: "Righto."

"It's the stuff that heals."

"Down she goes."

"It helps the night along."

"Fill them up again."

"Toodle-oo."

Then they would walk out of the crowded barroom, vaguely pleased with themselves. Walking slowly and erectly along the street they talked with assurance, a mutual respect for each other's opinion making it merely an exchange of information. They talked of the Englishman in Canada, comparing his lot with that of the Englishman in South Africa and India. They had never traveled but to ask what they knew of strange lands would have made one feel uncomfortable; it was better to take it for granted that the Bowles boys knew all about the ends of the earth and had judged them carefully, for in their eyes was the light of far-away places. Once in a while, after walking a block or two, one of the brothers would say he would damn well like to see India and the other would say it would be simply topping.

After work and on Sundays they took a look at the places they had heard about in the city. One Sunday they got up in good time and took the boat to Niagara. Their father had written asking if they had seen the Falls and would they send some souvenirs. That day they had as nice a time as a man would want to have. Standing near the pipe-rail a little way from the hotel that overlooks the Falls they watched the waterline just before the drop, smooth as a long strip of beveled glass, and Harry compared it favorably with a cataract in the Himalayas and a giant waterfall in Africa, just above the Congo. They took a car along the gorge and getting off near the whirlpool, picked out a little hollow near a big rock at the top of the embankment where the grass was lush and green. They stretched themselves out with hats tilted over their eyes for sunshades. The river whirled below. They talked about the funny ways of Mr. Brownson and his short fat legs and about the crazy women who fainted at the lifted hand of the faith healer who was in the city for a week. They liked the distant rumble of the Falls. They agreed to try and save a lot of money and go west to the Pacific in a year's time. They never mentioned trying to get a raise in pay.

Afterwards they each wrote home about the trip, sending the souvenirs.

Neither one was doing well on the paper. Harry wasn't much good because he hated writing the plain copy and it was hard for him to be strictly accurate. He liked telling a good tale but it never occurred to him that he was deliberately lying. He imagined a thing and felt it to be true. But it never occurred to Alfred to depart from the truth. He was accurate but lazy, never knowing when he was really working. He was taken off night police and for two weeks helped a man do courts at the City Hall. He got to know the boys at the press gallery, who smiled at his naïve sincerity and thought him a decent chap, without making up their minds about him. Every noon hour Harry came to the press gallery and the brothers, sitting at typewriters, wrote long letters about the country and the people, anything interesting, and after exchanging letters, tilted back in their swivel chairs, laughing out loud. Neither, when in the press gallery, seemed to write anything for the paper.

Some of the men tried kidding Alfred, teasing him about women, asking if he found the girls in this country to his liking; but he seemed to enjoy it more than they did. Seriously he explained that he had never met a girl in this country, but they looked very nice. Once Alfred and Bun Brophy, a red-headed fellow with a sharp tongue who did City Hall for the paper, were alone in the gallery. Brophy had in his hands a big picture of five girls in masquerade costumes. Without explaining that he loved one of the girls Brophy asked Bowles which of the lot was the prettiest.

"You want me to settle that," said Alfred, grinning and waving his pipe. He very deliberately selected a demure little girl with a shy smile.

Brophy was disappointed. "Don't you think this one is pretty?" – a colorful, bold-looking girl.

"Well, she's all right in her way, but she's too vivacious. I'll take this one. I like them kittenish," Alfred said.

Brophy wanted to start an argument but Alfred said it was neither here nor there. He really didn't like women.

"You mean to say you never step out?" Brophy said.

"I've never seemed to mix with them," he said, adding that the whole business didn't matter because he liked men much better.

The men in the press room heard about it and some suggested nasty things to Alfred. It was hard to tease him when he wouldn't be serious. Sometimes they asked if he took Harry out walking in the evenings. Brophy called them the heavy lovers. The brothers didn't mind because they thought the fellows were having a little fun.

In the fall Harry was fired. The editor in a nice note said that he was satisfied Mr. H.W. Bowles could not adapt himself to their methods. But everybody wondered why he hadn't been fired sooner. He was no good on the paper.

The brothers smiled, shrugged their shoulders and went on living together. Alfred still had his job. Every noon hour in the City Hall press room they were together, writing letters.

Time passed and the weather got cold. Alfred's heavy coat came from the Old Country and he gave his vest and a thin sweater to Harry, who had only a light spring coat. As the weather got colder Harry buttoned his coat higher up on his throat and even though he looked cold he was neat as a pin with his derby and cane.

Then Alfred lost his job. The editor, disgusted, called him a fool. For the first time since coming over last spring he felt hurt, something inside him was hurt and he told his brother about it, wanting to know why people acted in such a way. He said he had been doing night police. On the way over to No. 1 station very late Thursday night he had met two men from other papers. They told him about a big fire earlier in the evening just about the time when Alfred was accustomed to going to the hotel to have a drink with his brother. They were willing to give all the details and Alfred thankfully shook hands with them and hurried back to the office to write the story. Next morning the assistant city editor phoned Alfred and asked how it was the morning papers missed the story. Alfred tried to explain but Mr. Brownson said he was a damn fool for not phoning the police and making sure instead of trying to make the paper look like a pack of fools printing a fake story. The fellows who had kidded him said that too. Alfred kept asking his brother why the fellows had to do it. He seemed to be losing a good feeling for people.

Still the brothers appeared at noontime in the press room. They didn't write so many letters. They were agreeable, cheerful, on good terms with everybody. Bun Brophy every day asked how they were doing and they felt at home there. Harry would stand for a while watching the checker game always in progress, knowing that if he stood staring intently at the black and red squares, watching every deliberate move, he would be asked to sit in when it was necessary that one of the players make the rounds in the hall. Once Brophy gave Harry his place and walked over to the window where Alfred stood watching the fleet of automobiles arranged in a square in the courtyard. The police wagon with a load of drunks was backing toward the cells.

"Alfie, I often wonder how you guys manage," he said.

"Oh, first rate."

"Well, you ought to be in a bad way by now."

"Oh, no, we have solved the problem," said Alfie in a grand way, grinning. There was a store in their block, he said, where a package of tobacco could be got for five cents; they did their own cooking and were able to live on five dollars a week. "What about coming over and having tea with us some-times?" Alfred said.

Brophy, abashed, suggested the three of them go over to the café and have a little toast. Harry talked volubly on the way over and while having coffee. He was really a better talker than his brother. They sat in an armchair lunch, gripped the handles of their thick mugs, and talked about religion. The brothers were sons of a Baptist minister but never thought of going to church. It seemed that Brophy had traveled a lot during wartime and afterward in Asia Minor and India. He was telling them about a great golden temple of the Sikhs at Amritsar and Harry listened carefully, asking many questions. Then they talked about newspapers until Harry started talking about the East, slowly feeling his way. All of a sudden he told about standing on a height of land near Amritsar, looking down at a temple. It couldn't have been so but he would have it that Brophy and he had seen the same temple and he described the country in the words Brophy had used.

Alfred liked listening to his brother but he said: "Religion is a funny business. I tell you it's a funny business." Alfred had a casual way of making a cherished belief or opinion seem unimportant, a way of dismissing even the bright yarns of his brother.

After that afternoon in the café Brophy never saw Harry. Alfred came often to the City Hall but never mentioned his brother. Someone said maybe Harry had a job but Alfred laughed and said no such luck in this country, explaining casually that Harry had a bit of a cold and was resting up. In the passing days Alfred came only once in a while to the City Hall, writing his letter without enthusiasm.

The press men would have tried to help the brothers if they had heard Harry was sick. They were entirely ignorant of the matter. On a Friday afternoon at three-thirty Alfred came into the gallery and, smiling apologetically, told Brophy that his brother was dead; the funeral was to be in three-quarters of an hour; would he mind coming? It was pneumonia, he added. Brophy, looking hard at Alfred, put on his hat and coat and they went out.

It was a poor funeral. The hearse went on before along the way to the Anglican cemetery that overlooks the ravine.

One old cab followed behind. There had been a heavy snow in the morning, and the slush on the pavement was thick. Alfred and Brophy sat in the old cab, silent. Alfred was leaning forward, his chin resting on his hands, the cane acting as a support, and the heavy pimples stood out on the lower part of his white face. Brophy was uncomfortable and chilly but he mopped his shining forehead with a big handkerchief. The window was open and the air was cold and damp.

Alfred politely asked how Mrs. Brophy was doing. Then he asked about Mr. Brownson.

"Oh, he's fine," Brophy said. He wanted to close the window but it would have been necessary to move Alfred so he sat huddled in the corner, shivering.

Alfred asked suddenly if funerals didn't leave a bad taste in the mouth and Brophy, surprised, started talking absently about that golden temple of the Sikhs in India. Alfred appeared interested until they got to the cemetery. He said suddenly he would have to take a look at the temple one fine day.

They buried Harry Bowles in a grave in the paupers' section on a slippery slope of the hill. The earth was hard and chunky and it thumped down on the coffin case. It snowed a little near the end.

On the way along the narrow, slippery footpath up the hill Alfred thanked Brophy for being thoughtful enough to come to the funeral. There was little to say. They shook hands and went different ways.

After a day or two Alfred again appeared in the press room. He watched the checker game, congratulated the winner and then wrote home. The men were sympathetic and said it was too bad about his brother. He smiled cheerfully and said they were good fellows. In a little while he seemed to have convinced them that nothing important had really happened.

His last cent must have gone to the undertaker, for he was particular about paying bills, but he seemed to get along all right. Occasionally he did a little work for the paper, a story from a night assignment when the editor thought the staff was being overworked.

One afternoon at two-thirty in the press gallery Brophy saw the last of Alfred, who was sucking his pipe, his feet up on a desk, wanting to be amused. Brophy asked if anything had turned up. In a playful, resigned tone, his eye on the big clock, Alfred said he had until three to join the Air Force. They wouldn't take him, he said, unless he let them know by three.

Brophy said, "How will you like that?"

"I don't fancy it."

"But you're going through."

"Well, I'm not sure. Something else may come along."

No one saw him after that, but he didn't join the Air Force. Someone in the gallery said that wherever he went he probably wrote home as soon as he got there.

1927

# AMUCK IN THE BUSH

G us Rapp, who worked in Howard's lumberyard near the Spruceport dock on Georgian Bay, lived with his old man in a rough-cast cottage two doors along the road from the boss's house. The road faced the yard and the bay. He had worked in the lumberyard as a laborer for five years, loafing a lot when the sun was hot. The boss didn't fire him because he looked after his old man. Gus didn't like the boss, Sid Walton, but liked watching Mrs. Walton, who often brought her husband a jug of iced tea on a hot day.

One day Gus was unloading planks from a boxcar on the siding at the board platform near the general office. The sun was hot on the platform and burned through the boots of the men piling lumber.

The lumberyard was on an inlet at the southern pier below the shipyard and the old tinned and weathered brown grain elevator. The inlet's waterline at the lumberyard had gone back fifty feet, and smooth flat rock and small rocks baked in the sun. Piles of lumber with sloping tops were back from the shoreline. The low brick buildings of the milling plant were at the foot of the pier. On the water side of the plant sawdust was heaped up and packed down. Farther back from the lumberyard the long road, curving down from the station, followed the shoreline south beyond the town and the wooded picnic park, farther along skirting the bush at Little River, all the way to the rifle ranges.

Gus Rapp, sweating a lot and chewing his mustache, could stand in the boxcar door, looking up the street to the station and over the town to the blue mountains, where a red sun always set brilliantly.

Gus was working in the boxcar, kneeling on the lumber close to the roof. The boxcar had a stuffy smell of damp fresh wood. He was on his knees swinging the eight-by-two planks loose, shoving them down to the door where they slid into the hands and close to the hips of two men, who trudged across the platform, piling the planks on two sawhorses. By craning his neck to one side Gus could see through the door the wide-brimmed straw hat, the strong neck, and the thick shoulders of Sid Walton, who kept telling the men to show a little life. Gus didn't feel much like working. The planks slid down slowly. He wanted to lie flat on his belly and look out through a wide crack in the car to the milling plant, where little kids in bathing suits were jumping down from the roof into the sawdust.

Walton yelled to get to work. Gus swore to himself. It was hot and he was sleepy and it would have been fine to sit with his back against the side of the car. Walton yelled and Gus yelled back. Sid told Gus to trade places with one of the men. Gus made sure where Walton stood on the platform and swung a plank loose, sliding it far down, swinging it in a wide curve. A man yelled and Walton ducked. Gus stood sullenly in the boxcar door, his brown arm wiping his brown face, his hair and forehead damp. He jumped down to the platform.

"You damn hunkie," Walton yelled, running at Gus. He picked up an axe handle and whacked him hard three times across the back. Gus went down on his knees and hollered but got up kicking out. He tried to pick up a plank but the men grabbed him. They held him and he yelled, "You big son of a bitch." Sid was bigger than Gus and stood there laughing, legs wide apart, his big hands on his hips. Gus's back hurt and he rubbed his shoulder.

The boss said seriously, "All right, Rapp, you can clear out for good."

Gus picked up his coat and cursed some more on the way over to the time office. He left the yard and went down past the station, cutting across the tracks north of the water tower, intending to drink squirrel whiskey in Luke Horton's flour-and-feed store at the end of Main Street. His brown sweater was tucked in at his belt, he carried his coat, and his overalls were rolled four inches above his heavy boots.

He was alone with Luke in the room back of the store that smelt of dog biscuits and chicken feed. Gus sat at the small table feeling good, on the whiskey. Luke sat opposite, kidding him, nodding his bald head sympathetically and stroking his hairy arms.

"I can kick hell out of Walton," Gus said finally.

"Sure you can, he's not so much."

"Well, stick around, I'm going to."

"Sid'll be up at the park at the ball game tonight," Luke said.

"Damn the ball game."

"Don't you want to have a go at him?"

"I'll get him alone when he won't know what hit him."

"Mrs. Walton'll be there too, Gus."

"I'd as leave have a go at her, Luke."

31

Gus drank the whiskey out of a big cup and his long mustache got wet. He left Horton's place sucking his mustache. He hurried back past the lumberyard to his house near Walton's place on the road by the bay. It hurt his head thinking how much he hated Walton. Let him put his hand on a gun and he'd maybe go down to the yard. He wasn't drunk, just feeling pretty good.

He went in the house and came out of the back door with the gun. Standing on the porch, he looked over into Walton's place. He didn't hurry back to the yard as he thought he would. He stood on the porch watching Mrs. Walton's big hips and firm back. She didn't speak to Gus because Sid had been having trouble with him, but wondered why he wasn't working. She and her six-year-old Anna were going berry picking. He saw Mrs. Walton take a blue sweater coat from a nail in the porch and Anna brought a pail and two wooden boxes from the woodshed.

Gus went around his side entrance to watch Mrs. Walton go down the road with the girl. He hardly thought about going back to the lumberyard. He sat on the front steps for twenty minutes, his head in his hands, spitting at a bug crawling on the picket walk and thinking about grabbing and hiding the kid that always became Mrs. Walton when he thought about it very much. "That'll make Walton sweat all right," he thought, and got up quickly, happy to go swinging along the road beyond the town to the berry patch in the bush. He thought about stealing the kid but liked following Mrs. Walton. She had full red lips and a lot of black hair bunched over her ears.

Mrs. Walton passed out of sight behind a bunch of girls in automobiles on the road near the wooded picnic park. He hurried. In sight of the line of spruce trees back from the bay, he saw Mrs. Walton help the kid across the plank over the shallow Little River and follow the path into the bush.

She kept to the path and he followed through the trees, getting excited. He didn't think much about the kid but felt he would take her away all right.

It was shady yet warm in the bush. The afternoon sun was strong. Brownish-green leaves were beginning to fall from the trees on the path. The berry patch was at the southwest fringe of the bush. Mrs. Walton walked slowly with a strong stride, her wide-brimmed hat flapping regularly. It was warm in the bush and small noises sounded loud but it was cooling to look back through the trees to the blue waterline of the bay. Anna at times left her mother and played among the trees, hiding behind a big rock, calling to her that she couldn't find her. Many huge rounded rocks were in the bush. Gus followed carefully.

The trees thinned out at the fringe of the bush and the berry patch. No one else was berry picking. Mrs. Walton quickly started to work. The berries were black and heavy and fell with a soft little thud in the bottom of the pail. Gus, his side straight against a tree, watched her working, filling the small box, then dumping it into the pail close to her right leg. He watched until the pail was nearly three-quarters full. The little girl at the bush to the left was filling her box slowly and eating the berries. Gus dropped his coat and stepped from behind a tree, leaning his weight back off his step on the twigs. He thought he wanted to grab the kid, but sneaked up behind Mrs. Walton, her shoulder dipping up and down with the picking. He was behind her, flinging his arms around her waist, pulling back heavily. The berries sprayed from the box.

"You got to let me have the kid," he said.

She squealed, frightened at first, but seeing and knowing him, she got mad. "Let me go, Gus Rapp, you big fool. Just you wait," she said.

Gus said nothing and stopped thinking. He tried to trip and throw her down but she dropped to her knees, gripping hard at his belt and yelling to the girl to run. He banged her on the mouth and leaned forward and down heavily on her shoulders. The kid got as far as a big rock and stood screeching at him.

"You damn kid, shut up," he yelled.

The woman kicked and scratched so he flopped down, smothering her, jerking her hands from his belt, getting her between his legs. She yelled, "Anna, Anna," but one big hand was on her throat, squeezing. Her clothes ripped and she rolled, but he held, hard pressing, bending her stiff back until the kid ran up and got hold of his ankle just above the thick boot, pulling; his arm swung free and caught the kid by the throat, slamming her down hard, choking her. He tugged and the woman's sweater came away. Twisting around and holding her arm, he grunted, "You got to lie there," three times. His legs were thick and heavy and she got weaker. His arms were hard and heavy but she bit deep into his forearm and he hollered, "God damn it." He could hardly hold on. She was a big strong woman and the kid was yelling. Snarling, he jerked loose, spinning around and pulling at his gun. He felt crazy and didn't know why he was doing it. He jumped up shooting, three shots; and one grazed her forehead, gashing her cheek, and one went into a log. Then he ran at the kid to stop her yelling, taking her by the neck. Mrs. Walton said not very loud, "Don't kill my little girl," so he shot at the woman to kill, but missed.

The kid got up and started to run. Gus took a jump at the woman, knocking her over easily, but didn't know what

34

he wanted. He couldn't help thinking what his boss, Sid Walton, would do about it. Mrs. Walton got up slowly. He was scared, and said, "You better lie there." Her skirt was torn and blood was on her leg. He wanted to run away. She zigzagged through the trees after her girl, pushing the hair out of her eyes and crying softly as she ran. Gus hesitated, watching her, then ran the other way, through the bush away from the town.

He ran and stumbled through the bush, quite sober and scared, his heart pounding heavily as he banged into little trees, his shaky legs hardly knowing where to go. He wanted to get through the bush to the bay and along the road to the rifle ranges where he could maybe swipe a boat. After running until he was tired, he stopped suddenly and thought it was no use trying. He looked around the bush and down to the bay. Between him and the lakeshore road was a line of trees, branches and tops covered with thick old vines that kids used for tree tag. He climbed a tree to the vines, his feet slashing through green shoots, but the thick, springy wood held him. He twined the vines round his legs, resting most of his weight on a branch near the top. The branch swayed and he sweated and cursed and shivered, waiting for the dark. He looked through the leaves up the road and away over the town at the orange sky on the blue mountains, and at the still waters of the bay and the fading skyline.

It got dark and no one came near the tree. He felt better but very stiff and still shaky. It would fool everybody to go back to the town, he muttered. He slid down the vines and started running, his feet thudding steadily, his breath whistling.

Where the road went back from the shoreline he left it, going down by the waterworks and back of Harvey's fishing-station. The big shadow of the wooded picnic park was ahead and he was glad to go because they'd think it a silly place to look. The streetlights seemed bright and gave him a funny feeling over his stomach. Maybe he should have gone looking for a boxcar down at the station, but he ran on to the lumberyard. There was no moon and he was sure the lumber was piled too high. He went through the lumberyard and over to the elevator. The *Mississippi*, with a cargo of grain, was docked. He crawled along the pier but boards were rotten farther out and missing in places. The moon came out and the lapping water underneath the pier scared him so much he lay flat on his belly, breathing drunkenly, trying to pray. "Holy Mary, Holy Mary, Holy Mary, you can do it. I used to go to church, I used to go with the old lady." A light was lit on the *Mississippi* and then two more. A pain was in his side but he went slinking back along the pier and out again to the lakeshore road. It was a shame having to pass his own house, and he thought of the old man sleeping in there.

Gus was surprised to feel hungry. He went along the side entrance of a house with a big veranda and crept into the garden where he pulled carrots and onions, stuffing them into his pockets. The back door opened and in the light he hugged the ground and shivered and puked and lay very still. But the door closed.

He took the road again, running along trying to eat the carrot, and puffing hard. The carrot had a bad taste. He wanted to get around the town and up to the hills. A night bird screeched and his teeth chattered so much he had to drop the carrot. He slowed to a walk.

At a bend in the road near Bell's grocery store he saw a shadow humped at the foot of a lamppost and the hump became a man getting up from the gutter. Two other men came at him and Gus took three jumps forward. "Oh, I thought you was a bear," he said. He didn't have a chance to run. One of the men was Walton with his big hands, and John Woods got ready to slug him, but he slumped loosely in their arms. He said hoarsely, "I don't want to die, Mr. Walton. Please, Mr. Walton, for Christ sake." Sid put his hand over Gus's mouth and squeezed until he spluttered and shut up. "Truss the skunk up, boys," he said. They bound his hands and put three ropes around his waist and shoulders, the ropes five feet long, a man at the end of each rope. They twisted the ropes around Gus and the lamppost while Joel Hurst went in the grocery store to phone for the police car. Gus couldn't cry, he was so scared of Walton. There was a gray streak of light in the sky across the bay.

The Bells and their four kids came out half dressed, forming a circle around Gus. Lights appeared in the windows of other houses. People were hearing that Gus was caught. Leaning his weight forward on the ropes, he stared hard at the bat that swooped and darted around the light overhead. The police car came along and they had no trouble with him. As Gus got in, the kids yelled and threw stones and sticks at him.

1927

# A COUNTRY PASSION

T he paper was not interesting and at the end of the column he did not remember what he had been reading, so he tossed the paper on the porch, and slumped back in the chair, looking over into Corley's back yard.

A clump of lilac trees prevented him from seeing directly through the open door to Corley's kitchen. Jim Cline, sitting on the porch, could see two wire bird-cages on Corley's back veranda. The faint smell of lilacs pleased him.

Jim got up, leaning over the porch rail and sucked in his upper lip. The moustache tickled him, and he rubbed his hand quickly across his bearded face. Ettie Corley came out and sat down on the back steps. Ettie was sixteen but so backward for her age she had had to quit school. Jim was twenty-nine years older than Ettie. In two days' time Ettie was to go away to an institution in Barrie. Jim had wanted to marry her but the minister, who had reminded him that he had been in jail four times, would not marry them, so he had come to an agreement with her anyway.

Jim rubbed the toe-cap of his right boot against the heel of his left. His boots were thick and heavy. He repaired them himself and could not get the soles on evenly. His brother Jake came out and picked up the paper. Jake saw Jim's forehead wrinkling and knew something was worrying him. One of the canaries in a cage on Corley's veranda started to sing and Jake looked over and saw Ettie.

"It ain't no good, Jim."

"Eh?"

"What's the matter?"

"Aw, lay off, Jake."

"Heard up town today they're thinkin' of ropin' you in on somethin' pretty bad."

"They roped me in a few times before, didn't they, Jake?"

"Well, it's done you no good."

"Awright, it's done me no good."

"It'll be serious."

"Who's going to touch me around here?"

Turning away in disgust he looked through the lilac leaves. Jake thrust his hands in his pockets, then drew out the right one and examined the palm attentively.

"The sun's hitting the porch," Jim said suddenly. "I think I'll go in." The sun shone on his thick neck. He turned around, shaking his head, and blinked his eyes in the sun.

"Didn't I buy Corley's coal last winter? Where'd Ettie be now if it weren't for me? Where's her sister gone, running around like a little mink somewhere?"

He went in the house, right through the kitchen to the hall and out to the front steps, and looked around, surprised to find himself facing the street so unexpectedly, then he stared down at a broken picket in the walk. As he looked at the one broken picket in particular, he wondered how he could fix things up with Ettie. Stepping down to the walk he pulled the broken picket from the scantling and tossed it out to the road. Dust formed in a small cloud and drifted toward the green grass on the other side of the road.

He walked across the front of the house and stood at the corner, waving his hand at Ettie. She saw him and came out to the sidewalk and down to Cline's veranda.

"What do ya want, Jim?"

"What's up, do you know?"

"I'm kind of scared. They got it out of me."

"They won't do nothin'; that's all right."

"Can't we beat it, Jim?"

"No use, you can't beat it."

She was a big girl for her age, and her mouth was hanging open, and her dress was four inches above her knees, and her hair uncombed. Jim didn't notice that her hair wasn't combed. He was so eager to explain something to her, an idea that might be carried to a point where everything would be satisfactory, but words wouldn't come readily. It was a feeling inside him but he had no words for it. He felt himself getting hold of a definite thought. Last winter he had wanted to give her some underwear after discovering she had made some herself out of sacking but she had protested strongly against such extravagance.

"I'm going to give you something to wear before you go 'way, Ettie."

"Aw no, Jim."

"I'm going to get the car out and we'll go down-street and get some."

Half grinning she wiped away a strand of hair from her face. She looked worried, moistening her lips, and she leaned against the thick poplar tree while he went around the house to get the car. He had a slouchy stride, his wide shoulders swinging as he walked.

The car rocked and swayed coming up the driveway. Ettie got into the car. Passing Corleys', Jim drove slowly without looking at Ettie. Mrs. Corley came out to the sidewalk, wiping her hands in her apron, shaking her head jerkily. She watched the car turn the corner, then went into the house quickly, her loose shoes scraping on the steps.

At the Elton Avenue bridge Jim stopped the car while Noble's cow crossed, its tail swishing against the rear mudguard. Tommie Noble, following a few paces behind, glanced at Jim and Ettie, then turned his head away. "Co Boss," he said, cutting at the cow with a gad. The car jerked forward, Ettie bounced back, her head hitting Jim's shoulder.

They drove down Main Street and Jim parked the car outside Hunt's dry-goods store. Until the car stopped in front of the store Jim had imagined himself going in with Ettie, but he merely took hold of her by the wrist, giving her an idea of the things he thought she should buy. Ettie giggled a little till Jim took seven dollars out of his pocket and counted it carefully. "Aw gee, Jim, you'd be good to me," she said.

She got out of the car and walked timidly across the sidewalk to the store. The door closed behind her and Jim fidgeted to get a more comfortable position, one foot thrust over the car door, his eyes closed. Ettie would just about be talking to a clerk, he thought, and imagined the woman taking down from a shelf many flimsy articles for a girl. He hoped Ettie would not buy the first shown to her instead of taking time to pick out pale blue, or cream, or even pink, which would be a nice color for a girl. Jim opened his eyes, looking down the street. Three kids, swinging wet bathing-suits, were coming along the street.

Smiling prettily, Ettie crossed over to the car and Jim kicked the door open with his heel. She had the bundle under her arm. "Oh, boy," she said, climbing into the car. Jim looked at her, her cheeks flushed, eyes bright, and grinning. He started the car. She would become a fine woman later on, he thought.

"We'll be getting along," he said cheerfully.

"Ain't it too bad we got to go home?"

"Aw hell, Ettie."

The car turned out to the middle of the road, and backed up, and Jim saw the sheriff, Ned Bickle, getting out of a car at the curb. Jack Spratt and Henry Tompkins were with him. The three men, walking alertly, approached Jim's car.

"Get out of the car, Jim," the sheriff said.

"What's the matter, Ned?" Jim said suspiciously, though appearing very friendly. Ned had arrested him three times, twice for stealing chickens, once when he had got into a fight at Clayton's blind pig, but it had required at least three men to hold him. The sheriff weighed two hundred and twenty-five pounds. His hard hat was pushed well back on his head, a two-days' growth of hair was on his face. Jim did not look directly at either Tompkins or Spratt, though aware of them as if they had been just a few feet from him many times before.

"Now Jim, there's a couple of charges against you. You know how it is, Jim."

"Awright, go on, don't get tongue-tied."

"Well, it's about Ettie, Jim."

"What about her?"

"Her old woman's had a lot to say."

Jim leaned over the steering-wheel, staring at the sheriff, then glancing casually at Ettie, was suddenly disappointed and bewildered. He straightened up, his back erect, resentful, his neck getting red, his moustache twitching till his lower lip moved up and held it. His left foot shot out and the door flew open, catching Tompkins in the middle, forcing him back two or three paces.

Jim jumped out, but tripped on the running-board and lurched forward, bumping blindly against Tompkins and spinning half-way round. Tompkins wrapped his arms around Jim's back and held on as Jim tried to swing him off. Twice he swung his shoulders, and one of Tompkins' arms lost its grip. Only someone had Jim's feet. He yelled and kicked out with his free foot, the boot sinking into something soft, but a huge weight was on his shoulders, forcing him down slowly, his knees bending gradually, his feet stationary, his legs held tightly together. They had him. Jim knew when they had him in such a way he couldn't move. Always they tried to get him the same way. He toppled over on his back and the road bricks hurt his shoulder-blades.

"Just a minute now till I get the cuffs out," the sheriff said.

The cuffs went on easily. Jim stretched out on the road, twisted his head till he could see Ettie, who was standing up in the car, leaning over the seat, crying and yelling, "Leave him alone, do ya hear, leave him alone."

They hoisted Jim to his feet. He walked willingly to the sheriff's car. People who had come out of the stores to stand on the curb now formed a ring around the police car. "Aw leave the guy alone," somebody yelled. Ned Bickle pushed Jim into the back seat and got in beside him. Tompkins stepped into the driver's seat. Spratt went over to Jim's car to drive Ettie home.

"This is about the worst you been in yet," Bickle said to Jim as the car passed the dry-goods store. The sheriff, puffing a little, was smiling contentedly, feeling good-natured.

"Yeah."

"I'm afraid you'll do a long stretch, Jim."

"What for? What gets into you guys?"

"Seduction and abduction we're calling it, Jim."

"Aw lay down."

Under the maple trees in front of the jail the car stopped. The leaves of the tree were so low they scraped against Jim's bare head as he stood up to get out. The jail was a one-storey brick building, four cells and a yard with a twelve-foot brick wall. Jim had been in jail three times but had never remained there more than fifteen days.

Tompkins and Spratt followed Jim and the sheriff into the cell and leaned against the wall, very serious while Ned was taking the handcuff from his own wrist, then from Jim's wrist. Jim, rubbing his wrist, looked at the bare walls, many names written there, his own over at the corner, underneath the window.

"Who else is around?" Jim asked.

"Willie Hopkins."

"What for?"

"Stealing three barrels of wine from old man Stanley's cellar."

Jim sat down on the bed and they went out, locking the door carefully. He leaned forward, his elbows on his knees, his chin cupped in his hands, staring at three iron bars in the small window. Sitting there on the bed he felt all right till he remembered that an hour ago he had been sitting on his back porch looking at the lilacs. He got up and walked around the room, his thoughts confused, and when he tried thinking slowly his head seemed to ache. He sat down on the bed to forget all about it, stretching his legs out, his arms behind his head. The sun shone through the window, forming barred squares of light on the opposite wall.

A tap on the door aroused him. "Heh, Jim." Dannie Parker, the guard, was smiling at him. "Do you want to take some exercise in the yard?"

"Not now," Jim said mildly.

"Ain't you feeling well?"

"Awright."

"Suit yourself then, I thought you'd like to, that's all."

Jim lay on the bed till Dannie brought him some supper, cold beef, potatoes, and maple syrup. The meat and potatoes he ate greedily, and liked the maple syrup so much he coaxed Dannie to give him an extra saucerful and promised to play checkers after supper.

For fifteen minutes Jim waited for Dannie to return with the checker-board. Then he heard Dan's voice and another voice. The Rev. Arthur Sorrel, a plump, agreeable little man with a small nose, the minister who had refused to marry Ettie and Jim, came into the cell with Dannie.

"Well, Mr. Cline," he said.

"Well," Jim said soberly.

"I thought we might want to talk things over."

"Maybe I'd better get another chair," Dan said.

"Don't bother. I'll stand, or perhaps sit on the bed."

Dan went away. Jim folded his arms across his chest and glared at the minister, who sat down on the edge of the bed.

"I want you to understand, Jim, that I'll do all in my power to help you. I'm not against you." The minister scratched his head thoughtfully, rubbing his cheek with the palm of his hand. "But there's not much I can do for you," he added.

"There's only one thing I want to know," Jim said.

"What's that?"

"If I'm guilty, what'll I get for it?"

"Oh, I don't know, I'm sure. I mean I can't say for certain but I'm afraid it will be life and lashes. That's the usual thing."

Jim jumped up. "Life?"

"And lashes, yes. But I can do all in my power to have them go easy on the lashes."

"Life, eh?"

"I'm afraid so."

Jim sat down, then stretched out on the bed, vaguely aware that the minister was talking but not interested in following the words.

"Ettie is going down to Barrie tomorrow and she'll be with the Ladies of Charity and I wouldn't wonder if she grew up to be a decent woman."

Jim, staring at the ceiling, did not answer.

"Of course she's had the worst home in town and something should have been done about it long ago," he said.

Jim did not answer.

The minister got up, slightly irritated, and called through the door to Dannie, who let him out.

Turning over on the bed Jim rubbed his forehead on the pillow. The minister had said he would get life and he had helped Corleys and bought coal for them last winter. Everybody in town knew he had bought coal and food and some men had said the Corley kid would be lucky if he married her. Jim sat up, feeling uneasy. He had almost hit upon an idea that would be a solution for everything. Everybody knew it would be best for Ettie to marry him, and Ettie wanted to, and he could go to work, but the people who had arrested him couldn't understand it. Fiercely indignant, he felt himself getting excited. If he could get out he could explain his idea to everybody and get people behind him. Jim walked over to the window, and looked out over the yard to the tall brick building, the waterworks.

A key turned in the door. "How about the checkers now?" Dannie Parker said.

"I got a headache, Dannie. Can't I go out in the yard a while?"

"Wouldn't you like a little game first?"

"I feel kinda rotten, Dannie."

"Did Sorrel bother you?"

"No, I just feel punk."

"All right, just as you say."

Dannie left him alone in the yard. It was about half past seven Daylight Saving Time and the sun was striking the tops of the trees. Jim walked the length of the yard without looking at the walls. Walking back, his eye followed the top line of the wall. He wasn't thinking of anything, just watching the wall. It was very old. He could remember when it was built twenty-five years ago. Cracks and crevices were spoiling it. One long crevice ran the full height of the wall.

Slyly he looked around at the jail, though he kept on walking. Passing the crevice, he saw that there was room for his boot three feet above the ground.

The second time he passed the crevice he turned quickly, jammed in his boot, reached up, hoisting himself to the wall top. He dropped over to the street. No one in sight. He started to run. As he ran down the street he tried to concentrate on the idea of doing something definite that would explain his feeling for Ettie, and appeal to the whole town. The idea had come to him back in the cell but it was necessary to get home first. He passed Hanson's grocery store, then the Catholic church, and the caretaker watering the lawn yelled at him.

He ran across the bridge and on to Corley's house. Mrs. Corley was sitting on the veranda. Seeing her, he stopped, shaking drops of sweat from his forehead and pulling his shirt open at the throat. "Now you keep out of this, do you hear, you old bat," he said. She stood up, remained motionless, then squealing, ran in the door, slamming it. "Scared as a rabbit," Jim said to himself. He laughed out loud. He walked around his own house and in the back way. The evening paper was on the porch.

No one was in the house. In the front room he sat down on the sofa, breathing deeply, fascinated by the heavy beating of his heart. He was ready to go on with the idea of getting people behind him but did not know how to go about it. He stood up angrily, rubbing his forehead. His own head was to blame. There was a way, only he couldn't see it and make use of it.

He stepped into the hall to the telephone and called up the sheriff, Ned Bickle. "Is that you, Ned? This is Jim Cline. You'd better keep away from me. I'm out and I'm going to stay out."

Jim didn't hear what the sheriff said. Walking away from the phone he felt much better. He went upstairs to get a Mauser revolver from the bureau drawer. He put it in his back pocket. No one would bother him, but it was better to have it. Downstairs he felt helpless, wondering how it was the idea seemed so simple back in the cell.

A car drew up on the road. Jim heard the car and turned to run out of the back door. He rubbed his chin, assuring himself he should go out of the front door. He opened the door and stood there on the veranda. Ned Bickle jumped out of the car, pointing a gun.

Jim half opened his mouth, getting ready to give an explanation, then looked stupidly at the barrel of the gun. He couldn't think of anything to say. Hunching his shoulders, he resentfully clenched his fists, leaning forward, his forehead wrinkled. He half turned on one heel, his hand moving toward his hip.

"Stick 'em up, Jim."

Jim straightened up and let his muscles relax. His mouth closed abruptly; there was no way of getting people behind him. Shaking his head he grinned sheepishly, holding out his hands. Ned slipped on the cuffs.

It was getting dark and crickets were singing along the road. Jim got in the back seat between two men. "You ought to be ashamed of yourself, Jim," Ned said.

1928

# ANCIENT LINEAGE

T he young man from the Historical Club with a green magazine under his arm got off the train at Clintonville. It was getting dark but the station lights were not lit. He hurried along the platform and jumped down on the sloping cinder path to the sidewalk.

Trees stood alongside the walk, branches dropping low, leaves scraping occasionally against the young man's straw hat. He saw a cluster of lights, bluish-white in the dusk across a river, many for a small town. He crossed the lift-lock bridge and turned on to the main street. A hotel was at the corner.

At the desk a bald-headed man in a blue shirt, the sleeves rolled up, looked critically at the young man while he registered. "All right, Mr. Flaherty," he said, inspecting the signature carefully.

"Do you know many people around here?" Mr. Flaherty asked.

"Just about everybody."

"The Rowers?"

"The old lady?"

"Yeah, the old lady."

"Sure, Mrs. Anna Rower. Around the corner to the left, then turn to the right on the first street, the house opposite the Presbyterian church on the hill."

"An old family?" suggested the young man.

"An old-timer all right." The hotel man made it clear by a twitching of his lips that he was a part of the new town, canal, water power, and factories.

Mr. Flaherty sauntered out and turned to the left. It was dark and the street had the silence of small towns in the evening. Turning a corner he heard girls giggling in a doorway. He looked at the church on the hill, the steeple dark against the sky. He had forgotten whether the man had said beside the church or across the road, but could not make up his mind to ask the fellow who was watering the wide church lawn. No lights in the shuttered windows of the rough-cast house beside the church. He came down the hill and had to yell three times at the man because the water swished strongly against the grass.

"All right, thanks. Right across the road," Mr. Flaherty repeated.

Tall trees screened the square brick house. Looking along the hall to a lighted room, Mr. Flaherty saw an old lady standing at a sideboard. "She's in all right," he thought, rapping on the screen door. A large woman of about forty, dressed in a blue skirt and blue blouse, came down the stairs. She did not open the screen door.

"Could I speak to Mrs. Anna Rower?"

"I'm Miss Hilda Rower."

"I'm from the University Historical Club."

"What did you want to see Mother for?"

Mr. Flaherty did not like talking through the screen door. "I wanted to talk to her," he said firmly.

"Well, maybe you'd better come in."

He stood in the hall while the large woman lit the gas in the front room. The gas flared up, popped, showing fat hips and heavy lines on her face. Mr. Flaherty, disappointed, watched her swaying down the hall to get her mother. He carefully inspected the front room, the framed photographs of dead Conservative politicians, the group of military men hanging over the old-fashioned piano, the faded greenish wallpaper and the settee in the corner.

An old woman with a knot of white hair and good eyes came into the room, walking erectly. "This is the young man who wanted to see you, Mother," Miss Hilda Rower said. They all sat down. Mr. Flaherty explained he wanted to get some information concerning the Rower genealogical tree for the next meeting of his society. The Rowers, he knew, were a pioneer family in the district, and descended from William the Conqueror, he had heard.

The old lady laughed thinly, swaying from side to side. "It's true enough, but I don't know who told you. My father was Daniel Rower, who came to Ontario from Cornwall in 1830."

Miss Hilda Rower interrupted. "Wait, Mother, you may not want to tell about it." Brusque and businesslike, she turned to the young man. "You want to see the family tree, I suppose."

"Oh, yes."

"My father was a military settler here," the old lady said.

"I don't know but what we might be able to give you some notes," Miss Hilda spoke generously.

"Thanks awfully, if you will."

"Of course you're prepared to pay something if you're going to print it," she added, smugly adjusting her big body in the chair.

Mr. Flaherty got red in the face; of course he understood,

but to tell the truth he had merely wanted to chat with Mrs. Rower. Now he knew definitely he did not like the heavy nose and unsentimental assertiveness of the lower lip of this big woman with the wide shoulders. He couldn't stop looking at her thick ankles. Rocking back and forth in the chair she was primly conscious of lineal superiority; a proud unmarried woman, surely she could handle a young man, half-closing her eyes, a young man from the university indeed. "I don't want to talk to her about the university," he thought.

Old Mrs. Rower went into the next room and returned with a framed genealogical tree of the house of Rower. She handed it graciously to Mr. Flaherty, who read, "The descent of the family of Rower, from William the Conqueror, from Malcom 1st, and from the Capets, Kings of France." It bore the imprimatur of the College of Arms, 1838.

"It's wonderful to think you have this," Mr. Flaherty said, smiling at Miss Hilda, who watched him suspiciously.

"A brother of mine had it all looked up," old Mrs. Rower said.

"You don't want to write about that," Miss Hilda said, crossing her ankles. The ankles looked much thicker crossed. "You just want to have a talk with Mother."

"That's it," Mr. Flaherty smiled agreeably.

"We may write it up ourselves someday." Her heavy chin dipped down and rose again.

"Sure, why not?"

"But there's no harm in you talking to Mother if you want to, I guess."

"You could write a good story about that tree," Mr. Flaherty said, feeling his way.

"We may do it some day but it'll take time," she smiled complacently at her mother, who mildly agreed.

Mr. Flaherty talked pleasantly to this woman, who was so determined he would not learn anything about the family tree without paying for it. He tried talking about the city, then tactfully asked old Mrs. Rower what she remembered of the Clintonville of seventy years ago. The old lady talked willingly, excited a little. She went into the next room to get a book of clippings. "My father, Captain Rower, got a grant of land from the Crown and cleared it," she said, talking over her shoulder. "A little way up the Trent River. Clintonville was a small military settlement then . . ."

"Oh, Mother, he doesn't want to know all about that," Miss Hilda said impatiently.

"It's very interesting indeed."

The old woman said nervously, "My dear, what difference does it make? You wrote it all up for the evening at the church."

"So I did too," she hesitated, thinking the young man ought to see how well it was written. "I have an extra copy." She looked at him thoughtfully. He smiled. She got up and went upstairs.

The young man talked very rapidly to the old lady and took many notes.

Miss Rower returned. "Would you like to see it?" She handed him a small gray booklet. Looking quickly through it, he saw it contained valuable information about the district.

"The writing is simply splendid. You must have done a lot of work on it."

"I worked hard on it," she said, pleased and more willing to talk.

"Is this an extra copy?"

"Yes, it's an extra copy."

"I suppose I might keep it," he said diffidently.

She looked at him steadily. "Well . . . I'll have to charge you twenty-five cents."

"Sure, sure, of course, that's fine." He blushed.

"Just what it costs to get them out," the old lady explained apologetically.

"Can you change a dollar?" He fumbled in his pocket, pulling the dollar out slowly.

They could not change it but Miss Rower would be pleased to go down to the corner grocery store. Mr. Flaherty protested. No trouble, he would go. She insisted on asking the next-door neighbor to change it. She went across the room, the dollar in hand.

Mr. Flaherty chatted with the nice old lady and carefully examined the family tree, and wrote quickly in a small book till the screen door banged, the curtains parted, and Miss Hilda Rower came into the room. He wanted to smirk, watching her walking heavily, so conscious of her ancient lineage, a virginal mincing sway to her large hips, seventy-five cents' change held loosely in drooping fingers.

"Thank you," he said, pocketing the change, pretending his work was over. Sitting back in the chair he praised the way Miss Rower had written the history of the neighborhood and suggested she might write a splendid story of the family tree, if she had the material, of course.

"I've got the material, all right," she said, trying to get comfortable again. How would Mr. Flaherty arrange it and where should she try to sell it? The old lady was dozing in the rocking chair. Miss Rower began to talk rather nervously about her material. She talked of the last title in the family and the Sir Richard who had been at the court of Queen Elizabeth.

Mr. Flaherty chimed in gaily, "I suppose you know the O'Flahertys were kings in Ireland?"

She said vaguely, "I daresay, I daresay," conscious only of an interruption to the flow of her thoughts. She went on talking with hurried eagerness, all the fine talk about her ancestors bringing her peculiar satisfaction. A soft light came into her eyes and her lips were moist.

Mr. Flaherty started to rub his cheek, and looked at her big legs, and felt restive, and then embarrassed, watching her closely, her lower lip hanging loosely. She was talking slowing, lazily, relaxing in her chair, a warm fluid oozing through her veins, exhausting but satisfying her.

He was uncomfortable. She was liking it too much. He did not know what to do. There was something immodest about it. She was close to forty, her big body relaxed in the chair. He looked at his watch and suggested he would be going. She stretched her legs graciously, pouting, inviting him to stay a while longer, but he was standing up, tucking his magazine under his arm. The old lady was still dozing. "I'm so comfortable," Miss Rower said, "I hate to move."

The mother woke up and shook hands with Mr. Flaherty. Miss Rower got up to say good-bye charmingly.

Halfway down the path Mr. Flaherty turned. She was standing in the doorway, partly shadowed by the tall trees, bright moonlight filtering through leaves touching soft lines on her face and dark hair.

He went down the hill to the hotel unconsciously walking with a careless easy stride, wondering at the change that had come over the heavy, strong woman. He thought of taking a walk along the river in the moonlight, the river on which old Captain Rower had drilled troops on the ice in the winter of 1837 to fight the rebels. Then he thought of having a western sandwich in the café across the road from the hotel. That big woman in her own way had been hot stuff.

In the hotel he asked to be called early so he could get the first train to the city. For a long time he lay awake in the fresh, cool bed, the figure of the woman whose ancient lineage had taken the place of a lover in her life, drifting into his thoughts and becoming important while he watched on the wall the pale moonlight that had softened the lines of her face, and wondered if it was still shining on her bed, and on her throat, and on her contented, lazily relaxed body.

1928

# A REGRET FOR YOUTH

The first time Mrs. Jerry Austin's husband went away, she cried and wrote a long letter home, but in two months' time he came back. They had dinner and agreed never to quarrel again and he promised not to feel restless any more. The second time he left her, she didn't bother looking for a job. She told the landlady, Mrs. Oddy, that Mr. Austin had gone traveling and was doing well. Mrs. Oddy, who had red hair, a toothy accent and a loud voice, said that whenever Mr. Oddy did any traveling she liked to keep him company, but after all, it was none of her business.

Mrs. Austin had paid a month's rent in advance. She was friendly with Mrs. Oddy, who occasionally invited her to go motoring. Mr. and Mrs. Oddy sat in the front seat and Mrs. Austin sat in the back seat. Mr. Oddy was in the civil service, a good job, but his wife got twice as much money from her three rooming houses. Mr. Oddy always drove the car as fast as possible along Lakeshore Drive and Mrs. Oddy made a long conversation over her shoulder about a trip she had planned for Europe next year.

In the long summer evenings Mrs. Austin was sometimes

lonesome. She sat on the front step till dusk talking to Mrs. Oddy, then she went upstairs to her kitchen to sit down at the window and look out through the leaves on the tree across the street to the well-kept school ground, the shadowed building and the few stars coming out over the roof of the school. Four men standing underneath a lamppost at the corner were trying to make harmony with their voices, but only one fellow had a good voice, the others were timid. She listened, leaning out of the window, hoping they would follow through with the next piece instead of laughing in the middle of it. She heard a loud laugh and the men moved farther down the street, singing softly, lazily. Disappointed, she pulled down the blind and turned on the light.

She heard the Oddys talking downstairs, Mrs. Oddy's voice loud and sharp because her husband was a little deaf. She talked to everybody as though they were a little deaf. That was mainly the trouble with Mrs. Oddy. Mrs. Austin got out her ironing board, adjusting the electric plug in the wall. She patted the board two or three times, hesitating till she decided she didn't feel like ironing at the moment, so she went to her bedroom and looked at herself in the large expensive mirror her mother had given her. Mrs. Austin patted her hair, the knot at the back of the neck, and the wave at the side. She had fine, fair hair. Her nose wasn't a good nose and she was too plump for her height. She was only thirty but looked at least five years older. Her legs were short and plump but shaped nicely at the ankles. She wanted to get thin but couldn't diet for more than five days at a time.

She combed her hair carelessly, staring in the mirror, not concentrating but simply passing time, pleasant thoughts in her head. In the next room she heard a noise and knew the young man, Mr. Jarvis, would be going out soon. She hoped he would speak to her as he passed the open door and maybe ask her to go for a walk. Before Jerry went away she had thought of Mr. Jarvis only occasionally, after a quarrel usually, and had been unhappy when she found herself thinking too often of him. Now that Jerry had left her she enjoyed having long imaginary conversations with the young man and was glad her ankles were slender. She was at least eight years older than he, and really didn't know him very well but liked his small hands, and his slim body, and was sure he had a good education, and would probably wear spats in the winter. Once she had given him a cup of tea and another time had made his bed. She liked making his bed. Vaguely she thought of Jerry, missing him merely because she was used to him. The idea of his walking in the door didn't excite her at all.

She knotted her hair again and returned to the ironing board. Mr. Jarvis, going along the hall, passed the open door and called, "How's the little lady tonight?"

"Fine and dandy," she said.

He passed quickly and she caught only a glimpse of him, but his shoes were shiny and his suit well pressed. She thought of going downstairs and suggesting to Mrs. Oddy that they ask the young man to go motoring with them some night, but realized that Mr. Oddy, who didn't like Jarvis, would say something unpleasant. Oddy had often said the young fellow was too deep for him.

At the end of the month Mrs. Austin had a hard time paying the rent. The landlady suggested Jerry was indeed a peculiar traveling man, and the suggestion irritated Mrs. Austin, so she took twenty-one dollars out of the bank and for three dollars sold a small bookcase to a second-hand dealer who called at the house once a week for rags, bones, and bottles. At four o'clock in the afternoon, Mrs. Oddy, not quite so friendly now, came upstairs to examine critically Mrs. Austin's furniture. She offered to buy the mirror because it was an awkward size and not much use to anybody. Mrs. Austin said her husband might object. Mrs. Oddy eagerly disagreed for she had been waiting a long time to talk plainly about Mr. Austin. She talked rapidly, waving her arms till Mrs. Austin said, "For heaven's sake, Mrs. Oddy, you'll have a hemorrhage if you don't watch out."

But afterward she cried, eager to leave the city and go home, but was ashamed to tell the folks Jerry had left her again. Besides, Jerry would be back soon. Stretched out on the bed, she dabbed her nose with a handkerchief and was glad she had at least been dignified with Mrs. Oddy, practically insisting the woman mind her own business. She got up and looked out of the window at the clean streets in the sunlight. She decided to go out for a walk; many people passing on the street would be company for her.

She took off her housedress and before putting on her blue serge suit with the coat that was a little tight, she stood in front of the mirror, patting her sides and hips critically, dissatisfied. She needed another corset, she thought. She had only a few dollars in the bank, and a little food in the house, but was worried mainly about having a good strong corset. She nodded vigorously at her image in the mirror, many angry words that she might have used to Mrs. Oddy coming into her head.

It was a hot day, there was bright sunlight and men were carrying their coats. She walked all the way downtown. In one of the department stores she bought a corset and arranged to have it sent C.O.D. It was five o'clock before she started to walk home. At her corner she saw Mr. Jarvis getting off the streetcar. He raised his hat, slowing down so that they could walk home together. She talked eagerly about Mrs. Oddy and about being a little lonesome. He had many splendid words he could use carelessly. Nearly all the words pleased her and made her feel happy. He was carrying a yellow slicker though it didn't look like rain, carrying it neatly hooked under his arm close to his hip. She liked his clean fedora at a jaunty angle on his head and was sorry his mouth turned down a little at the corners.

Opposite the Women's Christian Temperance Union they turned the corner. Some boys were playing catch on the road and over in the schoolyard girls were playing baseball.

"I don't think I'll go right up," she said. "I think I'll sit on the steps a while and watch the kids play."

"Want some company?" He grinned at her.

"Oh, I nearly always like company."

They sat on the stone alongside the steps. Mr. Jarvis went on talking, enjoying his own jokes and Mrs. Austin's laughter. For a while she tried watching the girls playing, her eyes following white and red blouses and light and dark skirts on the green grass across the road, and she listened to high-pitched shouting, but losing interest in the game, she wondered how she could keep him talking.

She saw Mr. Oddy turn the corner, a paper under his arm. He came along the street, a big man. He turned up the walk. He nodded curtly and went in the house.

"That guy's an egg," Mr. Jarvis said.

"A what?"

"Boiled a little too long."

"I don't like him much myself."

Mr. Jarvis, getting up, held open the door, and followed her upstairs where he smiled good-naturedly and said good evening. She heard him going downstairs.

She took off her hat and coat and smiled at herself in the mirror. She fingered her hair. For the first time in months she looked closely at her hair and was glad it was so nice. She smiled and knew she wouldn't feel lonesome for some time. She moved around the room, glancing in the mirror to catch glimpses of herself, pretending she was not alone. She ate some supper and found herself comparing Mr. Jarvis with Jerry. She didn't think of Jerry as her husband, simply as a man she had known a long time before he had gone away.

Three days after the walk along the street with Mr. Jarvis she wrote home to tell her mother Jerry had gone away again. Her mother said in a long letter that Jerry was a good-for-nothing who would never amount to a hill of beans in this world, and enclosed was the railroad fare home, if she wanted to come. There was some gossip in the letter about people she had known, two or three girls she had known at school were married and had babies. Thinking of these girls with their babies made her feel bad. Rather than go home and meet these people she would try and get a job in one of the department stores. She put the money for the railroad fare in the bank.

She went downtown but it was hard to get a job because of summer holidays and the slack time in all the big stores. In the evening, wondering what she could sell to the second-hand dealer, she selected two chairs. She put the chairs in a corner, and standing a few feet away, her hands on her hips, made up her mind to pay rent by the week from now on. Mrs. Oddy rapped on the door and wanted to know how Mrs. Austin was getting on with the rent money.

"At the end of the month I'll start paying by the week," Mrs. Austin said.

"Oh, that's up to you, of course."

"Yes, it's up to me."

"Are you sure you can get it? Of course it's none of my business."

"I'll get it all right."

Mrs. Oddy looked around the room and saw the chairs in the corner. Not sure of herself, she said, "Maybe you'll need to be selling something soon."

"Just a thing or two. I don't know what's the matter with Jerry, he should be back any day now." She knew she didn't want Jerry to come back.

"Well, if you're selling stuff, I'll always take that mirror for a fair price."

"Oh, no thanks."

"How much do you want for it?"

"I really wouldn't sell it."

"No?"

"Really no."

Mrs. Oddy, sucking her lips, said mildly, "The girls across the hall say you're a bit cuckoo, you and the mirror, I mean."

"Well, I certainly like the nerve of those hussies."

"Oh, I don't know, they say you're looking for a husband in the mirror."

"Very clever."

"I thought so myself."

The girls across the hall had seen her combing her hair a few times, Mrs. Oddy explained. Mrs. Austin, listening politely, became indignant. Mrs. Austin had intended to speak fiercely but said, "The mirror is company for me in a way."

Mrs. Oddy laughed good-humoredly. "We do have some queer people around here, quaint, I mean. You and the uppish Mr. Jarvis. We'll find out a thing or two about him yet and out he'll go."

Mr. Jarvis had been two days late paying his room rent, she explained.

"What's the matter with him?" she asked.

"There's something fishy."

"How do you mean, Mrs. Oddy?"

"For one thing, where does he work?"

"I don't know. Do you?"

"He doesn't work, that's the point, and he's so superior."

"I don't think so."

"And much above everyone else around here, a mighty suspicious character, I tell you."

Mrs. Oddy went out. When the door was closed Mrs. Austin started to laugh at her, a suspicious woman, a ridiculous woman with a long tongue and a loud voice, but suddenly remembering the girls across the hall she felt unhappy. Two waitresses found her amusing; commonplace girls with huge hands who took off their coats as soon as they got into the house and sat around in their vests. She had never seen Mr. Jarvis without his jacket on. Then she worried Mr. Jarvis would go away and there were things she wanted to say to him. Before going to bed that evening she combed her hair, smiling at herself in the mirror, wondering if she would be able to find the right words so she could tell him how much she liked him and would be happy if she could please him. For the first time she looked carefully at the mirror, the handsome oak frame, the wide bevel. She laughed out loud, thinking of Mrs. Oddy and the girls across the hall.

A week later Mrs. Oddy told her that Mr. Jarvis was again late with his rent and that they had come to a definite conclusion about him, and Mr. Oddy was going to give him so many hours to get out. Mr. Oddy had two minds to go over to a police station and see if the young man had a record.

Mrs. Austin waited for Mr. Jarvis to come home at five-thirty that evening. She imagined herself talking to him till she had convinced him she really loved him and they would be happy together in another city after she divorced Jerry. She was excited, feeling timidly that there was an understanding between them so she could talk freely.

He came up the stairs about half past five. Mrs. Austin heard Mrs. Oddy follow him upstairs. Then Mr. Oddy came up slowly. Mrs. Austin opened her door. Mrs. Oddy was saying, "My husband has something to say to you, young man."

"That's unusual," Mr. Jarvis said.

"I've got nothing much to say," Mr. Oddy said. "You'd better clear out, that's all. This ain't a charity circus."

"No."

"You heard me."

"All right. You mind telling me what's eating you?"

"You got two hours to get out," Oddy said. "I know all about you, I had you looked up."

"You're a stupid man, Mr. Oddy."

"Don't worry about that," Oddy said.

"You're a great ox, Mr. Oddy."

Mrs. Austin, stepping out in the hall, looked coldly at Mrs. Oddy and put her hands on her hips.

"You just can't help being ridiculous, Mrs. Oddy," she said.

"Well, I like your nerve, Mrs. Austin," the landlady said. "An abandoned woman like you," she said. "We've too many people like you. The house'll get a bad name." Mrs. Austin said she would certainly leave the house the next day.

Alone in her room, Mrs. Austin sat down to write home. She was excited and felt she wouldn't really go home at all. She lay awake in bed wondering if she would be able to talk to Mr. Jarvis before he went away.

At noontime the next day he rapped at her door. He smiled and said he heard her say she was going home and he would like to escort her to the train station. He was polite and good-humored. The train didn't go till four, she said. He offered to come at three. When he had gone she phoned an express company and arranged to have her furniture shipped home. She worked hard for an hour packing and cleaning. She dressed slowly and carefully. She took many deep breaths. She put on the blue serge suit and wore a small green felt hat fitting her head snugly.

At three o'clock he called. She hurried around the room, fussing, and getting herself excited. He said not to hurry, they had lots of time to walk to the station. They walked along the street, talking agreeably, a stout little woman in a green felt hat, and a short blue coat a little tight around the waist, trying not to feel much older than the neatly dressed fellow. She let herself think they were going away together. She didn't think he would actually get on the train but it seemed as if he ought to. They talked about the Oddys. He said he would have a new job next week. When she saw the clock at the station tower she was uneasy because she couldn't bring the conversation to a point where she could explain her feeling for him.

"I'm glad I met you at the Oddy's, anyway," she said.

"Well, it was a relief to meet you," he said sincerely. He added that very few women knew how to mind their own business.

In the station she bought her ticket, fumbling in her purse for coins. She felt that something was slipping away from her. "He ought to speak to me," she said to herself fiercely, then felt foolish for thinking it.

"It's funny the Oddys had something against both of us," she said. He laughed boyishly and helped her on the train.

"What did they have against you?" he said.

"They thought I was seeing things in the mirror. How about you?"

"I was holding something back, something up my sleeve, I guess."

"Funny the way they linked us together," she said shyly.

"Yeah."

"Don't you think it was funny?"

"Yeah, you bet. The old dame was seeing things, not you."

She stood on the last step, looking down at him and smiling awkwardly. She got confused when the train moved. "You're a good sport," he said, "I have an aunt just like you."

He waved cheerfully. "Good luck, Mrs. Austin."

"Good luck," she repeated vaguely.

"Goodbye."

"Goodbye."

1928

# A PREDICAMENT

Father Francis, the youngest priest at the cathedral, was hearing confessions on a Saturday afternoon. He stepped out of the confessional to stretch his legs a moment and walked up the left aisle toward the flickering red light of the Precious Blood, mystical in the twilight of the cathedral. Father Francis walked back to the confessional, because too many women were waiting on the penitent bench. There were not so many men.

Sitting again in the confessional, he said a short prayer to the Virgin Mary to get in the mood for hearing confessions. He wiped his lips with his handkerchief, cleared his throat, and pushed back the panel, inclining his ear to hear a woman's confession. The panel slid back with a sharp grating noise. Father Francis whispered his ritual prayer and made the sign of the cross. The woman hadn't been to confession for three months and had missed mass twice for no good reason. He questioned her determinedly, indignant with this woman who had missed mass twice for no good reason. In a steady whisper he told her the story of an old woman who had crawled on the ice to get to mass. The woman hesitated, then told about missing her morning prayers. . . . "Yes, my child yes, my child . . ." "And about certain thoughts . . ." "Now, about these thoughts; let's look at it in this way . . ." He gave the woman absolution and told her to say the beads once for her penance.

Closing the panel on the women's side he sat quietly for a moment in the darkness of the confessional. He was a young priest, very interested in confessions.

Father Francis turned to the other side of the confessional, pushing back the panel to hear some man's confession. Resting his chin on his hand after making the sign of the cross, he did not bother trying to discern the outline of the head and shoulders of the man kneeling in the corner.

The man said in a husky voice: "I wanna get off at the corner of King and Yonge Street."

Father Francis sat up straight, peering through the wire work. The man's head was moving. He could see his nose and his eyes. His heart began to beat unevenly. He sat back quietly.

"Cancha hear me, wasamatter, I wanna get off at King and Yonge," the man said insistently, pushing his nose through the wire work.

On the man's breath there was a strong smell of whiskey. Father Francis nervously slid the panel back into position. As the panel slid into place he knew it sounded like the closing of doors on a bus. There he was hearing confessions, and a drunken man on the other side of the panel thought him a conductor on a bus. He would go into the vestry and tell Father Marlow.

Father Francis stepped out of the confessional to look around the cathedral. Men and women in the pews and on the penitents' benches wondered why he had come out of the confessional twice in the last few minutes when so many were waiting. Father Francis wasn't feeling well, that was the trouble. Walking up the aisle, he rubbed his smooth cheek with his hand, thinking hard. If he had the man thrown out he might be a tough customer and there would be a disturbance. There would be a disturbance in the cathedral. Such a disturbance would be sure to get in the papers. Everything got in the papers. There was no use telling it to anybody. Walking erectly he went back to the confessional. Father Francis was sweating.

Rubbing his shoulder-blades uneasily against the back of the confessional, he decided to hear a woman's confession. It was evading the issue – it was a compromise, but it didn't matter; he was going to hear a woman's confession first.

The woman, encouraged by many questions from Father Francis, made an extraordinarily good confession, though sometimes he did not seem to be listening very attentively. He thought he could hear the man moving. The man was drunk – drunkenness, the over-indulgence of an appetite, the drunken state. Scholastic psychology. Cardinal Mercier's book on psychology had got him through the exam at the seminary.

"When you feel you're going to tell a lie, say a short prayer to Mary the mother of God," he said to the woman.

"Yes, father."

"Some lies are more serious than others."

"Yes, father."

"But they are lies just the same."

"I tell mostly white lies," she said.

"They are lies, lies, lies, just the same. They may not endanger your soul, but they lead to something worse. Do you see?"

"Yes, father."

"Will you promise to say a little prayer every time?"

Father Francis could not concentrate on what the woman was saying. But he wanted her to stay there for a long time. She was company. He would try and concentrate on her. He could not forget the drunken man for more than a few moments.

The woman finished her confession. Father Francis, breathing heavily, gave her absolution. Slowly he pushed back the panel – a street-car, a conductor swinging back the doors on a street-car. He turned deliberately to the other side of the confessional, but hesitated, eager to turn and hear another confession. It was no use – it couldn't go on in that way. Closing his eyes he said three "Our Fathers" and three "Hail, Marys," and felt much better. He was calm and the man might have gone.

He tried to push back the panel so it would not make much noise, but moving slowly, it grated loudly. He could see the man's head bobbing up, watching the panel sliding back.

"Yes, my son," Father Francis said deliberately.

"I got to get off at King and Yonge," the man said stubbornly.

"You better go, you've got no business here."

"Say, there, did you hear me say King and Yonge?"

The man was getting ugly. The whiskey smelt bad in the confessional. Father Francis drew back quickly and half closed the panel. That same grating noise. It put an idea into his head. He said impatiently: "Step lively there; this is King and Yonge. Do you want to go past your stop?"

"All right, brother," the man said slowly, getting up clumsily.

"Move along now," Father Francis said authoritatively.

"I'm movin'; don't get so huffy," the man said, swinging aside the curtains of the confessional, stepping out to the aisle.

Father Francis leaned back in the confessional and nervously gripped the leather seat. He began to feel very happy. There were no thoughts at all in his head. Suddenly he got up and stepped out to the aisle. He stood watching a man going down the aisle swaying almost imperceptibly. The men and women in the pews watched Father Francis curiously, wondering if he was really unwell because he had come out of the confessional three times in a half-hour. Again he went into the confessional.

At first Father Francis was happy hearing the confessions, but he became restive. He should have used shrewd judgment. With that drunken man he had gone too far, forgotten himself in the confessional. He had descended to artifice in the confessional to save himself from embarrassment.

At the supper-table he did not talk much to the other priests. He had a feeling he would not sleep well that night. He would lie awake trying to straighten everything out. The thing would first have to be settled in his own conscience. Then perhaps he would tell the bishop.

1928

# AN ESCAPADE

Snow fell softly and the sidewalks were wet. Mrs. Rose Carey had on her galoshes and enjoyed the snow underfoot. She walked slowly, big flakes falling on her lamb coat and clinging to her hair, the falling snow giving her, in her warm coat, a feeling of self-indulgence. She stood on the corner of Bloor and Yonge, an impressive woman, tall, stout, good-looking for forty-two, and waited for the traffic light. Few people were on this corner at half past eight, Sunday evening. A policeman, leaning against a big plate-glass window, idly watched her cross the road and look up to the clock on the fire hall and down the street to the theater lights, where Reverend John Simpson held Sunday service. She had kept herself late, intending to enter the theater unnoticed, and sit in a back seat, ready to leave as soon as the service was over. Bothered by her own shyness, she remembered that her husband had asked if Father Conley was speaking tonight in the cathedral.

Under the theater lights someone said to her: "This way, lady. Step this way, right along now."

She stopped abruptly, watching the little man with a

long nose and green sweater, pacing up and down in front of the entrance, waving his hands. He saw her hesitating and came close to her. He had on a flat black hat, and walked with his toes turned out. "Step lively, lady," he muttered, wagging his head at her.

She was scared and would have turned away but a man got out of a car at the curb and smiled at her. "Don't be afraid of Dick," he said. The man had grey hair and a red face and wore a tie pin in a wide black tie. He was going into the theater.

"Run along, Dick," he said and, turning to Mrs. Carey, he explained: "He's absolutely harmless. They call him Crazy Dick."

"Thank you very much," Mrs. Carey said.

"I hope he didn't keep you from going in," he said, taking off his hat. He had a generous smile.

"I didn't know him, that was all," she said, feeling foolish as he opened the door for her.

The minister was moving on stage and talking quietly. She knew it was the minister because she had seen his picture in the papers and recognized the Prince Albert coat and the four-in-hand tie with the collar open at the throat. She took three steps down the aisle, fearfully aware that many people were looking at her, and sat down, four rows from the back. Only once before had she been in a strange church, when a friend of her husband's had got married, and it hadn't seemed like church. She unbuttoned her coat, leaving a green and black scarf lying across her full breasts, and relaxed in the seat, getting her big body comfortable. Someone sat down beside her. The man with the grey hair and red face was sitting beside her. She was annoyed, she knew she was too aware of his closeness. The minister walked the length of the platform, his voice pleasant and soothing. She tried to follow the flow of words but was too restless. She had come in too late, that was the trouble. So she tried concentrating, closing her eyes, but thought of a trivial and amusing argument she had had with her husband. The minister was trying to describe the afterlife and some of his words seemed beautiful, but she had no intention of taking his religious notions seriously.

The seat was uncomfortable, and she stretched a little, crossing her legs at the ankles. The minister had a lovely voice, but so far he'd said nothing sensational, and she felt out of place in the theater and slightly ashamed.

The man on her right was sniffling. Puzzled, she watched him out of the corner of her eye, as he gently dabbed at his eyes with a large white handkerchief. The handkerchief was fresh and the creases firm. One plump hand held four corners, making a pad, and he was watching the minister intently.

She was anxious not to appear ill-bred, but a man, moved by the minister's words, or an old thought, was sitting beside her, crying. She did not glance at him again till she realized that his elbow was on the arm of her seat, supporting his chin, while he blinked and moved his head. He was feeling so bad she was uncomfortable, but thought that he looked gentlemanly, though feeling miserable. He was probably a nice man, and she was sorry for him.

She expected him to get up and go out. Other people were noticing him. A fat woman, in the seat ahead, craned her neck. Mrs. Carey wanted to slap her. The man put the handkerchief over his face and didn't lift his head. The minister was talking rapidly. Mrs. Carey suddenly felt absolutely alone in the theater. Impulsively she touched the man's arm, leaning toward him, whispering: "I'm awfully sorry for you, sir."

She patted his arm a second time, and he looked at her

helplessly, and went to speak, but merely shook his head and patted the back of her hand.

"I'm sorry," she repeated gently.

"Thank you very much."

"I hope it's all right now," she whispered.

He spoke quietly: "Something the minister said, it reminded me of my brother who died last week. My younger brother."

People in the row ahead were turning angrily. She became embarrassed, and leaned back in her seat, very dignified, and looked directly ahead, aware that the man was now holding her hand. Startled, she twitched, but he didn't notice. His thoughts seemed so far away. She reflected it could do no harm to let him hold her hand a moment, if it helped him.

She listened to the minister but didn't understand a word he was saying, and glanced curiously at the grey-haired man, who didn't look at her but still held her hand. He was handsome, and a feeling she had not had for years was inside her, her hand suddenly so sensitive. She closed her eyes. Then the minister stopped speaking and, knowing the congregation was ready to sing a hymn, she looked at his hand on hers, and at him. He had put away the handkerchief and now was smiling sadly. She avoided his eyes, removing her hand as she stood up to sing the hymn. Her cheeks were warm. She tried to stop thinking altogether. It was necessary to leave at once only she would have to squeeze by his knees to reach the aisle. She buttoned her coat while they were singing, ready to slip past him. She was surprised when he stepped out to the aisle, allowing her to pass, but didn't look at him. Erect, she walked slowly up the aisle, her eyes on the door. Then she heard steps and knew he was following. An usher held open the door and she smiled awkwardly. The usher smiled.

Outside, she took a few quick steps, then stood still, bewildered, expecting Crazy Dick to be on the street. She thought of the green sweater and funny flat hat. Through the doorway she saw the grey-haired man smiling at the usher and putting on his hat, the tie pin shining in the light. Tucking her chin into her high fur collar she walked rapidly down the street. It was snowing harder, driving along on a wind. When she got to a car stop she looked back and saw him standing on the sidewalk in front of the theater doors. A streetcar was coming. She was sure he took a few steps toward her, but she got on the car. The conductor said, "Fares please," but hardly glancing at him, she shook wet snow from her coat and sat down, taking three deep breaths, while her cheeks tingled. She felt tired, and her heart was thumping.

She got off the car at Shuter Street. She didn't want to go straight home, and was determined to visit the cathedral.

On the side street the snow was thick. Men from the rooming houses were shovelling the sidewalks, the shovels scraping on concrete. She lifted her eyes to the illuminated cross on the cathedral spire. The congregation had come out half an hour ago, and she felt lonely walking in the dark toward the light.

Inside the cathedral she knelt down halfway up the center aisle. She closed her eyes to pray, and remembered midnight mass in the cathedral, the Archbishop with his miter and staff, and the choir of boys' voices. A vestry door opened, a priest passed in the shadow beside the altar, took a book from a pew, and went out. She closed her eyes again and said many prayers, repeating her favorite ones over and over, but often she thought of her husband at home. She prayed hard so she could go home and not be bothered by anything that had happened in the theater. She prayed for

half an hour, feeling better gradually, till she hardly remembered the man in the theater, and fairly satisfied, she got up
and left the cathedral.

1928

# NOW THAT APRIL'S HERE

As soon as they got the money they bought two large black hats and left America to live permanently in Paris. They were bored in their native city in the Middle West and convinced that the American continent had nothing to offer them. Charles Milford, who was four years older than Johnny Hill, had a large round head that ought to have belonged to a Presbyterian minister. Johnny had a rather chinless faun's head. When they walked down the street the heads together seemed more interesting. They came to Paris in the late autumn.

They got on very quickly in Montparnasse. In the afternoons they wandered around the streets, looking in art gallery windows at the prints of the delicate clever unsubstantial line work of Foujita. Pressing his nose against the window Johnny said, "Quite a sound technique, don't you think, Charles?"

"Oh sound, quite sound."

They never went to the Louvre or the museum in the Luxembourg Gardens, thinking it would be in the fashion of tourists, when they intended really to settle in Paris. In the evenings they sat together at a table on the terrace of the café, and clients, noticing them, began thinking of them as "the two boys." One night, Fanny Lee, a blonde, fat American girl who had been an entertainer at Zelli's until she lost her shape, but not her hilarity, stepped over to the boys' table and yelled, "Oh, gee, look what I've found." They were discovered. Fanny, liking them for their quiet, well-mannered behavior, insisted on introducing them to everybody at the bar. They bowed together at the same angle, smiling so cheerfully, so obviously willing to be obliging, that Fanny was anxious to have them follow her from one bar to another, hoping they would pay for her drinks.

They felt much better after the evening with Fanny. Johnny, the younger one, who had a small income of $100 a month, was supporting Charles, who, he was sure, would one day become a famous writer. Johnny did not take his own talent very seriously; he had been writing his memoirs of their adventures since they were fifteen, after reading George Moore's *Confessions of A Young Man*. George Moore's book had been mainly responsible for their visit to Paris. Johnny's memoirs, written in a snobbishly aristocratic manner, had been brought up to the present and now he was waiting for something to happen to them. They were much happier the day they got a cheaper room on Boulevard Arago near the tennis court.

They were happy at the cafés in the evenings but liked best being at home together in their own studio, five minutes away from the cafés. They lay awake in bed together a long time talking about everything that happened during the day, consoling each other by saying the weather would be finer later on and anyway they could always look forward to the spring days next April. Fanny Lee, who really liked them, was extraordinarily friendly and only cost them nine or ten drinks an evening. They lay awake in bed talking about her, sometimes laughing so hard the bed springs squeaked. Charles, his large round head buried in the pillow, snickered gleefully listening to Johnny making fun of Fanny Lee.

Soon they knew everybody in the Quarter, though no one knew either of them very intimately. People sitting at the café in the evening when the lights were on, saw them crossing the road together under the street lamp, their bodies leaning forward at the same angle, and walking on tiptoe. No one knew where they were going. Really they weren't going anywhere in particular. They had been sitting at the café, nibbling pieces of sugar they had dipped in coffee, till Johnny said, "We're being seen here too much, don't you think, Charles?" And Charles said, "I think we ought to be seen at all the bars. We ought to go more often to the new bar." So they had paid for their coffee and walked over to a side-street bar panelled in the old English style, with a good-natured English bartender, and sat together at a table listening to the careless talk of five customers at the bar, occasionally snickering out loud when a sentence overheard seemed incredibly funny. Stan Mason, an ingenuous heavy drinker, who had cultivated a very worldly feeling sitting at the same bars every night, explaining the depth of his sophistication to the same people, saw the boys holding their heads together and yelled, "What are you two little goats snickering at?" The boys stood up, bowing to him so politely and seriously he was ashamed of himself and asked them to have a drink with him. The rest of the evening they laughed so charmingly at his jokes he was fully convinced they were the brightest youngsters who had come to the Quarter in years. He asked the boys if they liked Paris, and smiling at each other and raising their glasses together they said that architecturally it was a great improvement over America. They had never been in New York or any other large American city but had no use for American buildings. There was no purpose in arguing directly with them. Charles would simply have raised his eyebrows and glanced slyly at Johnny, who would have snickered with his fingers over his mouth. Mason, who was irritated, and anxious to make an explanation, began talking slowly about the early block-like houses of the Taos Indians and the geometrical block style of the New York skyscrapers. For ten minutes he talked steadily about the Indians and a development of the American spirit. The boys listened politely, never moving their heads at all. Watching them, while he talked, Mason began to feel uncomfortable. He began to feel that anything he had to say was utterly unimportant because the two boys were listening to him so politely. But he finished strongly and said, "What do you think?"

"Do you really believe all that's important?" Charles said.

"I don't know, maybe it's not."

"Well, as long as you don't think it important," Johnny said.

At home the boys sat on the edge of the bed, talking about Stan Mason and snickered so long they were up half the night.

They had their first minor disagreement in the Quarter one evening in November with Milton Simpson, a prosperous, bright and effeminate young American business man who was living in Paris because he felt vaguely that the best approach to life was through all the arts together. He was secretly trying to write, paint and compose pieces for the piano. The boys were at a small bar with a floor for dancing and an American jazz artist at the piano, and Simpson and his wife came in. Passing, Simpson brushed against Charles, who, without any provocation at all, suddenly pushed him away. Simpson pushed too and they stood there pushing each other. Simpson began waving his arms in circles, and the man at the piano threw his arms around Charles, dragging him away. Neither one of them could have hurt each other seriously and everybody in the room was laughing at them. Finally Simpson sat down and Charles, standing alone, began to tremble so much he had to put his head down on the table and cry. His shoulders were moving jerkily. Then everybody in the room was sorry for Charles. Johnny, putting his arm around him, led him outside. Simpson, whose thin straight lips were moving nervously, was so impressed by Charles's tears, that he and his wife followed them outside and over to the corner café where they insisted on sitting down with them at one of the brown oblong tables inside. Simpson bought the boys a brandy and his wife, who was interested in the new psychology, began to talk eagerly with Charles, evidently expecting some kind of an emotional revelation. The boys finished their brandies and Simpson quickly ordered another for them. For an hour the boys drank brandies and listened patiently and seriously to Simpson, who was talking ecstatically because he thought they were sensitive, sympathetic boys. They only smiled at him when he excitedly called them "sensitive organisms." Charles, listening wide-eyed, was nervously scratching his cheek with the nail of his right forefinger till the flesh was torn and raw.

Afterwards, undressing slowly at home, Johnny said, "Simpson is such a bore, don't you think so, Charles?"

"I know, but the brandies were very good." They never mentioned the fight at the bar.

"It was so funny when you looked at him with that blue-eyed Danish stare of yours," Johnny said, chuckling.

"People think I expect them to do tricks like little animals when I look at them like that," Charles explained.

Naked, they sat on the edge of the bed, laughing at Simpson's eagerness to buy them brandies, and they made so many witty sallies they tired themselves out and fell asleep.

For two weeks they weren't seen around the cafés. Charles was writing another book and Johnny was typing it for him. It was a literary two weeks for both of them. They talked about all the modern authors and Johnny suggested that not one of them since Henry James had half Charles's perception or subtle delicacy. Actually Charles did write creditably enough and everything he did had three or four good paragraphs in it. The winter was coming on and when this literary work was finished they wanted to go south.

No one ever knew how they got the money to go to the Riviera for the winter. No one knew how they were able to drink so much when they had only Johnny's hundred dollars a month. At Nice, where Stan Mason was living, they were very cheerful and Mason, admiring their optimism because he thought they had no money, let them have a room in his apartment. They lived with him till the evening he put his ear against the thin wall and heard them snickering, sitting on the edge of the bed. They were talking about him and having a good laugh. Stan Mason was hurt because he had thought them bright boys and really liked them. He merely suggested next morning that they would have to move since he needed the room.

The boys were mainly happy in Nice because they were looking forward to returning to Paris in April. The leaves would be on all the trees and people would be sitting outside on the terraces at the cafés. Everybody they met in Nice told them how beautiful it was in Paris in the early spring, so they counted upon having the happiest time they had ever had together. When they did leave Nice they owed many thousand francs for an hotel bill, payment of which they had avoided by tossing their bags out of the window at two o'clock in the morning. They even had a little extra money at the time, almost twenty dollars they had received from an elderly English gentleman, who had suggested, after talking to them all one morning, he would pay well to see the boys make a "tableau" for him. The old fellow was enthusiastic about the "tableau" and the boys had something to amuse them for almost two weeks.

They returned to Paris the first week in April. Now that April was here they had expected to have so much fun, but the weather was disagreeable and cold. This year the leaves were hardly on the trees and there was always rain in the dull skies. They assured each other that the dull days could not last because it was April and Paris was the loveliest city in the world in the early spring.

Johnny's father had been writing many irritable letters from England, where he was for a few months, and the boys decided it was an opportune time for Johnny to go and see him for a week. When he returned they would be together for the good days at the end of the month.

People were not very interested in Charles while Johnny was away. They liked him better when he was with Johnny. All week he walked around on tiptoe or sat alone at a corner table in the café. The two boys together seemed well mannered and bright, but Charles, alone, looked rather insignificant. Without thinking much about it he knew the feeling people had for him and avoided company, waiting impatiently for the days to pass, worrying about Johnny. He said to Stan Mason late one night, "I hope Johnny has enough sense not to pick up with a girl over in England."

"Why worry? Do it yourself now."

"Oh I do, too, only I don't take them as seriously as Johnny does. Not that I mind Johnny having a girl," he said, "only I don't want him to have a complicated affair with one."

The night Johnny returned to Paris they went around to all the bars and people, smiling, said, "There go the two boys." They were happy, nervously happy, and Charles was scratching his cheek with his nail. Later on they wanted to be entirely alone and left the café district and the crowds to walk down the narrow side streets to the Seine while Johnny, chuckling, related the disagreeable circumstances of his visit to his father. His father had contended that he was a wastrel who ought to be earning his own living, and Johnny had jeeringly pointed out that the old man had inherited his money without having to work for it. They were angry with each other, and the father had slapped Johnny, who retaliated by poking him in the jaw. That was the most amusing part of the story the boys talked about, walking along the left bank of the Seine opposite the Louvre. Casually Johnny told about a few affairs he had with cheap women in London, and Charles understood that these affairs had not touched him at all. It was a warm clear evening, the beginning of the real spring days in April, and the boys were happy walking by the river in the moonlight, the polished water surface reflecting the red and white lights on the bridges.

Near the end of the month Constance Foy, whom the boys had known at Nice, came to Paris, and they asked her to live with them. She was a simple-minded fat-faced girl with a boy's body and short hair dyed red, who had hardly a franc left and was eager to live with anybody who would keep her. For a week the three of them were happy in the big studio. The boys were proud of their girl and took her around to all the bars, buying drinks for her, actually managing to do it on the hundred dollars a month. In the nighttime they were impartial and fair about Constance, who appeared to have all her enthusiasm for the one who, at the moment, was making love to her. But she said to Stan Mason one evening, "I don't know whether or not I ought to be there messing up that relationship."

"Aren't the three of you having a good time?"

"Good enough, but funny things are happening."

The boys were satisfied till Charles began to feel that Johnny was making love to Constance too seriously. It was disappointing, for he had never objected to having her in the studio, and now Johnny was so obvious in his appreciation of her. Charles, having this feeling, was now unable to touch her at all, and resented Johnny's unabated eagerness for her. It was all the same to Constance.

Before the end of the month the two boys were hardly speaking to each other, though always together at the cafés in the evening. It was too bad, for the days were bright and clear, the best of the April weather, and Paris was gay and lively. The boys were sad and hurt and sorry but determined to be fair with each other. The evening they were at the English bar, sitting at one of the table beer barrels, Charles had a hard time preventing himself crying. He was very much in love with Johnny and felt him slipping away. Johnny, his fingers over his mouth, sometimes shook his head but didn't know what to say.

Finally they left the bar to walk home. They were going down the short, quiet street leading to the Boulevard.

"What are you going to do about Constance?" Charles said.

"If it's all the same to you I'll have her to myself."

"But what are you going to do with her?"

"I don't know."

"You'd let a little tart like that smash things," Charles said, shaking his hand at Johnny.

"Don't you dare call her a tart."

"Please, Johnny, don't strike at me."

But Johnny who was nearly crying with rage swung his palm at Charles, hitting him across the face. Stan Mason had just turned the corner at the Boulevard, coming up to the bar to have a drink, and saw the two of them standing there.

"What's wrong?" he said.

"I begged him, I implored him not to hit me," Charles said.

"Oh, I hit him, I hit him, I hit him, what'll I do?" Johnny said, tears running down his cheeks.

They stood there crying and shaking their heads, but would not go home together. Finally Charles consented to go with Stan to his hotel and Johnny went home to Constance.

Charles stayed with Mason all week. He would not eat at all and didn't care what he was drinking. The night Mason told him Johnny was going back to America, taking Constance with him, he shook his head helplessly and said, "How could he hit me, how could he hit me, and he knew I loved him so much."

"But what are you going to do?"

"I don't know."

"How are you going to live?"

"I'll make enough to have a drink occasionally."

At the time, he was having a glass of Scotch, his arm trembling so weakly he could hardly lift the glass.

The day Johnny left Paris it rained and it was cold again, sitting at the café in the evening. There had been only one really good week in April. The boys always used to sit at the cafés without their hats on, their hair brushed nicely. This evening Charles had to go home and get his overcoat and the big black hat he had bought in America. Sitting alone at his table in the cool evening, his overcoat wrapped around him, and the black hat on, he did not look the same at all. It was the first time he had worn the hat in France.

1929

# THE FAITHFUL WIFE

Until a week before Christmas George worked in the station restaurant at the lunch counter. The weather was extraordinarily cold, then the sun shone strongly for a few days, though it was always cold again in the evenings. There were three other men working at the counter. They had a poor reputation. Women, unless they were careless and easygoing, never started a conversation with them over lunch at noontime. The girls at the station always avoided the red-capped negro porters and the countermen.

George was working there till he got enough money to go back home for a week and then start late in the year at college. He had wiry brown hair receding on his forehead and bad upper teeth, but he was very polite and open. Steve, the plump Italian with the waxed black moustache, who had charge of the restaurant, was very fond of George.

Many people passed the restaurant window on the way to the platform and the trains. The four men got to know some of them. Girls, brightly dressed, loitered in front of the open door, smiling at George, who saw them so often he knew their first names. Other girls, with a few minutes to spare before going back to work, used to walk up and down the tiled tunnel to the waiting room, loafing the time away, but they never glanced in at the countermen. It was cold outside, the streets were slippery, and it was warm in the station, that was all.

George watched one girl every day at noon hour. The others had also noticed her, and two or three times she came in for a cup of coffee, but she was so gentle, and aloofly pleasant, and so unobtrusively beyond them, they were afraid to try and amuse her with easy cheerful talk. George wished she had never seen him in the restaurant behind the counter, though he knew she had not noticed him at all. Her cheeks were usually rosy from the cold wind outside. When she went out of the door to walk up and down for a few minutes, an agreeable expression on her face, she never once looked back at the restaurant. George, pouring coffee, did not expect her to look back. She was about twenty-eight, pretty, rather shy, and dressed plainly and poorly in a thin, blue cloth coat. Then, one day she had on a fawn felt hat. She smiled politely at him when having a cup of coffee, and as long as possible he stood opposite her, cleaning the counter with a damp cloth.

The last night he worked at the station he went out at about half past eight in the evening, for he had an hour to himself, and then he would work till ten o'clock. In the morning he was going home, so he walked out of the station and down the side street to the docks, and was having only pleasant thoughts, passing the warehouses, looking out over the dark cold lake and liking the tang of the wind on his face. Christmas was only a week away. The falling snow was melting when it hit the sidewalk. He was glad he was through with the job at the restaurant.

An hour later, back at the counter, Steve said, "A dame just phoned you, George, and left her number."

"You know who she was?"

"No, you got too many girls, George. Don't you know the number?"

"Never saw it before."

He called the number and did not recognize the voice that answered. A woman was asking pleasantly if he remembered her. He said he did not. She said she had had a cup of coffee that afternoon at noontime, and added that she had worn a blue coat and a fawn-colored felt hat, and even though she had not spoken to him, she thought he would remember her.

"Good Lord," he said.

She wanted to know if he would come and see her at ten-thirty that evening. He said he would, and hardly heard her giving the address. Steve and the others started to kid him brightly, but he was too astonished, wondering how she had found out his name, to bother with them. As they said good-bye to him and elbowed him in the ribs, urging him to celebrate on his last night in the city, Steve shook his head and pulled the ends of his moustache down into his lips.

The address the girl had given him was only eight blocks away, so he walked, holding his hands clenched in his pockets, for he was cold and uncertain. The brownstone, opposite a public school on a side street, was a large old rooming house. A light was in a window on the second storey over the door. Ringing the bell he didn't really expect anyone to answer, and was surprised when the girl opened the door.

"Good evening," he said shyly.

"Come upstairs," she said smiling and practical.

In the front room he took off his overcoat and hat and sat down, noticing, out of the corner of his eye, that she was slim and had nice fair hair and lovely eyes. But she was moving nervously. He had intended to ask at once how she'd found out his name, but forgot as soon as she sat down opposite him on a camp bed and smiled shyly. She had on a red woollen sweater, fitting tightly at the waist. Twice he shook his head, unable to get used to having her there opposite him, nervous and expectant. The trouble was she'd always seemed so aloof.

"You're not very friendly," she said awkwardly.

"Yes I am. I am."

"Why don't you come over here and sit beside me?"

He sat beside her on the camp bed, smiling stupidly. He was slow to see that she was waiting for him to put his arms around her. He kissed her eagerly and she held on to him, her heart thumping, and she kept on holding him, closing her eyes and breathing deeply every time he kissed her. He became very eager and she got up suddenly, walking up and down the room, looking at the cheap alarm clock on a bureau. The room was clean but poorly furnished.

"What's the matter?" he said.

"My girlfriend, the one I room with, she'll be home in twenty minutes."

"Come here anyway."

"Please sit down, please do," she said.

He sat down beside her. When he kissed her she did not object but her lips were dry, her shoulders were trembling and she kept watching the clock. Though she was holding his wrist so tightly her nails dug into the skin, he knew she would be glad when he had to go. He kissed her again and she drew her left hand slowly over her lips.

"You really must be out of here before Irene comes home," she said.

"But I've only kissed and hugged you and you're wonderful." He noticed the red ring mark on her finger.

"You sure you're not waiting for your husband to come home?" he said irritably.

Frowning, looking away, she said, "Why do you have to say that?"

"There's a ring mark on your finger."

"I can't help it," she said, and began to cry quietly. "I am waiting for my husband to come home. He'll be here at Christmas."

"Too bad. Can't we do something about it?"

"I love my husband. I do, I really do, and I'm faithful to him too."

"Maybe I'd better go," he said, feeling ridiculous.

"He's at a sanitarium. He got his spine hurt in the war, then he got tuberculosis. He's pretty bad. They've got to carry him around. We want to love each other every time we meet, but we can't."

"That's tough, poor kid. I suppose you've got to pay for him."

"Yes."

"You have many men?"

"I don't want any."

"They come here to see you."

"No, no. I don't know what got into me. I liked you, and felt a little crazy."

"I'll slide along. What's your first name?"

"Lola. You'd better go now."

"Couldn't I see you again?" he said suddenly.

"No, you're going away tomorrow," she said, smiling confidently.

"So you've got it all figured out. Supposing I don't go?"

"Please, you must."

Her arms were trembling when she held his overcoat. She wanted him to go before Irene came home.

"You didn't give me much time," he said flatly.

"No. You're a lovely guy. Kiss me."

"You got that figured out too."

"Just kiss and hold me once more, George." She held on to him as if she did not expect to be embraced again for a long time, and he said, "I think I'll stay in the city a while longer."

"It's too bad. You've got to go. We can't see each other again."

In the poorly lighted hall she looked lovely, her cheeks were flushed. As he went out of the door and down the walk to the street he remembered that he hadn't asked how she had found out his name. Snow was falling lightly and there were hardly any footprints on the sidewalk. All he could think of was that he ought to go back to the restaurant and ask Steve for his job again. Steve was fond of him. But he knew he could not. "She had it all figured out," he muttered, turning up his coat collar.

1929

# THE CHISELER

O ld Poppa Tabb was never really cut out to be a manager for a fighter. He seemed too short and too fat, although he'd only got soft around the waist during the last year as Billy got a lot of work in the small clubs, fighting at the flyweight limit. If it hadn't been for his old man, Billy would have been a chesty little bum standing at night on street corners spitting after cops when they passed. The old man and Billy were both the same size – five foot two in their bare feet – only the old man weighed one hundred and thirty-five pounds and Billy one hundred and twelve.

Poppa Tabb had always wanted his son to amount to something and didn't like the stories he heard about his son being chased by policemen. It hurt him when Billy was sent down for three months for tripping a cop and putting the boots to him. So he thought his son might want to be a fighter and he made an arrangement with a man named Smooth Cassidy, who was very experienced with young fighters, to act as Billy's trainer and handler, and he himself held the contract as the manager. After Billy started fighting in the small clubs, Poppa Tabb bought two white sweaters with "Billy Tabb" on the back in black letters, one for himself and one for Smooth Cassidy. It was at this time that Poppa Tabb began to get a little fat around the waist. He used to sit over in the sunlight by the door of the fire hall and tell the firemen about Billy. He used to sit there and talk about "me and Billy," and have a warm glowing feeling down deep inside.

Late at night he used to wait for Billy to come home from drinking parties with fast white women. He waited, walking up and down the narrow hall of their flat, and he shook his head and imagined that Billy had gotten into an accident. When Billy came in and started to take off his shoes, Poppa Tabb, sitting opposite him, was so worried he said: "I don't want you strolling your stuff so late, Billy."

Billy looked at him. Standing up and coming closer, he said to his old man: "You tryin' to get on me?"

"No, only I know what's good for you, son."

"Yeah. Maybe I know what's good for me. Maybe I know you ain't so good for me."

"There some things you got to do, Billy."

Billy raised his fist. "You want something? You want some of this?"

"You don't go hitting me, Billy."

"Say you want some and I smack you. Or get off me."

After that, when Billy came in late Poppa Tabb just looked at his bright sharp eyes and smelled the cologne on his clothes and couldn't say anything to him. He only wished that Billy would tell him everything. He wanted to share the exciting times of his life and have the same feeling, talking to him, that he got when he held up the water pail and handed the sponge to Smooth Cassidy when he was ringside.

Billy did so well in the small clubs that bigger promoters offered him work. But they always talked business with Smooth

Cassidy, and Poppa Tabb felt they were trying to leave him out. Just before Billy fought Frankie Genaro, the flyweight champion, who was willing to fight almost anyone in town because the purses for flyweights were so small, Poppa Tabb heard stories that Dick Hallam, who liked owning pieces of fighters, was getting interested in Billy and taking him out to parties. At nights now Billy hardly ever talked to his old man, but still expected him to wait on him like a servant.

Old Poppa Tabb was thinking about it the afternoon of the Genaro fight and he was so worried he went downtown looking for Billy, asking the newsboys at the corner, old friends of Billy's, if they had seen him. In the afternoon, Billy usually passed by the newsstand and talked with the boys till smaller kids came along and whispered, staring at him. Poppa Tabb found Billy in a diner looking to see if his name had gotten into the papers, thrusting big forkfuls of chocolate cake into his wide mouth. The old man looked at him and wanted to rebuke him for eating the chocolate cake but was afraid, so he said: "What's happening Billy?"

"Uh," Billy said.

The old man said carefully: "I don't like this here talk about you stepping around too much with that Hallam guy."

"You don't?" Billy said, pushing his fine brown felt hat back on his narrow brow and wrinkling his forehead. "What you going do 'bout it?"

"Well, nothing, I guess, Billy."

"You damn right," Billy said flatly. Without looking up again he went on eating cake and reading the papers intently as if his old man hadn't spoken to him at all.

The Genaro fight was an extraordinary success for Billy. Of course, he didn't win. Genaro, who was in his late thirties, went into a kind of short waltz and then clutched and held on when he was tired, and when he was fresh and strong he used a swift pecking left hand that cut the eyes. But Billy liked a man to come in close and hold on, for he put his head on Genaro's chest and flailed with both hands, and no one could hold his arms. Once he got in close, his arms worked with a beautiful tireless precision, and the crowd, liking a great body-puncher, began to roar, and Poppa Tabb put his head down and jumped around, and then he looked up at Billy, whose eye was cut and whose lips were thick and swollen. It didn't matter whether he won the flyweight title, for soon he would be a bantamweight, and then a featherweight, the way he was growing.

Everybody was shouting when Billy left the ring, holding his bandaged hands up high over his head, and he rushed up the aisle to the dressing room, the crowd still roaring as he passed through the seats and the people who tried to touch him with their hands. His gown had fallen off his shoulders. His seconds were running on ahead shouting: "Out of the way! Out of the way!" and Billy, his face puffed, his brown body glistening under the lights, followed, looking straight ahead, his wild eyes bulging. The crowd closed in behind him at the door of the dressing room.

Poppa Tabb had a hard time getting through the crowd for he couldn't go up the aisle as fast as Billy and the seconds. He was holding his cap tightly in his hands. He had put on a coat over his white 'Billy Tabb' sweater. His thin hair was wet as he lurched forward. The neckband of his shirt stuck up from under the sweater and a yellow collar-button shone in the lamplight. "Let me in, let me in," he kept saying, almost hysterical with excitement. "It's my kid, that's my kid." The policeman at the door, who recognized him, said: "Come on in, Pop."

Billy Tabb was stretched out on the rubbing-table and his handlers were gently working over him. The room smelled of liniment. Everybody was talking. Smooth Cassidy was sitting at the end of the table, whispering with Dick Hallam, a tall thin man wearing well-pressed trousers. Old Poppa Tabb stood there blinking and then moved closer to Billy. He did not like Hallam's gold rings and his pearl-grey felt hat and his sharp nose. Old Poppa Tabb was afraid of Hallam and stood fingering the yellow collar-button.

"What's happening, Pop?" Hallam said, smiling expansively.

"Nothing," Pop said, hunching his shoulders and wishing Billy would look at him. They were working on Billy's back muscles and his face was flat against the board. His back rose and fell as he breathed deeply.

"Have a cigar, Pop!" Hallam said.

"No thanks."

"No? My man, I got some good news for you," he said, flicking the end of his nose with his forefinger.

"You got no good news for me," Poppa Tabb said, still wishing Billy would look up at him.

"Sure I do. Billy gonna be big in a few months and I'm gonna take his contract over – most of it, anyway – and have Cassidy look after him. So he won't be needing you no more."

"What you say?" Old Poppa Tabb said to Cassidy.

"It's entirely up to you, Poppa Tabb," Cassidy said, looking down at the floor.

"Yes sir, Billy made good tonight and I'm going to take a piece of him," Hallam said, glancing down at the shiny toes of his shoes. "The boy'll get on when I start looking after him. I'll get stuff for him you couldn't touch. He needs my influence. A guy like you can't expect to go on taking a big cut on Billy."

"So you going to butt in?" Poppa Tabb said.

"Me butt in? That's ripe, seeing you never did nothing but butt in on Billy."

"I'm sticking with Billy," Poppa Tabb said. "You ain't taking no piece of him."

"Shut your face," Billy said, looking up suddenly.

"Shut your face is right," Hallam said. "You're through buttin' in."

"You don't fool me none, Hallam. You just after a cut on Billy."

"You just another old guy trying to chisel on his son," Hallam said scornfully.

Billy was sitting up listening, his hands held loosely in his lap. The room was hot and smelled of sweat. Old Poppa Tabb, turning, went to put his hand on Billy's shoulder. "Tell him to beat it, Billy," he said.

"Keep your hands off. You know you been butting in all my life."

"Sure I have, Billy. I been there 'cause I'm your pop, Billy. You know how it's always been with me. I don't take nothing from you. I don't take a red cent. I just stick with you, Billy. See? We been big together."

"You never went so big with me," Billy said.

"Ain't nothing bigger with me than you, Billy. Tell this hustler to run." Again, he reached to touch Billy's shoulder.

"You insult my friend, you got no call," Billy said. He swung a short right to his father's chin. Poppa Tabb sat down on the floor. He was ready to cry but kept on looking at Billy, who was glaring at him.

"Goddamn, he your old man," Hallam said.

"He can get out. I done with him."

"Sure you are. He'll get out."

They watched Smooth Cassidy help Poppa Tabb get up. "What you going to do about this?" Smooth Cassidy was muttering to him. "You ought to be able to do something, Poppa."

Old Poppa Tabb shook his head awkwardly. "No, there's nothing, Smooth."

"But he your boy, and it's up to you."

"Nothing's up to me."

"It all right with you, Poppa, then it all right with me," Cassidy said, stepping back.

Old Poppa Tabb, standing there, seemed to be waiting for something. His jaw fell open. He did not move.

"Well, that be that," Hallam said. He took a cigar out of his pocket, looked at it and suddenly thrust it into Poppa Tabb's open mouth. "Have a cigar," he said.

Poppa Tabb's teeth closed down on the cigar. It was sticking straight out of his mouth as he went out, without looking back. The crowd had gone and the big building was empty. It was dark down by the ring. He didn't look at anything. The unlighted cigar stuck out of his mouth as he went out the big door to the street.

1930

# THE RED HAT

It was the kind of hat Frances had wanted for months, plain and little and red with the narrow brim tacked back, which would look so smart and simple and expensive. There was really very little to it, it was so plain, but it was the kind of felt hat that would have made her feel confident of a sleek appearance. She stood on the pavement, her face pressed up close against the shop window, a slender, tall, and good-looking girl wearing a reddish woolen dress clinging tightly to her body. On the way home from work, the last three evenings, she had stopped to look at the hat. And when she had got home she had told Mrs. Foley, who lived in the next apartment, how much the little hat appealed to her. In the window were many smart hats, all very expensive. There was only one red felt hat, on a mannequin head with a silver face and very red lips.

Though Frances stood by the window a long time she had no intention of buying the hat, because her husband was out of work and they couldn't afford it; she was waiting for him to get a decent job so that she could buy clothes for herself. Not that she looked shabby, but the fall weather was a little cold, a sharp wind sometimes blowing gustily up the avenue, and in the twilight, on the way home from work with the wind blowing, she knew she ought to be wearing a light coat. In the early afternoon when the sun was shining brightly she looked neat and warm in her woolen dress.

Though she ought to have been on her way home Frances couldn't help standing there, thinking she might look beautiful in this hat if she went out with Eric for the evening. Since he had been so moody and discontented recently she now thought of pleasing him by wearing something that would give her a new kind of elegance, of making him feel cheerful and proud of her and glad, after all, that they were married.

But the hat cost fifteen dollars. She had eighteen dollars in her purse, all that was left of her salary after shopping for groceries for the week. It was ridiculous for her to be there looking at the hat, which was obviously too expensive for her, so she smiled and walked away, putting both hands in the small pockets of her dress. She walked slowly, glancing at two women who were standing at the other end of the big window. The younger one, wearing a velvet coat trimmed with squirrel, said to the other: "Let's go in and try some of them on."

Hesitating and half turning, Frances thought it would be quite harmless and amusing if she went into the shop and tried on the red hat, just to see if it looked as good on her as it did on the mannequin head. It never occurred to her to buy the hat.

In the shop, she walked on soft, thick, gray carpet to the chair by the window, where she sat alone for a few minutes, waiting for one of the saleswomen to come to her. At one of the mirrors an elderly lady with bleached hair was fussing with many hats and talking to a deferential and patient saleswoman. Frances, looking at the big dominant woman with the bleached hair and the expensive clothes, felt embarrassed, because she thought it ought to be apparent to everyone in the shop, by the expression on her face, that she had no intention of taking a hat.

A deep-bosomed saleswoman, wearing black silk, smiled at Frances, appraising her carefully. Frances was the kind of customer who might look good in any one of the hats. At the same time, while looking at her, the saleswoman wondered why she wasn't wearing a coat, or at least carrying one, for the evenings were often chilly.

"I wanted to try on the little hat, the red one in the window," Frances said.

The saleswoman had decided by this time that Frances intended only to amuse herself by trying on hats, so when she took the hat from the window and handed it to Frances she smiled politely and watched her adjusting it on her head. Frances tried the hat and patted a strand of fair hair till it curled by the side of the brim. And then, because she was delighted to see that it was as attractive on her as it had been on the mannequin head with the silver face, she smiled happily, noticing in the mirror that her face was the shape of the mannequin face, a little long and narrow, the nose fine and firm, and she took out her lipstick and marked her lips. Looking in the mirror again she felt elated and seemed to enjoy a kind of freedom. She felt elegant and a little haughty. Then she saw the image of the deep-bosomed and polite saleslady.

"It is nice, isn't it?" Frances said, wishing suddenly that she hadn't come into the store.

"It is wonderfully becoming to you, especially to you."

And Frances said suddenly: "I suppose I could change it, if my husband didn't like it."

"Of course."

"Then I'll take it."

Even while paying for the hat and assuring herself that it would be amusing to take it home for the evening, she had a feeling that she ought to have known when she first came into the store that she intended to take the hat home. The saleswoman was smiling. Frances, no longer embarrassed, thought with pleasure of going out with Eric and wearing the hat, tucking the price tag up into her hair. In the morning she could return it.

But as she walked out of the store there was a hope way down within her that Eric would find her so charming in the red hat he would insist she keep it. She wanted him to be freshly aware of her, to like the hat, to discover its restrained elegance. And when they went out together for the evening they would both share the feeling she had had when first she had looked in the shop window. Frances, carrying the box, hurried, eager to get home. The sharp wind had gone down. When there was no wind on these fall evenings it was not cold, and she would not have to wear a coat with her woolen dress. It was just about dark now and all the lights were lit in the streets.

The stairs in the apartment house were long, and on other evenings very tiring, but tonight she seemed to be breathing lightly as she opened the door. Her husband was sitting by the table lamp, reading the paper. A black-haired man with a well-shaped nose, he seemed utterly without energy, slumped down in the chair. A slight odor of whiskey came from him. For four months he had been out of work and some of the spirit had gone out of him, as if he felt that he could never again have independence, and most of the afternoon he had been standing in the streets by the theaters, talking with actors who were out of work.

"Hello, Eric boy," she said, kissing him on the head.

"'Lo, Frances."

"Let's go out and eat tonight," she said.

"What with?"

"Bucks, big boy, a couple of dollar dinners."

He had hardly looked at her. She went into the bedroom and took the hat out of the box, adjusting it on her head at the right angle, powdering her nose and smiling cheerfully. Jauntily she walked into the living room, swinging her hips a little and trying not to smile too openly.

"Take a look at the hat, Eric. How would you like to step out with me?"

Smiling faintly, he said: "You look snappy, but you can't afford a hat."

"Never mind that. How do you like it?"

"What's the use if you can't keep it."

"Did you ever see anything look so good on me?"

"Was it bargain day somewhere?"

"Bargain day! Fifteen bucks at one of the best shops!"

"You'd bother looking at fifteen-dollar hats with me out of work?" he said angrily, getting up and glaring at her.

"I would."

"It's your money. You do what you want."

Frances felt hurt, as if for months there had been a steady pressure on her, and she said stubbornly: "I paid for it. Of course, I can take it back if you insist."

"If I insist," he said, getting up slowly and sneering at her as though he had been hating her for months. "*If I insist.* And you know how I feel about the whole business."

Frances felt hurt and yet strong from indignation, so she shrugged her shoulders, saying, "I wanted to wear it tonight."

His face was white, his eyes almost closed. Suddenly he

grabbed hold of her by the wrist, twisting it till she sank down on one knee.

"You'll get rid of that hat or I'll break every bone in your body. I'll clear out of here for good."

"Eric, please."

"You've been keeping me, haven't you?"

"Don't, Eric."

"Get your fifteen-buck hat out of my sight. Get rid of it, or I'll get out of here for good."

He snatched the hat from her head, pulling it, twisting it in his hands, then throwing it on the floor. He kicked it across the room. "Get it out of here or we're through."

The indignation had gone out of Frances. She was afraid of him; afraid, too, that he would suddenly rush out of the room and never come back, for she knew he had thought of doing it before. Picking up the hat she caressed the soft felt with her fingers, though she could hardly see it with her eyes filled with tears. The felt was creased, the price tag had been torn off, leaving a tiny tear at the back.

Eric was sitting there, watching her.

The hat was torn and she could not take it back. She put it in the box, wrapping the tissue paper around it, and then she went along the hall to Mrs. Foley's apartment.

Mrs. Foley, a smiling, fat woman with a round, cheerful face, opened the door. She saw Frances was agitated and felt sorry for her. "Frances, dear, what's the matter with you?"

"You remember the hat I was telling you about? Here it is. It doesn't look good on me. I was disappointed and pulled it off my head and there's a tiny tear in it. Maybe you'd want it."

Mrs. Foley thought at once that Frances had been quarreling with her husband. Mrs. Foley held up the hat and looked at it shrewdly. Then she went back into her bedroom and tried it on. The felt was good, and though it had been creased, it was quite smooth now. "Of course, I never pay more than five dollars for a hat," she said. The little felt hat did not look good on her round head and face.

"I hate to offer you five dollars for it, Frances, but . . ."

"All right. Give me five dollars."

As Mrs. Foley took the five dollars from her purse, Frances said suddenly: "Listen, dear, if I want it back next week you'll sell it back to me for five?"

"Sure I will, kid."

Frances hurried to her own apartment. Though she knew Eric could not have gone out while she was standing in the hall, she kept on saying to herself: "Please, Heaven, please don't let me do anything to make him leave me while he's feeling this way."

Eric, with his arms folded across his chest, was looking out of the window. Frances put the five dollars Mrs. Foley had given her, and the three dollars left over from her salary, on the small table by Eric's chair. "I sold it to Mrs. Foley," she said.

"Thanks," he said, without looking at her.

"I'm absolutely satisfied," she said, softly and sincerely.

"All right, I'm sorry," he said briefly.

"I mean I don't know what makes you think I'm not satisfied – that's all," she said.

Sitting beside him she put her elbow on her knee and thought of the felt hat on Mrs. Foley's head: it did not look good on her; her face was not the shape of the long silver face of the mannequin head. As Frances thought of the way the hat had looked on the head in the window she hoped vaguely that something would turn up so that she could get it back from Mrs. Foley by the end of the week. And just thinking of it, she felt that faint haughty elation; it was a plain little red hat, the kind of hat she had wanted for months, elegant and expensive, a plain felt hat, so very distinctive.

1931

# SISTER BERNADETTE

When Sister Bernadette, who had charge of the maternity ward in the hospital, wasn't rebuking a nurse in training for some petty fault, she was having a sharp disagreement with a doctor. She was a tall woman with a pale face; she looked very handsome in her starched white headpiece. To her, the notion that her nun's habit might be protecting her from sharp retorts from the nurses was intolerable. But she simply couldn't hold a grudge against anybody, and if she had a tiff with a nurse she would wait till she saw the girl passing in the corridor and say innocently, "I hear you're offended with me," as she offered the warmest, jolliest smile. When young nurses in training, who were having a bit of idle gossip, saw the sister's tall, gaunt form, so formidable in the black robes, coming toward them, they often felt like a lot of half-guilty schoolgirls as they smiled good-naturedly. Of course Sister Bernadette had sympathy for all the women who were suffering and bearing children and she was like a mother to them, but it was the small things in the ward that were most important to her. If she saw a man in the corridor carrying a parcel carefully, she would watch him go into a patient's room, wait till he had departed, then rush into the room and look around to try and guess at once what might have been in the parcel. It was not hard for her to guess correctly, for she seemed to know every object in each private room. All the mothers liked her but were a bit afraid of her. Sometimes forgetting that women were paying expensive doctors to look after them, she would give her own instructions and insist they be carried out completely, as if she knew more about the patients than the doctors did. There was a Doctor Mallory, a short dark fellow with a broad face, a shifting, far-away expression in his eyes, and a kind of warm, earthy tenderness in his manner, who often quarreled bitterly with Sister Bernadette because she ordered a patient of his to take a medicine he had not recommended. He did not know that Sister Bernadette loved him for quarrelling openly with her instead of being just cuttingly polite because she was a nun.

One day Doctor Mallory, looking very worried, waited in the corridor, watching Sister Bernadette's tall form with the dark robes coming toward him. When he looked into her face he couldn't help smiling, there was so much fresh, girlish contentment in her expression. But this time he spoke with a certain diffidence as he said, "Sister, I'd like to talk with you a minute."

"Please do, Doctor," she said. "You're not offended again, surely?"

"Oh no, not this time," he said, smiling warmly. "I wanted to tell you about a patient of mine I'd like to bring to the hospital to have her baby."

"Now, don't tell me you're so afraid of me you have to ask my permission to bring a patient here?" she said, laughing.

"Not at all. Only this girl doesn't want to come. She's ashamed. She's of a good family. I know all about her. But she's not married and won't come here under her own name. I said I'd speak to you and you'd fix it up, Sister. Won't you?"

Sister Bernadette frowned. The doctor was smiling at her, as if he couldn't be fooled by a harsh refusal. It gave her pleasure to think that he was so sure of her sympathetic nature. But she said sharply, "It's against the rules to register anybody under a false name, you know that, Doctor."

"I know it, that's why I wanted to speak to you, Sister."

With ridiculous sternness Sister Bernadette said, "What do I care? Do what you want to do. Register the woman as Mrs. Macsorley, or anything else, it's all the same to me," and she turned and walked away as though greatly offended. The doctor, chuckling, watched her hurrying along the corridor without looking back.

Sister Bernadette could hardly wait to see Doctor Mallory's new patient. Five minutes after the woman was brought to the hospital, Sister Bernadette was in the room looking at her with eager curiosity and speaking in a soft reassuring voice. The patient was only a girl with big scared blue eyes and fluffy blond hair whose confidence had been completely destroyed by her predicament. Sister Bernadette was desperately afraid that the young girl, who had been such a sinner and who was now suffering and disgraced, would be afraid of a woman like herself, a nun, who had given her life entirely to God. For some reason she wanted this scared girl to love her. That night, while the baby was being born, Sister Bernadette was in the corridor many times.

During the two weeks the girl remained at the hospital she was treated with a special attention by the nurses who thought she was an old friend of Sister Bernadette. No one suspected that Mrs. Macsorley wasn't married. Sister Bernadette got a good deal of pleasure realizing that she and the doctor were the only ones who shared the secret. Every morning she paid a visit to Mrs. Macsorley's room talking about everything on earth, praised the baby, and tried to make the girl feel at home by strutting about like a blunt, good-natured farm woman. The fair-haired, blue-eyed girl, who was really a self-possessed, competent person, was so impressed by the sister's frank, good-natured simplicity, she sent word out to the baby's father that there was no reason why he shouldn't come to see her.

When Sister Bernadette was introduced to the father, a well-dressed soft-spoken, tall man, she shook hands warmly, called him Mr. Macsorley and showed the baby to him. His embarrassment disappeared at once. He felt so much at ease with Sister Bernadette during that first visit that he decided to come every day at noontime. At first Sister Bernadette was delighted by the whole affair; it seemed so much like the kind of thing that was always going on in her ward, making her world seem so rich with experience that she didn't care whether she ever went outside the hospital. But when she heard that the girl's lover was a married man, it bothered her to see that he was still so attentive. Though she honestly liked the man and liked the girl too, she said to Doctor Mallory with awkward sincerity, "I don't like to see that man coming to see the girl so much. Evidently they're still in love."

"Does he come often?"

"Every day. And they are both so sure of themselves."

"It isn't very nice. It isn't fair to you," the doctor said.

"No, no, I don't mean that," Sister Bernadette said. "But you know that man is married and has two children. I just mean that the girl at least ought to respect his wife and children and not let him be so devoted to her." Then Sister Bernadette began to feel self-conscious as though the doctor was misunderstanding her. "Don't misinterpret me," she said at once. "The girl can run around with single men as much as she likes and come here as often as she likes as far as I'm concerned . . ."

"I'll tell them about it," the doctor said.

"No. Please don't. You'd better not say anything," she said.

Then it was time for Mrs. Macsorley to leave the hospital. Doctor Mallory came to Sister Bernadette and explained that he, himself, was going to find someone to adopt the baby. Coaxing and pleading, he asked if it wouldn't be all right to leave the baby in the hospital nursery for two days at the most.

Such a request didn't actually worry Sister Bernadette, but she snapped at the doctor, "It's absolutely against the rules of the hospital to leave a baby who's in good health in that nursery after the mother has gone." In the brief argument that followed she was short- and hot-tempered, and in the end she said, "All right, have your way, but only for one day, mind."

She didn't think it necessary to worry till the baby had been left in the nursery for a week. Doctor Mallory was trying very hard to get someone to adopt the baby girl. Sister Bernadette began to think that the child would remain in her nursery till she, herself, did something about it. Every time she looked at the brown-eyed baby she was reminded that she had done wrong in letting the mother register at the hospital under another name. After all, it was just vanity, her eagerness to have the doctor believe her a good-natured person, that was now causing trouble. Perhaps she ought to reveal the whole matter to the Mother Superior, she thought. In her prayers in the morning and in her evening prayers she asked that someone be found who would take the baby at once.

In the evenings, after ten o'clock feeding-time, she would go into the nursery when the lights were turned down looking at one small crib after another with an expert eye that made the nurse in charge wary. But she stood by Baby Macsorley's crib, frowning, puzzled by her own uneasiness. She lifted the baby up as though to see it for the first time. The baby was wearing a little pink sweater coat one of the nurses had knitted. Sister Bernadette knew that Baby Macsorley had become the pet of the nursery. Only last night one of the nurses had performed a mock marriage between the baby and another fine baby boy who was being taken home that day. When she put the baby back into the crib she found herself kissing her on the forehead and patting her back, as she hoped, quickly, that no one had seen her.

As soon as she saw Doctor Mallory next day she blurted out, "If you don't get that baby out of here by tomorrow, I'll throw it in the snowbank."

Doctor Mallory was a bit afraid of her now, for he knew that she was a determined woman, so he said, pleading, "Wait till tomorrow. I'm trying to get one particular lady to adopt it. Wait till tomorrow. I'm working with her."

"You'll have to work faster, that's all," Sister Bernadette said, without even smiling.

Instead of one day, she waited two days longer, but now she was so angry that whenever she went into the nursery and saw the baby, she felt herself resenting the young mother with the candid blue eyes and the baby blond curls and the bold straightforward lover who came so openly to the hospital and felt no shame. Once Sister Bernadette picked the baby up and then put it down hastily for she felt with disgust that the sordidness in the life of the mother and father might be touching her through the baby and disturbing her too much. "I can't go on thinking of those people," she muttered, "the baby goes out of here tomorrow."

But Doctor Mallory was avoiding her and she didn't have a chance to speak to him for three days. She saw him turn a corner and duck into an elevator. "Doctor," she called, "listen to me. I'm going to put that baby in the rear seat of your car and let you drive off with it. We're through with it."

"Why, what's the trouble now, Sister?" he said.

"It's demoralizing my nursery. I'll not have it," she said. "It's the pet of the whole place. Every nurse that goes in there at night picks it up. The baby's been here too long, I tell you."

"But just thinking about it surely doesn't bother you?"

"It certainly does. It's staring me in the face every moment."

"Here's some cheerful news then. Maybe you'll be rid of the baby tomorrow. I'm getting an answer from the lady I wanted to adopt it tonight."

"Honestly, Doctor, you don't know how glad I am to hear that," she said, taking a deep breath.

There was such light-hearted relief within Sister Bernadette when she entered the nursery that night that she had a full, separate smile for each baby as she moved, a tall, black-robed figure, among the cribs. When she stood beside Baby Macsorley's crib, she began to chuckle, feeling it might now be safe to let the baby have some of the warm attention she had sometimes wanted to give. She seemed to know this baby so much better than all the other babies. Humming to herself, she picked up the baby, patted her on the back and whispered, "Are you really going away tomorrow, darling?"

Carrying the baby over to the window she stood there looking down at the city which was spread out in lighted streets with glaring electric signs and moving cabs, the life of a great city at night moving under her eyes. Somewhere, down there, she thought, the bold young girl with the confident eyes and her lover were going their own way. As she held their baby in her arms, she muttered, frowning, "But perhaps they really are in love. Maybe they're out dancing." The girl and her lover belonged to the life down there in the city. "But that man ought to be home with his wife," she thought uneasily.

Sister Bernadette began to think of herself as a young girl again. For the first time in years she was disturbed by dim, half-forgotten thoughts: "Oh, why do I want so much to keep this one baby? Why this one?" Her soul, so chaste and aloof from the unbridled swarm in the city streets, was now over-whelmed by a struggle between something of life that was lost and something bright and timeless within her that was gained. But she started to tremble all over with more unhappiness than she had ever known. With a new, mysterious warmth, she began to hug the child that was almost hidden in her heavy black robes as she pressed it to her breast.

1932

# A SICK CALL

Sometimes Father Macdowell mumbled out loud and took a deep wheezy breath as he walked up and down the room and read his office. He was a huge old priest, white-headed except for a shiny baby-pink bald spot on the top of his head, and he was a bit deaf in one ear. His florid face had many fine red interlacing vein lines. For hours he had been hearing confessions and he was tired, for he always had to hear more confessions than any other priest at the cathedral; young girls who were in trouble, and wild but at times repentant young men, always wanted to tell their confessions to Father Macdowell, because nothing seemed to shock or excite him, or make him really angry, and he was even tender with those who thought they were most guilty.

While he was mumbling and reading and trying to keep his glasses on his nose, the house girl knocked on the door and said, "There's a young lady here to see, father. I think it's about a sick call."

"Did she ask for me especially?" he said in a deep but slightly cracked voice.

"Indeed she did, father. She wanted Father Macdowell and nobody else."

So he went out to the waiting-room, where a girl about thirty years of age, with fine brown eyes, fine cheek-bones, and rather square shoulders, was sitting daubing her eyes with a handkerchief. She was wearing a dark coat with a gray wolf collar. "Good evening, father," she said. "My sister is sick. I wanted you to come and see her. We think she's dying."

"Be easy, child; what's the matter with her? Speak louder. I can hardly hear you."

"My sister's had pneumonia. The doctor's coming back to see her in an hour. I wanted you to anoint her, father."

"I see, I see. But she's not lost yet. I'll not give her extreme unction now. That may not be necessary. I'll go with you and hear her confession."

"Father, I ought to let you know, maybe. Her husband won't want to let you see her. He's not a Catholic, and my sister hasn't been to church in a long time."

"Oh, don't mind that. He'll let me see her," Father Macdowell said, and he left the room to put on his hat and coat.

When he returned, the girl explained that her name was Jane Stanhope, and her sister lived only a few blocks away. "We'll walk and you tell me about your sister," he said. He put his black hat square on the top of his head, and pieces of white hair stuck out awkwardly at the sides. They went to the avenue together.

The night was mild and clear. Miss Stanhope began to walk slowly, because Father Macdowell's rolling gait didn't get him along the street very quickly. He walked as if his feet hurt him, though he wore a pair of large, soft, specially constructed shapeless shoes. "Now, my child, you go ahead and tell me about your sister," he said, breathing with difficulty, yet giving the impression that nothing could have happened to the sister which would make him feel indignant.

There wasn't much to say, Miss Stanhope replied. Her sister had married John Williams two years ago, and he was a good, hard-working fellow, only he was very bigoted and hated all church people. "My family wouldn't have anything to do with Elsa after she married him, though I kept going to see her," she said. She was talking in a loud voice to Father Macdowell so that he could hear her.

"Is she happy with her husband?"

"She's been very happy, father. I must say that."

"Where is he now?"

"He was sitting beside her bed. I ran out because I thought he was going to cry. He said if I brought a priest near the place he'd break the priest's head."

"My goodness. Never mind, though. Does your sister want to see me?"

"She asked me to go and get a priest, but she doesn't want John to know she did it."

Turning into a side street, they stopped at the first apartment house, and the old priest followed Miss Stanhope up the stairs. His breath came with great difficulty. "Oh dear, I'm not getting any younger, not one day younger. It's a caution how a man's legs go back on him," he said. As Miss Stanhope rapped on the door, she looked pleadingly at the old priest, trying to ask him not to be offended at anything that might happen, but he was smiling and looking huge in the narrow hallway. He wiped his head with his handkerchief.

The door was opened by a young man in a white shirt with no collar, with a head of thick, black, wavy hair. At first he looked dazed, then his eyes got bright with excitement when he saw the priest, as though he were glad to see someone he could destroy with pent-up energy. "What do you mean, Jane?" he said. "I told you not to bring a priest around here. My wife doesn't want to see a priest."

"What's that you're saying, young man?"

"No one wants you here."

"Speak up. Don't be afraid. I'm a bit hard of hearing," Father Macdowell smiled rosily. John Williams was confused by the unexpected deafness in the priest, but he stood there, blocking the door with sullen resolution as if waiting for the priest to try to launch a curse at him.

"Speak to him, father," Miss Stanhope said, but the priest didn't seem to hear her; he was still smiling as he pushed past the young man, saying, "I'll go in and sit down, if you don't mind, son. I'm here on God's errand, but I don't mind saying I'm all out of breath from climbing those stairs."

John was dreadfully uneasy to see he had been brushed aside, and he followed the priest into the apartment and said loudly, "I don't want you here."

Father Macdowell said, "Eh, eh?" Then he smiled sadly. "Don't be angry with me, son," he said. "I'm too old to try and be fierce and threatening." Looking around, he said, "Where's your wife?" and he started to walk along the hall, looking for the bedroom.

John followed him and took hold of his arm. "There's no sense in your wasting your time talking to my wife, do you hear?" he said angrily.

Miss Stanhope called out suddenly, "Don't be rude, John."

"It's he that's being rude. You mind your business," John said.

"For the love of God let me sit down a moment with her, anyway. I'm tired," the priest said.

"What do you want to say to her? Say it to me, why don't you?"

Then they both heard someone moan softly in the adjoining room, as if the sick woman had heard them. Father Macdowell, forgetting that the young man had hold of his arm, said, "I'll go in and see her for a moment, if you don't mind," and he began to open the door.

"You're not going to be alone with her, that's all," John said, following him into the bedroom.

Lying on the bed was a white-faced, fair girl, whose skin was so delicate that her cheek-bones stood out sharply. She was feverish, but her eyes rolled toward the door, and she watched them coming in. Father Macdowell took off his coat, and as he mumbled to himself he looked around the room, at the mauve-silk bed-light and the light wall-paper with the tiny birds in flight. It looked like a little girl's room. "Good evening, father," Mrs. Williams whispered. She looked scared. She didn't glance at her husband. The notion of dying had made her afraid. She loved her husband and wanted to die loving him, but she was afraid, and she looked up at the priest.

"You're going to get well, child," Father Macdowell said, smiling and patting her hand gently.

John, who was standing stiffly by the door, suddenly moved around the big priest, and he bent down over the bed and took his wife's hand and began to caress her forehead.

"Now, if you don't mind, my son, I'll hear your wife's confession," the priest said.

"No, you won't," John said abruptly. "Her people didn't want her and they left us together, and they're not going to separate us now. She's satisfied with me." He kept looking down at her face as if he could not bear to turn away.

Father Macdowell nodded his head up and down and sighed. "Poor boy," he said. "God bless you." Then he looked at Mrs. Williams, who had closed her eyes, and he saw a faint tear on her cheek. "Be sensible, my boy," he said. "You'll have to let me hear your wife's confession. Leave us alone a while."

"I'm going to stay right here," John said, and he sat down on the end of the bed. He was working himself up and staring savagely at the priest. All of a sudden he noticed the tears on his wife's cheeks, and he muttered as though bewildered, "What's the matter, Elsa? What's the matter, darling? Are we bothering you? Just open your eyes and we'll get out of the room and leave you alone till the doctor comes." Then he turned and said to the priest, "I'm not going to leave you here with her, can't you see that? Why don't you go?"

"I could revile you, my son. I could threaten you; but I ask you, for the peace of your wife's soul, leave us alone." Father Macdowell spoke with patient tenderness. He looked very big and solid and immovable as he stood by the bed. "I liked your face as soon as I saw you," he said to John. "You're a good fellow."

John still held his wife's wrist, but he rubbed one hand through his thick hair and said angrily, "You don't get the point, sir. My wife and I were always left alone, and we merely want to be left alone now. Nothing is going to separate us. She's been content with me. I'm sorry, sir; you'll have to speak to her with me here, or you'll have to go."

"No; you'll have to go for a while," the priest said patiently.

Then Mrs. Williams moved her head on the pillow and said jerkily, "Pray for me, father."

So the old priest knelt down by the bed, and with a sweet unruffled expression on his florid face he began to pray.

At times his breath came with a whistling noise as though a rumbling were inside him, and at other times he sighed and was full of sorrow. He was praying that young Mrs. Williams might get better, and while he prayed he knew that her husband was more afraid of losing her to the Church than losing her to death.

All the time Father Macdowell was on his knees, with his heavy prayer book in his two hands, John kept staring at him. John couldn't understand the old priest's patience and tolerance. He wanted to quarrel with him, but he kept on watching the light from overhead shining on the one baby-pink bald spot on the smooth, white head, and at last he burst out, "You don't understand, sir! We've been very happy together. Neither you nor her people came near her when she was in good health, so why should you bother her now? I don't want anything to separate us now; neither does she. She came with me. You see you'd be separating us, don't you?" He was trying to talk like a reasonable man who had no prejudices.

Father Macdowell got up clumsily. His knees hurt him, for the floor was hard. He said to Mrs. Williams in quite a loud voice, "Did you really intend to give up everything for this young fellow?" and he bent down close to her so he could hear.

"Yes, father," she whispered.

"In Heaven's name, child, you couldn't have known what you were doing."

"We loved each other, father. We've been very happy."

"All right. Supposing you were. What now? What about all eternity, child?"

"Oh, father, I'm very sick and I'm afraid." She looked up to try to show him how scared she was, and how much she wanted him to give her peace.

He sighed and seemed distressed, and at last he said to John, "Were you married in the church?"

"No, we weren't. Look here, we're talking pretty loud and it upsets her."

"Ah, it's a crime that I'm hard of hearing, I know. Never mind, I'll go." Picking up his coat, he put it over his arm; then he sighed as if he were very tired, and he said, "I wonder if you'd just fetch me a glass of water. I'd thank you for it."

John hesitated, glancing at the tired old priest, who looked so pink and white and almost cherubic in his utter lack of guile.

"What's the matter?" Father Macdowell said.

John was ashamed of himself for appearing so sullen, so he said hastily, "Nothing's the matter. Just a moment. I won't be a moment." He hurried out of the room.

The old priest looked down at the floor and shook his head; and then, sighing and feeling uneasy, he bent over Mrs. Williams, with his good ear down to her, and he said, "I'll just ask you a few questions in a hurry, my child. You answer them quickly and I'll give you absolution." He made the sign of the cross over her and asked if she repented for having strayed from the Church, and if she had often been angry, and whether she had always been faithful, and if she had ever lied or stolen – all so casually and quickly as if it hadn't occurred to him that such a young woman could have serious sins. In the same breath he muttered, "Say a good act of contrition to yourself and that will be all, my dear." He had hardly taken a minute.

When John returned to the room with the glass of water in his hand, he saw the old priest making the sign of the cross. Father Macdowell went on praying without even looking up at John. When he had finished, he turned and said, "Oh, there

ANCIENT LINEAGE AND OTHER STORIES

you are. Thanks for the water. I needed it. Well, my boy, I'm sorry if I worried you."

John hardly said anything. He looked at his wife, who had closed her eyes, and he sat down on the end of the bed. He was too disappointed to speak.

Father Macdowell, who was expecting trouble, said, "Don't be harsh, lad."

"I'm not harsh," he said mildly, looking up at the priest. "But you weren't quite fair. And it's as though she turned away from me at the last moment. I didn't think she needed you."

"God bless you, bless the both of you. She'll get better," Father Macdowell said. But he felt ill at ease as he put on his coat, and he couldn't look directly at John.

Going along the hall, he spoke to Miss Stanhope, who wanted to apologize for her brother-in-law's attitude. "I'm sorry if it was unpleasant for you, father," she said.

"It wasn't unpleasant," he said. "I was glad to meet John. He's a fine fellow. It's a great pity he isn't a Catholic. I don't know as I played fair with him."

As he went down the stairs, puffing and sighing, he pondered the question of whether he had played fair with the young man. But by the time he reached the street he was rejoicing amiably to think he had so successfully ministered to one who had strayed from the faith and had called out to him at the last moment. Walking along with the rolling motion as if his feet hurt him, he muttered, "Of course they were happy as they were . . . in a worldly way. I wonder if I did come between them?"

He shuffled along, feeling very tired, but he couldn't help thinking, "What beauty there was to his staunch love for her!" Then he added quickly, "But it was just a pagan beauty, of course."

As he began to wonder about the nature of this beauty, for some reason he felt inexpressibly sad.

1932

# AN OLD QUARREL

M rs. Massey, a stout, kindly woman of sixty, full of energy for her age, and red-faced and healthy except for an occasional pain in her left leg which she watched very carefully, had come from Chicago to see her son who was a doctor. The doctor's family made a great fuss over her, and she felt in such good humor that she said suddenly one night: "I declare, I'll go and see Mary Woolens. I wonder what's happened to her? Find out where she lives for me."

She had grown up with Mary Woolens. Thirty years ago they had quarrelled, she had married and gone West, and they had not seen each other since.

So the next afternoon Mrs. Massey was back in her old neighborhood on the avenue at the corner of Christopher Street, staring around longingly for some familiar sight that might recall an incident in her childhood. Looking carefully to the right and left, she had darted forward across the street with a determined look on her face, for traffic now made her nervous, and had arrived on the other side breathless with relief.

She walked slowly along the street, taking one deep breath after another, and leaning forward to lift some of the weight off her feet. Her face was screwed up as she peered at the numbers on the houses, and as she stopped to put on her glasses she was smiling eagerly like a woman who nurses a secret.

If she had closed her eyes and stood there, she could have remembered vividly almost every word of her quarrel with Mary Woolens. Mary had been a foolish, rather homely girl who found herself in love with a deceitful man who kept on promising to marry her while he borrowed her money. Then Mary had borrowed a hundred dollars from her, and it turned out that she had given it to the fellow, who had gone away, and of course Mary was not able to pay the money back. There had been so much bitterness. She had wanted to have the man arrested. For a while Mary and she seemed to hate each other, then their friendship was over.

Now, walking along the street, Mrs. Massey was full of shame to think there had been a quarrel about money. It seemed now that they both had been mean and spiteful, and she couldn't bear to think Mary might not know that she had forgiven her long ago. "This must be the place here," she said, looking up at a brownstone house. For a moment she felt awkward and still a bit ashamed, then she went up the steps, feeling like a self-possessed, well-dressed woman in good circumstances.

It was a clean-looking house with a little sign advertising small apartments and a few rooms for rent. As Mrs. Massey rang the bell in the hall, she peered up the stairs, waiting, and then saw a woman in a plain dark blue dress and with astonishingly white hair coming toward her. This woman, who had a pair of earnest blue eyes and a mild, peaceful expression, asked politely, "Were you wanting to see somebody?"

"I was wanting to see Miss Woolens," Mrs. Massey said. Then she said, "Goodness, you're Mary. Mary, don't you really know me?"

"I can't quite see you in that light. If you'd turn your head to the side. There now, well. Elsie Wiggins! It can't be Elsie Wiggins. I mean Elsie Massey."

The little white-haired woman was so startled that her hands, held up to her lips, began to shake. Then she was so pleased she could not move. "I never thought of such a thing in my life," she said. She was very flustered, so she cried out suddenly, "Oh, I'm so glad to see you; come in, please come in, Elsie," and she went hurrying along the hall to a room at the back of the house, while Mrs. Massey, following more slowly, smiled to herself with deep enjoyment.

And even when they were sitting in the big carpeted room with the old-fashioned couch and arm-chairs, she knew that Mary was still looking at her as though she were a splendid creature from a strange world. Mrs. Massey smiled with indulgent good humor. But Mary had no composure at all. "I just don't know what to say to you, Elsie. I'm so delighted to see you." Then darting up like a small bird, she said, "I'll put on the kettle and we'll have a cup of tea."

While she waited, Mrs. Massey felt a twinge of uneasiness, wondering how she would mention that she had long ago forgiven Mary, for she was sure that was what was making the poor woman so flustered, even though, so far, she was pretending there had never been bitterness between them. With a pot of tea on a tray, and beaming with childish warmth, Mary returned, saying, "I was just trying to count up the years since we last saw each other."

"It must be thirty years. Fancy that," Mrs. Massey said.

"But I've heard about you, Elsie. I once met a woman

who had lived in Chicago, and she told me that you had a son who was a doctor, and I read about some wonderful operation he performed in one of the hospitals here. It was in all the papers. You must be awfully proud, Elsie. Who does he look like?"

"They always said he looked like his father."

"Maybe so. But of course I always think of him as Elsie's boy."

"Has your health been good, Mary?"

"I've nothing to complain about. I don't look strong, do I? But outside of a pain in my head that the doctor says might be caused by an old tooth, I'm in good health. You look fine, though."

"Well, I am, and I'm not. I've a pain in the leg and sometimes a swelling here, just at the ankle, that may be from my heart. Never mind. Have the years been good to you, Mary? What's happened?"

"Why, nothing. Nothing at all, I suppose," Mary said, looking around the room as though puzzled. As she smiled, she looked sweet and frail. "I look after the house here. I learned to save my money," she said. All of a sudden she added, "Tell me all about your son, the doctor," and she leaned forward, as though seeking a confirmation of many things she might have dreamed. "I ought to pour the tea now," she said, "but you go right on talking. I'll hear everything you say."

Mrs. Massey began to talk quietly with a subdued pride about her son, and sometimes she looked up at Mary, who was pouring the tea with a thin trembling hand. The flush of excitement was still on Mary's face. Her chest looked almost hollow. She was a woman who, of course, had worked hard for years, every day wearing clothes that looked the same, seeing that her house was cleaned in the morning, going to the same stores every afternoon, and getting much pleasure out of a bit of lively gossip with a neighbor on the street.

"I need more hot water," she said now, and hurried to the kitchen with short steps, and then, when she returned, she stood there with a cup in her hand, lost in her thoughts. "Goodness," she said. "There are so many things to say I don't know what I'm doing."

Mrs. Massey continued to talk with gentle tolerance, remembering that her own life had been rich and fruitful, and having pity for Mary, who had remained alone. But when a bit of sunlight from the window shone on Mary's white head and thin face as she sat there with a teacup in her hand, her face held so much sweetness and gentleness that Mrs. Massey was puzzled, for Mary had been a rather homely girl.

"It upset me terribly to stand on the corner and feel so strange," Mrs. Massey was saying.

"Elsie, heavens above! I didn't ask about Will, your husband."

"Will? Why, Will's been dead for five years, Mary."

"Dead. Think of that. I hardly knew him. It seems like yesterday."

"We were married twenty-five years."

"You used to love him very much, didn't you, Elsie? I remember that. He was a good-living man, wasn't he?"

"He was a good man," Mrs. Massey said vaguely, and they both sat there, silent now, having their own thoughts.

Mary Woolens, the small white-haired one, was leaning forward eagerly, but Mrs. Massey, stout and red-faced, sighed, thinking of the long, steady years of married life; and though there had been children and some bright moments and some hopes fulfilled, she was strangely discontented now, troubled by a longing for something she could not see or understand.

Perhaps it was Mary's eagerness that was stirring her, but she aroused herself by thinking, "Has she forgotten I once told her I hated her? Won't she mention it at all?" And since she had been the one who had held the old grievance, she felt resentful, for the old mean quarrel had bothered her a long time, had filled her with shame so that she had been eager to forgive Mary; and now Mary seemed to have forgotten it.

She looked full into Mary's face, and then couldn't help wondering what was making her smile so happily. "What are you thinking of, Mary?" she asked.

"Do you remember how we grew up around here, and were little bits of kids together?"

"I sort of half remember."

"Do you remember when we were such little things, we used to sit together on the steps and you used to tell me all kinds of fairy stories, making them up. I'll bet you can't remember."

"I do remember," Mrs. Massey said, leaning forward eagerly. "There was another girl used to sit with us sometimes. Bertha, Bertha – oh, dear, now, what was it?"

"Bertha Madison. We wore big hair ribbons. I can remember some of the fairy stories now. The night I read about your son being the fine surgeon and performing that wonderful operation, I lay awake in bed thinking about you, and I remembered the stories. It used to seem so wonderful that you could make up such fine stories as you went along, and it seemed just right, when I thought about it, that your boy should be doing the things he was. I remember there was one story you kept carrying on, and like a whole lot of bright patches it was."

"I remember," Mrs. Massey said, holding on to her animation.

Mary looked up suddenly. Her face was flushed, her blue eyes were brilliant. She was looking up with a kind of desperate eagerness. With a rapt interest and mysterious delight, Mrs. Massey was leaning forward, her heavy face holding a little smile that kept her lips parted. They were both filled with delight, leaning close to each other, almost breathing together, while they were silent. Then, without any warning, Mary began to cry, shaking her head hopelessly from side to side, and dabbing at her eyes with a small handkerchief.

"Mary dear, Mary! What is the matter? Why are you crying?"

"I don't know," Mary said.

"You shouldn't go on like that, then," Mrs. Massey said, fretfully. But she, too, felt her eyes moistening. "Oh, dear, oh, dear, Mary," she said, rocking from side to side, "oh, dear, oh, dear." She tried bravely to smile, but it no longer seemed important that they had once quarrelled bitterly, or that her life had been full and Mary's quite barren – just that once they had been young together. A great deal of time had passed, and now they were both old.

1933

# TWO FISHERMEN

The only reporter on the town paper, *The Examiner*, was Michael Foster, a tall, long-legged, eager fellow, who wanted to go to the city some day and work on an important newspaper.

The morning he went to Bagley's Hotel, he wasn't at all sure of himself. He went over to the desk and whispered to the proprietor, "Did he come here, Mr. Bagley?"

Bagley said slowly, "Two men came here from this morning's train. They're registered." He put his spatulate forefinger on the open book and said, "Two men. One of them's a drummer. This one here, T. Woodley. I know because he was through this way last year and just a minute ago he walked across the road to Molson's hardware store. The other one . . . here's his name, K. Smith."

"Who's K. Smith?" Michael asked.

"I don't know. A mild, harmless looking little guy."

"Did he look like the hangman, Mr. Bagley?"

"I couldn't say that, seeing that I never saw one. He was awfully polite and asked where he could get a boat so he could

137

go fishing on the lake this evening, so I said likely down at Smollet's place by the powerhouse."

"Well, thanks. I guess if he was the hangman, he'd go over to the jail first," Michael said.

He went along the street, past the Baptist church to the old jail with the high brick fence around it. Two tall maple trees, with branches drooping low over the sidewalk, shaded one of the walls from the morning sunlight. Last night, behind those walls, three carpenters, working by lamplight, had nailed the timbers for the scaffold. In the morning, young Thomas Delaney, who had grown up in the town, was being hanged: he had killed old Mathew Rhinehart whom he had caught molesting his wife when she had been berry picking in the hills behind the town. There had been a struggle and Thomas Delaney had taken a bad beating before he had killed Rhinehart. Last night a crowd had gathered on the sidewalk by the lamppost, and while moths and smaller insects swarmed around the high blue carbon light, the crowd had thrown sticks and bottles and small stones at the out-of-town workmen in the jail yard. Billy Hilton, the town constable, had stood under the light with his head down, pretending not to notice anything. Thomas Delaney was only three years older than Michael Foster.

Michael went straight to the jail office, where the sheriff, Henry Steadman, a squat, heavy man, was sitting on the desk idly wetting his long moustache with his tongue. "Hello, Michael, what do you want?" he asked.

"Hello, Mr. Steadman, *The Examiner* would like to know if the hangman arrived yet."

"Why ask me?"

"I thought he'd come here to test the gallows. Won't he?"

"My, you're a smart young fellow, Michael, thinking of that."

"Is he in there now, Mr. Steadman?"

"Don't ask me. I'm saying nothing. Say, Michael, do you think there's going to be trouble? You ought to know. Does anybody seem sore at me? I can't do nothing. You can see that."

"I don't think anybody blames you, Mr. Steadman. Look here, can't I see the hangman? Is his name K. Smith?"

"What does it matter to you, Michael? Be a sport, go on away and don't bother us any more."

"All right, Mr. Steadman," Michael said, "just leave it to me."

Early that evening, when the sun was setting, Michael Foster walked south of the town on the dusty road leading to the powerhouse and Smollet's fishing pier. He knew that if Mr. K. Smith wanted to get a boat he would go down to the pier. Fine powdered road dust whitened Michael's shoes. Ahead of him he saw the power plant, square and low, and the smooth lake water. Behind him the sun was hanging over the blue hills beyond the town and shining brilliantly on square patches of farmland. The air around the powerhouse smelt of steam.

Out on the jutting, tumbledown pier of rock and logs, Michael saw a fellow without a hat, sitting down with his knees hunched up to his chin; a very small man who stared steadily far out over the water. In his hand he was holding a stick with a heavy fishing line twined around it and a gleaming copper spoon bait, the hooks brightened with bits of feathers such as they used in the neighborhood when trolling for lake trout. Apprehensively Michael walked out over the rocks toward the stranger and called, "Were you thinking of fishing, mister?" Standing up, the man smiled. He had a large head, tapering down to a small chin, a bird-like neck and a wistful smile. Puckering his mouth up, he said shyly to Michael, "Did you intend to go fishing?"

"That's what I came down here for. I was going to get a boat back at the boathouse there. How would you like it if we went together?"

"I'd like it first rate," the shy little man said eagerly. "We could take turns rowing. Does that appeal to you?"

"Fine. Fine. You wait here and I'll go back to Smollet's place and ask for a rowboat and I'll row around here and get you."

"Thanks. Thanks very much," the mild little man said, as he began to untie his line. He seemed very enthusiastic.

When Michael brought the boat around to the end of the old pier and invited the stranger to make himself comfortable so he could handle the line, the stranger protested comically that he ought to be allowed to row.

Pulling strongly on the oars, Michael was soon out in the deep water and the little man was letting the line out slowly. In one furtive glance, he had noticed that the man's hair, gray at the temples, was inclined to curl to his ears. The line was out full length. It was twisted around the little man's forefinger, which he let drag in the water. And then Michael looked full at him and smiled because he thought he seemed so meek and quizzical. "He's a nice little guy," Michael assured himself, and he said, "I work on the town paper, *The Examiner.*"

"Is it a good paper? Do you like the work?"

"Yes. But it's nothing like a first-class city paper and I don't expect to be working on it long. I want to get a reporter's job on a city paper. My name's Michael Foster."

"Mine's Smith. Just call me Smitty."

"I was wondering if you'd been over to the jail yet?"

Up to this time the little man had been smiling with the charming ease of a small boy who finds himself free, but now he became furtive and disappointed. Hesitating, he said, "Yes, I was over there first thing this morning."

"Oh, I just knew you'd go there," Michael said. They were a bit afraid of each other. By this time they were far out on the water which had a millpond smoothness. The town seemed to get smaller, with white houses in rows and streets forming geometric patterns, just as the blue hills behind the town seemed to get larger at sundown.

Finally Michael said, "Do you know this Thomas Delaney that's dying in the morning?" He knew his voice was slow and resentful.

"No. I don't know anything about him. I never read about them. Aren't there any fish at all in this old lake? I'd like to catch some," he said. "I told my wife I'd bring her home some fish." Glancing at Michael, he was appealing, without speaking, that they should do nothing to spoil an evening's fishing.

The little man began to talk eagerly about fishing as he pulled out a small flask from his hip pocket. "Scotch," he said, chuckling with delight. "Here, have a swig." Michael drank from the flask and passed it back. Tilting his head back and saying, "Here's to you, Michael," the little man took a long pull at the flask. "The only time I take a drink," he said, still chuckling, "is when I go on a fishing trip by myself. I usually go by myself," he added apologetically, as if he wanted the young fellow to see how much he appreciated his company.

They had gone far out on the water but they had caught nothing. It began to get dark. "No fish tonight, I guess, Smitty," Michael said.

"It's a crying shame," Smitty said. "I looked forward to coming up here when I found out the place was on the lake. I wanted to get some fishing in. I promised my wife I'd bring her back some fish. She'd often like to go fishing with me, but of course she can't because she can't travel around from place to place like I do. Whenever I get a call to go to some place, I always look at the map to see if it's by a lake or on a river, then I take my lines and hooks along."

"If you took another job, you and your wife could probably go fishing together," Michael suggested.

"I don't know about that. We sometimes go fishing together anyway." He looked away, waiting for Michael to be repelled and insist that he ought to give up the job. And he wasn't ashamed as he looked down at the water, but he knew Michael thought he ought to be ashamed. "Somebody's got to do my job. There's got to be a hangman," he said.

"I just meant that if it was such disagreeable work, Smitty."

The little man did not answer for a long time. Michael rowed steadily with sweeping, tireless strokes. Huddled at the end of the boat, Smitty suddenly looked up with a kind of melancholy hopelessness and said mildly, "The job hasn't been so disagreeable."

"Good God, man, you don't mean you like it?"

"Oh, no," he said, to be obliging, as if he knew what Michael expected him to say. "I mean you get used to it, that's all." But he looked down again at the water, knowing he ought to be ashamed of himself.

"Have you got any children?"

"I sure have. Five. The oldest boy is fourteen. It's funny, but they're all a lot bigger and taller than I am. Isn't that funny?"

They started a conversation about fishing rivers that ran into the lake farther north. They felt friendly again. The little man, who had an extraordinary gift for storytelling, made many quaint faces, puckered up his lips, screwed up his eyes and moved around restlessly as if he wanted to get up in the boat and stride around for the sake of more expression. Again he brought out the whiskey flask and Michael stopped rowing. Grinning, they toasted each other and said together, "Happy days." The boat remained motionless on the placid water. Far out, the sun's last rays gleamed on the waterline. And then it got dark and they could only see the town lights. It was time to turn around and pull for the shore. The little man tried to take the oars from Michael, who shook his head resolutely and insisted that he would prefer to have his friend catch a fish on the way back to the shore.

"It's too late now, and we have scared all the fish away," Smitty laughed happily. "But we're having a grand time, aren't we?"

When they reached the old pier by the powerhouse, it was full night and they hadn't caught a single fish. As the boat bumped against the rocks Michael said, "You can get out here, I'll take the boat around to Smollet's."

"Won't you be coming my way?"

"Not just now. I'll probably talk with Smollet a while."

The little man got out of the boat and stood on the pier looking down at Michael. "I was thinking dawn would be the best time to catch some fish," he said. "At about five o'clock. I'll have an hour and a half to spare anyway. How would you like that?" He was speaking with so much eagerness that Michael found himself saying, "I could try. But if I'm not here at dawn, you go on without me."

"All right. I'll go back to the hotel now."

"Good night, Smitty."

"Good night, Michael. We had a fine neighborly time, didn't we?"

As Michael rowed the boat around to the boathouse, he hoped that Smitty wouldn't realize he didn't want to be seen walking back to town with him. And later, when he was going along the dusty road in the dark and hearing all the crickets chirping in the ditches, he couldn't figure out why he felt so ashamed of himself.

At seven o'clock next morning Thomas Delaney was hanged in the town jail yard. There was hardly a breeze on that leaden gray morning and there were no small whitecaps out over the lake. It would have been a fine morning for fishing. Michael went down to the jail, for he thought it his duty as a newspaperman to have all the facts, but he was afraid he might get sick. He hardly spoke to all the men and women who were crowded under the maple trees by the jail wall. Everybody he knew was staring at the wall and muttering angrily. Two of Thomas Delaney's brothers, big, strapping fellows with bearded faces, were there on the sidewalk. Three automobiles were at the front of the jail.

Michael, the town newspaperman, was admitted into the courtyard by old Willie Mathews, one of the guards, who said that two newspapermen from the city were at the gallows on the other side of the building. "I guess you can go around there too, if you want to," Mathews said, as he sat down on the step. White-faced, and afraid, Michael sat down on the step with Mathews and they waited and said nothing.

At last the old fellow said, "Those people outside there are pretty sore, ain't they?"

"They're pretty sullen, all right. I saw two of Delaney's brothers there."

"I wish they'd go," Mathews said. "I don't want to see anything. I didn't even look at Delaney. I don't want to hear anything. I'm sick." He put his head against the wall and closed his eyes.

The old fellow and Michael sat close together till a small

procession came around the corner from the other side of the yard. First came Mr. Steadman, the sheriff, with his head down as though he were crying, then Dr. Parker, the physician, then two hard-looking young newspapermen from the city, walking with their hats on the backs of their heads, and behind them came the little hangman, erect, stepping out with military precision and carrying himself with a strange cocky dignity. He was dressed in a long black cut-away coat with gray striped trousers, a gates-ajar collar and a narrow red tie, as if he alone felt the formal importance of the occasion. He walked with brusque precision until he saw Michael, who was standing up, staring at him with his mouth open.

The little hangman grinned and as soon as the procession reached the doorstep, he shook hands with Michael. They were all looking at Michael. As though his work was over now, the hangman said eagerly to Michael, "I thought I'd see you here. You didn't get down to the pier at dawn?"

"No. I couldn't make it."

"That was tough, Michael. I looked for you," he said. "But never mind. I've got something for you." As they all went into the jail, Dr. Parker glanced angrily at Michael, then turned his back on him. In the office, where the doctor prepared to sign the certificate, Smitty was bending down over his fishing basket, which was in the corner. Then he pulled out two good-sized trout, folded in newspaper, and said, "I was saving these for you, Michael. I got four in an hour's fishing." Then he said, "I'll talk about that later if you'll wait. We'll be busy here, and I've got to change my clothes."

Michael went out to the street with Dr. Parker and the two city newspapermen. Under his arm he was carrying the fish, folded in the newspaper. Outside, at the jail door, Michael thought that the doctor and the two newspapermen were standing a little apart from him. Then the crowd, with their clothes all dust-soiled from the road, surged forward and the doctor said to them, "You might as well go home, boys. It's all over."

"Where's old Steadman?" somebody demanded.

"We'll wait for the hangman," somebody else shouted.

The doctor walked away by himself. For a while Michael stood beside the two city newspapermen, and tried to look as nonchalant as they were looking, but he lost confidence in them when he smelled whiskey. They only talked to each other. Then they mingled with the crowd, and Michael stood alone. At last he could stand there no longer looking at all those people he knew so well, so he, too, moved out and joined the crowd.

When the sheriff came out with the hangman and the guards, they got halfway down to one of the automobile before someone threw an old boot. Steadman ducked into one of the cars, as the boot hit him on the shoulder, and the two guards followed him. The hangman, dismayed, stood alone on the sidewalk. Those in the car must have thought at first that the hangman was with them for the car suddenly shot forward, leaving him alone on the sidewalk. The crowd threw small rocks and sticks, hooting at him as the automobile backed up slowly towards him. One small stone hit him on the head. Blood trickled from the side of his head as he looked around helplessly at all the angry people. He had the same expression on his face, Michael thought, as he had had last night when he had seemed ashamed and had looked down at the water. Only now, he looked around wildly, looking for someone to help him as the crowd kept pelting him. Farther and farther Michael backed into the crowd and all the time he felt dreadfully ashamed as though he were betraying Smitty, who last night had had such a good neighborly time with him. "It's different now, it's different," he kept thinking, as he held the fish in the newspaper tight under his arm. Smitty started to run toward the automobile, but James Mortimer, a big fisherman, shot out his foot and tripped him and sent him sprawling on his face.

Looking for something to throw, the fisherman said to Michael, "Sock him, sock him."

Michael shook his head and felt sick.

"What's the matter with you, Michael?"

"Nothing. I got nothing against him."

The big fisherman started pounding his fists up and down in the air. "He just doesn't mean anything to me at all," Michael said quickly. The fisherman, bending down, kicked a small rock loose from the roadbed and heaved it at the hangman. Then he said, "What are you holding there, Michael, what's under your arm? Fish? Pitch them at him. Here, give them to me." Still in a fury, he snatched the fish, and threw them one at a time at the little man just as he was getting up from the road. The fish fell in the thick dust in front of him, sending up a little cloud. Smitty seemed to stare at the fish with his mouth hanging open, then he didn't even look at the crowd. That expression on Smitty's face as he saw the fish in the road made Michael hot with shame and he tried to get out of the crowd.

Smitty had his hands over his head, to shield his face as the crowd pelted him, yelling, "Sock the little rat! Throw the runt in the lake!" The sheriff pulled him into the automobile. The car shot forward in a cloud of dust.

1934

# ONE SPRING NIGHT

They had been to an eleven-o'clock movie. Afterward, as they sat very late in the restaurant, Sheila was listening to Bob Davis, liking all the words he used and showing by the quiet gladness that kept coming into her face the deep enjoyment she felt in being with him. She was the young sister of his friend, Jack Staples. Every time Bob had been at their apartment, she had come into the room, they had laughed and joked with her, they had teased her about the new way she wore her clothes, watching her growing, and she had always smiled and answered them in a slow, measured way.

Bob had taken her out a few times when he had felt like having some girl to talk to who knew him and liked him. And tonight he was leaning back good-humoredly, telling her one thing and then another with the wise self-assurance he usually had when with her; but gradually, as he watched her, he found himself talking more slowly, his voice grew serious and much softer, and then finally he leaned across the table toward her as though he had just discovered that her neck was full and soft with her spring coat thrown open, and that her face under her little black straw hat tilted back on her head had a new, eager beauty. Her warm, smiling softness was so close to him that he smiled a bit shyly.

"What are you looking at, Bob?" she said.

"What is there about you that seems different tonight?" he said, and they both began to laugh lightly, as if sharing the same secret.

When they were outside, walking along arm in arm and liking the new spring night air, Sheila said quickly, "It's awfully nice out tonight. Let's keep walking a while, Bob," and she held his arm as though very sure of him.

"All right," he said. "We'll walk till we get so tired we'll have to sit on the curb. It's nearly two o'clock, but it doesn't seem to matter much, does it?"

Every step he took with Sheila leaning on his arm in this new way, and with him feeling now that she was a woman he hardly knew, made the excitement grow in him, and yet he was uneasy. He was much taller than Sheila and he kept looking down at her, and she always smiled back with frank gladness. Then he couldn't help squeezing her arm tight, and he started to talk recklessly about anything that came into his head, swinging his free arm and putting passionate eloquence into the simplest words. She was listening as she used to listen when he talked with her brother and father in the evenings, only now she wanted him to see how much she liked having it tonight all for herself. Almost pleading, she said, "Are you having a good time, Bob? Don't you like the streets at night, when there's hardly anybody on them?"

They stopped and looked along the wide avenue and up the towering, slanting faces of the buildings to the patches of night sky. Holding out her small, gloved hand in his palm, he patted it with his other hand, and they both laughed as though he had done something foolish but charming. The whole city was quieter now, the streets flowed away from them without direction, but there was always the hum underneath the silence like something restless and stirring and really touching them, as the soft, spring night air of the streets touched them, and at a store door he pulled her into the shadow and kissed her warmly, and when she didn't resist he kept on kissing her. Then they walked on again happily. He didn't care what he talked about; he talked about the advertising agency where he had gone to work the year before, and what he planned to do when he got more money, and each word had a feeling of reckless elation behind it.

For a long time, they walked on aimlessly like this before he noticed that she was limping. Her face kept on turning up to him, and she laughed often, but she was really limping badly. "What's the matter, Sheila? What's the matter with your foot?" he said.

"It's my heel," she said, lifting her foot off the ground. "My shoe has been rubbing against it." She tried to laugh. "It's all right, Bob," she said, and she tried to walk on without limping.

"You can't walk like that, Sheila."

"Maybe if we just took it off a minute, Bob, it would be all right," she said as though asking a favor of him.

"I'll take it off for you," he said, and he knelt down on one knee while she lifted her foot and balanced herself with her arm on his shoulder. He drew the shoe off gently.

"Oh, the air feels so nice and cool on my heel," she said. No one was coming along the street. For a long time he remained kneeling, caressing her ankle gently and looking up with his face full of concern. "Try and put it on now, Bob," she said. But when he pushed the shoe over her heel, she said, "Good heavens, it seems tighter than ever." She limped along for a few steps. "Maybe we should never have taken it off. There's a blister there," she said.

"It was crazy to keep walking like this," he said. "I'll call a taxi as soon as one comes along." They were standing by the curb, with her leaning heavily on his arm, and he was feeling protective and considerate, for with her heel hurting her, she seemed more like the young girl he had known. "Look how late it is. It's nearly four o'clock," he said. "Your father will be wild."

"It's terribly late," she said.

"It's my fault. I'll tell him it was all my fault."

For a while she didn't raise her head. When she did look up at him, he thought she was frightened. She was hardly able to move her lips. "What will they say when I go home at this hour, Bob?"

"It'll be all right. I'll go right in with you," he said.

"Wouldn't it be better . . . Don't you think it would be all right if I stayed the night with Alice – with my girl friend?"

She was so hesitant that it worried him, and he said emphatically, "It's nearly morning now, and anyway, your father knows you're with me."

"Where'll we say we've been till this hour, Bob?"

"Just walking."

"Maybe he won't believe it. Maybe he's sure by this time I'm staying with Alice. If there was some place I could go . . ." While she waited for him to answer, all that had been growing in her for such a long time was showing in the softness of her dark, eager face.

There was a breathless excitement in him and something like a slow unfolding that was all lost in guilty uneasiness. Then a half-ashamed feeling began to come over him and he began thinking of himself at the apartment, talking with Jack and the old man, and with Sheila coming in and listening with her eager face full of seriousness. "Why should you think there'll be trouble?" he said. "Your father will probably be in bed."

"I guess he will," she said quickly. "I'm silly. I ought to know that. There was nothing . . . I must have sounded silly." She began to fumble for words, and then her confusion was so deep that she could not speak.

"I'm surprised you don't know your father better than that," he said rapidly, as though offended. He was anxious to make it an argument between them over her father. He wanted to believe this himself, so he tried to think only of the nights when her father, with his white head and moustaches, had talked in his good-humored way about the old days in New York and the old eating places, but every one of these conversations, every one of these nights that came into his thoughts, had Sheila there, too, listening and watching. Then it got so that he could remember nothing of those times but her intense young face, which kept rising before him, although he had never been aware that he had paid much attention to her. So he said desperately, "There's the friendliest feeling in the world between your people and me. Leave it to me. We'll go back to the corner, where we can see a taxi."

They began to walk slowly to the corner, with her still limping though he held her arm firmly. He began to talk with a soft persuasiveness, eager to have her respond readily, but she only said, "I don't know what's the matter. I feel tired or something." When they were standing on the street corner, she began to cry a little. "Poor little Sheila," he said.

Then she said angrily, "Why 'poor little Sheila'? There's nothing the matter with me. I'm just tired." And they both kept looking up and down the street for a taxi.

Then one came, they got in, and he sat with his arm along the back of the seat, just touching her shoulder. He dared not tighten his arm around her, though never before had he wanted so much to be gentle with anyone; but with the street lights sometimes flashing on her face and showing the frightened, bewildered whiteness that was in it, he was scared to disturb her. His heart began to beat with slow heaviness and he was glad when the ride was over.

As soon as they opened the apartment door and lit the light in the living room, they heard her father come shuffling from his bedroom. His white moustaches were working up and down furiously as he kept wetting his lips, and his hair, which was always combed nicely, was mussed over his head because he had been lying down. "Where have you been till this hour, Sheila?" he said. "I kept getting up all the time. Where have you been?"

"Just walking with Bob," she said. "I'm dead tired, Dad. We lost all track of time." She spoke very calmly and then she smiled, and Bob saw how well she knew that her father loved her. Her father's face was full of concern while he peered at her, and she only smiled openly, showing no worry and saying, "Poor Daddy, I never dreamed you'd get up. I hope Jack is still sleeping."

"Jack said if you were with Bob, you were all right," Mr. Staples said. Glancing at Bob, he added curtly, "She's only eighteen, you know. I thought you had more sense."

"I guess we were fools to walk for hours like that, Mr. Staples," Bob said. "Sheila's got a big blister on her foot." Bob shook his head as if he couldn't understand why he had been so stupid.

Mr. Staples looked a long time at Sheila, and then he looked shrewdly at Bob; they were both tired and worried, and they were standing close together. Mr. Staples cleared his throat two or three times and said, "What on earth got into the pair of you?" Then he grinned suddenly and said, "Isn't it extraordinary what young people do? I'm so wide-awake now I can't sleep. I was making myself a cup of coffee. Won't you both sit down and have a cup with me? Eh, Bob?"

"I'd love to," Bob said heartily.

"You go ahead. I won't have any coffee. It would keep me awake," Sheila said.

"The water's just getting hot," Mr. Staples said. "It will be ready in a minute." Still chuckling and shaking his head, for he was glad Sheila had come in, he said, "I kept telling myself she was all right if she was with you, Bob." Bob and Mr. Staples grinned broadly at each other.

But when her father spoke like this, Sheila raised her head, and Bob thought that he saw her smile at him. He wanted to smile, too, but he couldn't look at her and had to turn away uneasily. And when he did turn to her again, it was almost pleadingly, for he was thinking "I did the only thing there was to do. It was the right thing, so why should I feel ashamed now?" and yet he kept on remembering how she had cried a little on the street corner. He longed to think of something to say that might make her smile agreeably – some gentle, simple, friendly remark that would make her feel close to him – but he could only go on remembering how yielding she had been.

Her father was saying cheerfully, "I'll go and get the coffee now."

"I don't think I'd better stay," Bob said.

"It'll only take a few minutes," Mr. Staples said.

"I don't think I'll wait," Bob said, but Mr. Staples, smiling and shaking his head, went on into the kitchen to get the coffee.

Bob kept on watching Sheila, who was supporting her head with her hand and frowning a little. There was some of the peacefulness in her face now that had been there days ago, only there was also a new, full softness; she was very quiet, maybe feeling again the way he had kissed her, and then she frowned again as though puzzled, as though she were listening and overhearing herself say timidly, "If there was some place I could go . . ."

Growing more and more uneasy, Bob said, "It turned out all right, don't you see, Sheila?"

"What?" she said.

"There was no trouble about coming home," he said.

As she watched him without speaking, she was not at all like a young girl. Her eyes were shining. All the feeling of the whole night was surging through her; she could hardly hold within her all the mixed-up feeling that was stirring her, and then her face grew warm with shame and she said savagely, "Why don't you go? Why do you want to sit there talking, talking, talking?"

"I don't know," he said.

"Go on. Please go. Please," she said.

"All right, I'll go," he muttered, and he got up clumsily, looking around for his hat and coat. As he started to go, his face got hot with humiliation. He longed to look back at her, and when she did not call out to him as he went, he was full of a wild resentment.

In the cold, early-morning light, with heavy trucks rumbling on the street, he felt terribly tense and nervous. He could hardly remember anything that had happened. Inside him there was a wide, frightening emptiness. He wanted to reach out desperately and hold that swift, ardent, yielding joy that had been so close to him. For a while he could not think at all. And then he felt that slow unfolding coming in him again, making him quick with wonder.

1934

# THE SNOB

It was at the book counter in the department store that John Harcourt, the student, caught a glimpse of his father. At first he could not be sure in the crowd that pushed along the aisle, but there was something about the color of the back of the elderly man's neck, something about the faded felt hat, that he knew very well. Harcourt was standing with the girl he loved, buying a book for her. All afternoon he had been talking to her with an anxious diligence, as if there still remained in him an innocent wonder that she should be delighted to be with him. From underneath her wide-brimmed straw hat, her face, so fair and beautifully strong with its expression of cool independence, kept turning up to him and sometimes smiled at what he said. That was the way they always talked, never daring to show much full, strong feeling. Harcourt had just bought the book, and had reached into his pocket for the money with a free, ready gesture to make it appear that he was accustomed to buying books for young ladies, when the white-haired man in the faded felt hat, at the other end of the counter, turned half toward him, and Harcourt knew he was standing only a few feet away from his father.

The young man's easy words trailed away and his voice became little more than a whisper, as if he were afraid that everyone in the store might recognize it. There was rising in him a dreadful uneasiness; something very precious that he wanted to hold seemed close to destruction. His father, standing at the end of the bargain counter, was planted squarely on his two feet, turning a book over thoughtfully in his hands. Then he took out his glasses from an old, worn leather case and adjusted them on the end of his nose, looking down over them at the book. His coat was thrown open, two buttons on his vest were undone, his grey hair was too long, and in his rather shabby clothes he looked very much like a working man, a carpenter perhaps. Such a resentment rose in young Harcourt that he wanted to cry out bitterly, "Why does he dress as if he never owned a decent suit in his life? He doesn't care what the whole world thinks of him. He never did. I've told him a hundred times he ought to wear his good clothes when he goes out. Mother's told him the same thing. He just laughs. And now Grace may see him. Grace will meet him."

So young Harcourt stood still, with his head down, feeling that something very painful was impending. Once he looked anxiously at Grace, who had turned to the bargain counter. Among those people drifting aimlessly by, getting in each other's way, using their elbows, she looked tall and splendidly alone. She was so sure of herself, her relation to the people in the aisles, the clerks behind the counter, the books on the shelves, and everything around her. Still keeping his head down and moving close, he whispered uneasily, "Let's go and have a drink somewhere, Grace."

"In a minute, dear," she said.

"Let's go now."

"In just a minute, dear," she repeated absently.

"There's not a breath of air in here. Let's go now."

"What makes you so impatient?"

"There's nothing but old books on that counter."

"There may be something here I've wanted all my life," she said, smiling at him brightly and not noticing the uneasiness in his face.

Harcourt had to move slowly behind her, getting closer to his father all the time. He could feel the space that separated them narrowing. Once he looked up with a vague, sidelong glance. But his father, red-faced and happy, was still reading the book, only now there was a meditative expression on his face, as if something in the book had stirred him and he intended to stay there reading for some time.

Old Harcourt had lots of time to amuse himself, because he was on a pension after working hard all his life. He had sent John to the university and he was eager to have him distinguish himself. Every night when John came home, whether it was early or late, he used to go into his father's and mother's bedroom and turn on the light and talk to them about the interesting things that had happened to him during the day. They listened and shared this new world with him. They both sat up in their nightclothes and, while his mother asked all the questions, his father listened attentively with his head cocked on one side and a smile or a frown on his face. The memory of all this was in John now, and there was also a desperate longing and a pain within him growing harder to bear as he glanced fearfully at his father, but he thought stubbornly, "I can't introduce him. It'll be easier for everybody if he doesn't see us. I'm not ashamed. But it will be easier. It'll be more sensible. It'll only embarrass him to see Grace." By this time he knew he was ashamed, but he felt that his shame was justified, for Grace's father had the smooth, confident manner of a man who had lived all his life among people who were rich and sure of themselves. Often, when he had been in Grace's home talking politely to her mother, John had kept on thinking of the plainness of his own home and of his parents' laughing, good-natured untidiness, and he resolved that he must make Grace's people admire him.

He looked up cautiously, for they were about eight feet away from his father, but at that moment his father, too, looked up and John's glance shifted swiftly over the aisle, over the counters, seeing nothing. As his father's blue, calm eyes stared steadily over the glasses, there was an instant when their glances might have met. Neither one could have been certain, yet John, as he turned away and began to talk to Grace hurriedly, knew surely that his father had seen him. He knew it by the steady calmness in his father's blue eyes. John's shame grew, and then humiliation sickened him as he waited and did nothing.

His father turned away, going down the aisle, walking erectly in his shabby clothes, his shoulders very straight, never once looking back.

His father would walk slowly along the street, he knew, with that meditative expression deepening and becoming grave.

Young Harcourt stood beside Grace, brushing against her soft shoulder, and made faintly aware again of the delicate scent she used. There, so close beside him, she was holding within her everything he wanted to reach out for, only now he felt a sharp hostility that made him sullen and silent.

"You were right, John," she was drawling in her soft voice. "It does get unbearable in here on a hot day. Do let's go now. Have you ever noticed that department stores after a time can make you really hate people?" But she smiled when she spoke, so he might see that she really hated no one.

"You don't like people, do you?" he said sharply.

"People? What people? What do you mean?"

"I mean," he went on irritably, "you don't like the kind of people you bump into here, for example."

"Not especially. Who does? What're you talking about?"

"Anybody could see you don't," he said recklessly. "You don't like simple, honest people, the kind of people you meet all over the city." He blurted the words out as if he wanted to shake her, but he was longing to say, "You wouldn't like my family. Why couldn't I take you home to have dinner with them? You'd turn up your nose at them, because they've no pretensions. As soon as my father saw you, he knew you wouldn't want to meet him. I could tell by the way he turned."

His father was on his way home now, he knew, and that evening at dinner they would meet. His mother and sister would talk rapidly, but his father would say nothing to him, or to anyone. There would only be Harcourt's memory of the level look in the blue eyes, and the knowledge of his father's pain as he walked away.

Grace watched John's gloomy face as they walked through the store, and she knew he was nursing some private rage, and so her own resentment and exasperation kept growing, and she said crisply, "You're entitled to your moods on a hot afternoon, I suppose, but if I feel I don't like it here, then I don't like it. You wanted to go yourself. Who likes to spend very much time in a department store on a hot afternoon? I begin to hate every stupid person that bangs into me, everybody near me. What does that make me?"

"It makes you a snob."

"So I'm a snob now?" she said angrily.

"Certainly you're a snob," he said. They were at the door and going out to the street. As they walked in the sunlight, in the crowd moving slowly down the street, he was groping for words to describe the secret thoughts he had always had about her. "I've always known how you'd feel about people I like who didn't fit into your private world," he said.

"You're a very stupid person," she said. Her face was flushed now, and it was hard for her to express her indignation, so she stared straight ahead as she walked along. They had never talked in this way, and now they were both quickly eager to hurt each other. With a flow of words, she started to argue with him, then she checked herself and said calmly, "Listen, John, I imagine you're tired of my company. There's no sense in having a drink together. I think I'd better leave you right here."

"That's fine," he said. "Good afternoon."

"Good-bye."

"Good-bye."

She started to go, she had gone two paces, but he reached out desperately and held her arm, and he was frightened, and pleading. "Please don't go, Grace."

All the anger and irritation had left him; there was just a desperate anxiety in his voice as he pleaded, "Please forgive me. I've no right to talk to you like that. I don't know why I'm so rude or what's the matter. I'm ridiculous. I'm very, very ridiculous. Please, you must forgive me. Don't leave me."

He had never talked to her so brokenly, and his sincerity, the depth of his feeling, began to stir her. While she listened, feeling all the yearning in him, they seemed to have been brought closer together by opposing each other than ever before, and she began to feel almost shy. "I don't know what's the matter. I suppose we're both irritable. It must be the weather," she said. "But I'm not angry, John."

He nodded his head miserably. He longed to tell her that he was sure she would have been charming to his father, but he had never felt so wretched in his life. He held her arm as if he must hold it or what he wanted most in the world would slip away from him, yet he kept thinking, as he would ever think, of his father walking away quietly with his head never turning.

1934

# THE RUNAWAY

In the lumberyard by the lake there was an old brick
building two stories high and all around the foundations
were heaped great piles of soft sawdust, softer than the
thick moss in the woods. There were many of these golden
mounds of dust covering the yard down to the lake. That
afternoon all the fellows followed Michael up the ladder to
the roof of the old building and they sat with their legs
hanging over the edge looking out at the whitecaps on the
water. Michael was younger than some of them but his legs
were long, his huge hands dangled awkwardly at his sides and
his thick black hair curled all over his head. "I'll stump you
all to jump down," he said, and without thinking about it he
shoved himself off the roof and fell on the sawdust where he
lay rolling and laughing.

"You're all stumped," he shouted, "you're all yellow,"
coaxing them to follow him. Still laughing, he watched them,
white-faced and hesitant, and then one by one they jumped
and got up grinning with relief.

In the hot afternoon sunlight they all lay on the sawdust
pile telling jokes till at last one said, "Come on up on the old

roof again and jump down." There wasn't much enthusiasm amongst them, but they all went up to the roof again and began to jump off in a determined, desperate way till only Michael was left and the others were all down below grinning up at him calling, "Come on, Mike. What's the matter with you?" Michael longed to jump down and be with them, but he remained on the edge of the roof, wetting his lips, with a silly grin on his face. It had not seemed such a long drop the first time. For a while they thought he was only kidding them, then they saw him clenching his fists, trying to count to ten and then jump, and when that failed, he tried to take a long breath and close his eyes.

In a while they began to jeer; they were tired of waiting and it was getting on to dinnertime. "Come on, you're yellow, you think we're going to sit here all night?" They began to shout, and when he did not move they began to walk away, still jeering. "Who did this in the first place? What's the matter with you guys?" he shouted.

But for a long time he remained on the edge of the roof, staring unhappily and steadily at the ground. He remained all alone for nearly an hour while the sun, a great orange ball getting bigger and bigger, rolled slowly over the dray line beyond the lake. His clothes were wet from nervous sweating. At last he closed his eyes, slipped off the roof, fell heavily on the pile of sawdust and lay there a long time. There were no sounds in the yard; the workmen had gone home. As he lay there he wondered why he had been unable to move; and then he got up slowly and walked home feeling deeply ashamed and wanting to avoid everybody.

He was so late that his stepmother said to him sarcastically, "You're big enough by this time surely to be able to get home in time for dinner. But if you won't come home, you'd better try staying in tonight." She was a well-built woman with a fair, soft skin and a little touch of gray in her hair and a patient smile. She was speaking now with a restrained, passionless severity, but Michael, with his dark face gloomy and sullen, hardly heard her; he was still seeing the row of grinning faces down below on the sawdust pile, and hearing them jeer at him.

As he ate his cold dinner he was rolling his brown eyes fiercely and sometimes shaking his big black head. His father, who was sitting in the armchair by the window, a huge man with his hair nearly all gone so that his smooth wide forehead rose in a shining dome, kept looking at him steadily. When Michael had finished eating and had gone out to the veranda, his father followed, sat down beside him, lit his pipe and said gently, "What's bothering you, son?"

"Nothing, Dad. There's nothing bothering me," Michael said, but he kept staring out at the gray dust drifting off the road.

His father kept coaxing and whispering in a voice that was amazingly soft for such a big man. As he talked his long fingers played with the heavy gold watch fob on his vest. He was talking about nothing in particular and yet by the tone of his voice he was expressing a marvelous deep friendliness that somehow seemed to become part of the twilight and then of the darkness. Michael began to like the sound of his father's voice, and soon he blurted out, "I guess by this time all the guys around here are saying I'm yellow. I'd like to be a thousand miles away." He told how he could not force himself to jump off the roof the second time. But his father lay back in the armchair laughing in that hearty, easy way that Michael loved to hear; years ago when Michael had been younger and he was walking along the paths in the evening, he used to try and laugh like his father only his voice was not deep enough and he would grin sheepishly and look up at the trees overhanging the paths as if someone hiding up there had heard him. "You'll be alright with the bunch, son," his father was saying. "I'm betting you'll lick any boy in town that says you're yellow."

But there was the sound of the screen door opening, and Michael's stepmother said in her mild, firm way, "If I've rebuked the boy, Henry, as I think he ought to be rebuked, I don't know why you should be humoring him."

"You surely don't object to me talking to Michael."

"I simply want you to be reasonable, Henry."

In his grave, unhurried way, Mr. Lount got up and followed his wife into the house and soon Michael could hear them arguing; he could hear his father's firm, patient voice floating clearly out to the street; then his stepmother's voice, mild at first, rising, becoming hysterical till at last she cried out wildly, "You're setting the boy against me. You don't want him to think of me as his mother. The two of you are against me. I know your nature."

As he looked up and down the street, Michael began to make prayers that no one would pass by who would think, "Mr. and Mrs. Lount are quarreling again." Alert, he listened for faint sounds on the cinder path, but he heard only the frogs croaking under the bridge opposite Stevenson's place and the faraway cry of a freight train passing behind the hills. "Why did Dad have to get married? It used to be swell on the farm," he thought, remembering how he and his father had gone fishing down at the glen. And then while he listened to the sound of her voice, he kept thinking that his stepmother was a fine woman, only she always made him uneasy because she wanted him to like her, and then when she found out that he couldn't think of her as his mother, she had grown resentful. "I like her and I like my father. I don't know why they quarrel. Maybe it's because Dad shouldn't have sold the farm and moved here. There's nothing for him to do." Unable to get interested in the town life, his father loafed all day down at the hotel or in Bailey's flour-and-feed store but he was such a fine-looking, dignified, reticent man that the loafers would not accept him as a crony.

Inside the house now, Mrs. Lount was crying quietly and saying, "Henry, we'll kill each other. We seem to bring out the very worst qualities in each other. I do all I can and yet you both make me feel like an intruder."

"It's just your imagination, Martha. Now stop worrying."

"I'm an unhappy woman. But I try to be patient. I try so hard, don't I, Henry?"

"You're very patient, dear, but you shouldn't be so suspicious of everybody, don't you see?" Mr. Lount was saying in the voice of a man trying to pacify an angry, hysterical wife.

Then Michael heard footsteps on the cinder path, and then he saw two long shadows: two women were approaching, and one tall, slender girl. When Michael saw this girl, Helen Murray, he tried to duck behind the veranda post, for he had always wanted her for his girl. He had gone to school with her. At night he used to lie awake planning remarkable feats that would so impress her she would never want to be far away from him. Now the girl's mother was calling, "Hello there, Michael," in a very jolly voice.

"Hello, Mrs. Murray," he said glumly, sure his father's or his mother's voice would rise again.

"Come on and walk home with us, Michael," Helen called. Her voice sounded so soft and her face in the dusk light seemed so round, white and mysteriously far away that Michael began to ache with eagerness. Yet he said hurriedly, "I can't. I can't tonight," speaking almost rudely as if he believed they only wanted to tease him.

As they went along the path and he watched them, he was really longing for that one bright moment when Helen would pass under the high corner light, though he was thinking with bitterness that he could already hear them talking, hear Mrs. Murray saying, "He's a peculiar boy, but it's not to be wondered at since his father and mother don't get along at all." And inside one of the houses someone had stopped playing a piano, maybe to hear one of the fellows who had been in the lumberyard that afternoon laughing and telling that young Lount was scared to jump off the roof.

Watching the corner, Michael felt that the twisting and pulling in the life in the house was twisting and choking him. "I'll get out of here. I'll go away." And he began to think of going to the city. He began to long for freedom in strange places where everything was new and fresh and mysterious. He began to breathe heavily at the thought of freedom. In the city he had an Uncle D'Arcy who sailed the lake boats in the summer months and in the winter went all over the south from one racetrack to another following the horses. "I ought to go down to the city tonight and get a job," he thought: but he did not move; he was still waiting for Helen Murray to pass under the light.

For most of the next day, too, Michael kept to himself. He was uptown once on a message, and he felt like running on the way home. With long sweeping strides he ran steadily on the paths past the shipyard, the church, the railway tracks, his face serious with determination.

But in the late afternoon when he was sitting on the veranda reading, Sammy Schwartz and Ike Hershfield came around to see him.

"Hello Mike, what's new with you?" they said, sitting on the steps.

"Sammy, hello, Ike. What's new with you?"

They began to talk to Michael about the colored family that had moved into the old roughcast shack down by the tracks. "The big coon kid thinks he's tough," Sammy said. "He offered to beat up any of us so we said he wouldn't have a snowball's chance with you."

"What did the nigger say?"

"He said he'd pop you one right on the nose if you came over his way."

"Let's go over," Michael said. "I'll tear his guts out for you."

They went out to the street, fell in step very solemnly, and walked over to the field by the tracks without saying a word. When they were about fifty paces away from the shack, Sammy said, "Wait here. I'll go get the coon," and he ran to the unpainted door of the white-washed house calling, "Art, Art, come on out." A big colored boy with closely cropped hair came out and put his hand up, shading his eyes from the sun. Then he went back into the house and came out again with a straw hat on his head. He was in his bare feet. The way he came walking across the field with Sammy was always easy to remember because he hung back a little, talking rapidly, shrugging his shoulders. When he came close to Michael he grinned, flashing his teeth, and said, "What's the matter with you white boys? I don't want to do no fighting." He looked scared.

"I'm going to do a nice job on you," Michael said.

The colored boy took off his straw hat and with great care laid it on the ground while all the time he was looking mournfully across the field and at his house, hoping maybe that somebody would come out. Then they started to fight, and Michael knocked him down four times, but he, himself, got a black eye and a cut lip. The colored boy had been so brave and he seemed so alone, licked and lying on the ground, that they sat down around him, praising him and making friends with him. Finding out that Art was a good ball player, a left-handed pitcher who specialized in a curve ball, they agreed they could use him, maybe, on the town team.

Lying there in the field, flat on his back, Michael liked it so much that he almost did not want to go away. Art was telling how he had always wanted to be a jockey but had got too big; he had a brother who could make the weight. Michael began to boast about his Uncle D'Arcy who went around to all the tracks in the winter making and losing money at places like Saratoga, Blue Bonnets and Tia Juana. It was a fine, friendly, eager discussion about faraway places.

It was nearly dinnertime when Michael got home; he went in the house sucking his cut lip and hoping his mother would not notice his black eye. But he heard no movement in the house. In the kitchen he saw his stepmother kneeling down in the middle of the floor with her hands clasped and her lips moving.

"What's the matter, Mother?" he asked.

"I'm praying," she said.

"What for?"

"For your father. Get down and pray with me."

"I don't want to pray."

"You've got to," she said.

"My lip's all cut. It's bleeding. I can't do it," he said.

Late afternoon sunshine coming through the kitchen window shone on his stepmother's graying hair, on her soft smooth skin and on the gentle, patient expression that was on her face. At that moment Michael thought that she was desperately uneasy and terribly alone, and he felt sorry for her even while he was rushing out of the back door.

He saw his father walking toward the woodshed, walking slow and upright with his hands held straight at his side and with the same afternoon sunlight shining so brightly on the high dome of his forehead. He went into the woodshed without looking back. Michael sat down on the steps and waited. He was afraid to follow. Maybe it was because of the way his father was walking with his head held up and his hands straight at his sides. Michael began to make a small desperate prayer that his father should suddenly appear at the woodshed door.

Time dragged slowly. A few doors away Mrs. McCutcheon was feeding her hens who were clucking as she called them. "I can't sit here till it gets dark," Michael was thinking, but he was afraid to go into the woodshed and afraid to think of what he feared.

"What's he doing in here, what's he doing?" Michael said out loud, and he jumped up and rushed to the shed and flung the door wide.

His father was sitting on a pile of wood with his head on his hands and a kind of beaten look on his face. Still scared, Michael called out, "Dad, Dad," and then he felt such relief he sank down on the pile of wood beside his father and looked up at him.

"What's the matter with you, son?"

"Nothing. I guess I just wondered where you were."

"What are you upset about?"

"I've been running. I feel all right."

So they sat there quietly till it seemed time to go into the house. No one said anything. No one noticed Michael's black eye or his cut lip.

Even after they had eaten Michael could not get rid of the fear within him, a fear of something impending. In a way he felt that he ought to do something at once, but he seemed unable to move; it was like sitting on the edge of the roof yesterday, afraid to make the jump. So he went back of the house and sat on the stoop and for a long time looked at the shed till he grew even more uneasy. He heard the angry drilling of a woodpecker and the quiet rippling of the little water flowing under the street bridge and flowing on down over the rocks into the glen. Heavy clouds were sweeping up from the horizon.

He knew now that he wanted to run away, that he could not stay there any longer, only he couldn't make up his mind to go. Within him was the same breathless feeling he had had when he sat on the roof staring down, trying to move. Now he walked around to the front of the house and kept going along the path as far as Helen Murray's house. After going around to the back door, he stood for a long time staring at the lighted window, hoping to see Helen's shadow or her body moving against the light. He was breathing deeply and smelling the rich heavy odors from the flower garden. With his head thrust forward he whistled softly.

"Is that you, Michael?" Helen called from the door.

"Come on out."

"What do you want?"

"Come on for a walk?"

For a moment she hesitated at the door, then she came toward him, floating in her white organdie party dress over the grass toward him. She was saying, "I'm dressed to go out. I can't go with you. I'm going down to the dance hall."

"Who with?"

"Charlie Delaney."

"All right," he said. "I just thought you might be doing nothing." As he walked away he called back to her, "So long, Helen."

It was then, on the way back to the house, that he felt he had to go away at once. "I've got to go. I'll die here. I'll write to Dad from the city."

No one paid any attention to him when he returned to the house. His father and stepmother were sitting quietly in the living room reading the paper. In his own room he took a little wooden box from the bottom drawer of his dresser and emptied it of twenty dollars and seventy cents, all that he had saved. He listened solemnly for sounds in the house, then he folded a clean shirt and stuffed a comb and a toothbrush into his pocket.

Outside he hurried along with his great swinging strides, going past the corner house, on past the long fence and the bridge and the church, and the shipyard, and past the last of the town lights to the highway. He was walking stubbornly, looking solemn and dogged. Then he saw the moonlight shining on the hay stacked in the fields, and when he smelled the oats and the richer smell of sweet clover he suddenly felt alive and free. Headlights from cars kept sweeping by and already he was imagining he could see the haze of bright light hanging over the city. His heart began to thump with eagerness. He put out his hand for a lift, feeling full of hope. He looked across the fields at the dark humps, cows standing motionless in the night. Soon someone would stop and pick him up. They would take him among a million new faces, rumbling sounds and strange smells. He got more excited. His Uncle D'Arcy might get him a job on the boats for the rest of the summer, maybe, too, he might be able to move around with him in the winter. Over and over he kept thinking of places with beautiful names, places like Tia Juana, Woodbine, Saratoga and Blue Bonnets.

1934

# THE BLUE KIMONO

It was hardly more than dawn when George woke up
suddenly. He lay wide awake listening to a heavy truck
moving on the street below; he heard one truck driver
shout angrily to another; he heard the noises of doors slamming, of women taking in the milk, of cars starting, and
sometime later on in the morning, he wondered where all
these people went when they hurried out briskly with so
much assurance.

Each morning he wakened a little earlier and was wide
awake. But this time he was more restless than ever and he
thought with despair. "We're unlucky, that's it. We've never
had any luck since we've come here. There's something you
can't put your hands on working to destroy us. Everything
goes steadily against us from bad to worse. We'll never have
any luck. I can feel it. We'll starve before I get a job."

Then he realized that his wife, Marthe, was no longer
in the bed beside him. He looked around the room that
seemed so much larger and so much emptier in that light and
he thought, "What's the matter with Marthe? Is it getting
that she can't sleep?" Sitting up, he peered uneasily into the

room's dark corners. There was a light coming from the kitch-enette. As he got out of bed slowly, with his thick hair stand-ing up straight all over his head, and reached for his slippers and dressing gown, the notion that something mysterious and inexorable was working to destroy them was so strong in him that he suddenly wanted to stand in front of his wife and shout in anger, "What can I do? You tell me something to do. What's the use of me going out to the streets today? I'm going to sit down here and wait, day after day." That time when they had first got married and were secure now seemed such a little faraway forgotten time.

In his eagerness to make his wife feel the bad luck he felt within him, he went striding across the room, his old, shape-less slippers flapping on the floor, his dressing gown only half pulled on, looking in that dim light like someone huge, reck-less, and full of sudden savage impulse, who wanted to pound a table and shout. "Marthe, Marthe," he called, "what's the matter with you? Why are you up at this time?"

She came into the room carrying their two-year-old boy. "There's nothing the matter with me," she said. "I got up when I heard Walter crying." She was a small, slim, dark woman with black hair hanging on her shoulders, a thin eager face, and large soft eyes, and as she walked over to the window with the boy she swayed her body as though she were humming to him. The light from the window was now a little stronger. She sat there in her old blue kimono holding the boy tight and feeling his head with her hand.

"What's the matter with him?" George said.

"I don't know. I heard him whimpering, so I got up. His head felt so hot."

"Is there anything I can do?" he said.

"I don't think so."

She seemed so puzzled, so worried and aloof from even the deepest bitterness within him, that George felt impatient, as if it were her fault that the child was sick. For a while he watched her rocking back and forth, always making the same faint humming sound, with the stronger light showing the deep frown on her face, and he couldn't seem to think of the child at all. He wanted to speak with sympathy, but he burst out, "I had to get up because I couldn't go on with my own thoughts. We're unlucky, Marthe. We haven't had a day's luck since we've come to this city. How much longer can this go on before they throw us out on the street? I tell you we never should have come here."

She looked up at him indignantly. He couldn't see the fierceness in her face because her head was against the window light. Twice he walked the length of the room, then he stood beside her, looking down at the street. There was now traffic and an increasing steady hum of motion. He felt chilled and his fingers grasped at the collar of his dressing gown, pulling it across his chest. "It's cold here, and you can imagine what it'll be like in winter," he said. And when Marthe again did not answer, he said sullenly, "You wanted us to come here. You wanted us to give up what we had and come to a bigger city where there were bigger things ahead. Where we might amount to something because of my fine education and your charming manner. You thought we didn't have enough ambition, didn't you?"

"Why talk about it now, George?"

"I want you to see what's happened to us."

"Say I'm responsible. Say anything you wish."

"All right. I'll tell you what I feel in my bones. Luck is against us. Something far stronger than our two lives is working against us. I was thinking about it when I woke up. I must have been thinking about it all through my sleep."

"We've been unlucky, but we've often had a good time, haven't we?" she said.

"Tell me honestly, have we had a day's luck since we got married?" he said brutally.

"I don't know," she said with her head down. Then she looked up suddenly, almost pleading, but afraid to speak.

The little boy started to whimper and then sat up straight, pushing away the blanket his mother tried to keep around him. When she insisted on covering him, he began to fight and she had a hard time holding him till suddenly he was limp in her arms, looking around the darkened room with the bright wonder that comes in a child's fevered eyes.

George watched Marthe trying to soothe the child. The morning light began to fall on her face, making it seem a little leaner, a little narrower and so dreadfully worried. A few years ago everybody used to speak about her extraordinary smile, about the way the lines around her mouth were shaped for laughter, and they used to say, too, that she had a mysterious, tapering, Florentine face. Once a man had said to George, "I remember clearly the first time I met your wife. I said to myself, 'Who is the lady with that marvelous smile?'"

George was now looking at this face as though it belonged to a stranger. He could think of nothing but the shape of it. There were so many angles in that light; it seemed so narrow. "I used to think it was beautiful. It doesn't look beautiful. Would anybody say it was beautiful?" he thought, and yet these thoughts had nothing to do with his love for her.

In some intuitive way she knew that he was no longer thinking of his bad luck, but was thinking of her, so she said patiently, "Walter seems to have quite a fever, George." Then he stopped walking and touched Walter's head, which was very hot.

"Here, let me hold him a while and you get something," he said. "Get him some aspirin."

"I'll put it in orange juice, if he'll take it," she said.

"For God's sake, turn on the light, Marthe," he called. "This ghastly light is getting on my nerves."

He tried talking to his son while Marthe was away. "Hello, Walter, old boy, what's the matter with you? Look at me, big boy, say something bright to your old man." But the little boy shook his head violently, stared vacantly at the wall a moment, and then tried to bury his face in his father's shoulder. So George, looking disconsolately around the cold room, felt that it was more barren than ever.

Marthe returned with the orange juice and the aspirin. They both began to coax Walter to take it. They pretended to be drinking it themselves, made ecstatic noises with their tongues as though it were delicious and kept it up till the boy cried, "Orange, orange, me too," with an unnatural animation. His eyes were brilliant. Then he swayed as if his spine were made of putty and fell back in his mother's arms.

"We'd better get a doctor in a hurry, George," Marthe said.

"Do you think it's that bad?"

"Look at him," she said, laying him on the bed. "I'm sure he's very sick. You don't want to lose him, do you?" and she stared at Walter, who had closed his eyes and was sleeping.

As Marthe in her fear kept looking up at George, she was fingering her old blue kimono, drawing it tighter around her to keep her warm. The kimono had been of a Japanese pattern adorned with clusters of brilliant flowers sewn in silk. George had given it to her at the time of their marriage; now he stared at it, torn as it was at the arms, with pieces of old padding hanging out at the hem, with the light-colored lining showing through in many places, and he remembered how, when the kimono was new, Marthe used to make the dark hair across her forehead into bangs, fold her arms across her breasts, with her wrists and hands concealed in the sleeve folds, and go around the room in the bright kimono, taking short, prancing steps, pretending she was a Japanese girl.

The kimono now was ragged and gone; it was gone, he thought, like so many bright dreams and aspirations they had once had in the beginning, like so many fine resolutions he had sworn to accomplish, like so many plans they had made and hopes they had cherished.

"Marthe, in God's name," he said suddenly, "the very first money we get, even if we just have enough to put a little down, you'll have to get a decent dressing gown. Do you hear?"

She was startled. Looking up at him in bewilderment, she swallowed hard, then turned her eyes down again.

"It's terrible to have to look at you in that thing," he muttered.

After he had spoken in this way he was ashamed, and he was able to see for the first time the wild terrified look on her face as she bent over Walter.

"Why do you look like that?" he asked. "Hasn't he just got a little fever?"

"Did you see the way he held the glass when he took the orange juice?"

"No. I didn't notice."

"His hand trembled. Earlier, when I first went to him, and gave him a drink I noticed the strange trembling in his hand."

"What does it mean?" he said, awed by the fearful way she was whispering.

"His body seemed limp and he could not sit up either. Last night I was reading about such symptoms in the medical column in the paper. Symptoms like that with a fever are symptoms of infantile paralysis."

"Where's the paper?"

"Over there on the table."

George sat down and began to read the bit of newspaper medical advice; over and over he read it, very calmly. Marthe had described the symptoms accurately; but in a stupid way he could not get used to the notion that his son might have such a dreadful disease. So he remained there calmly for a long time.

And then he suddenly realized how they had been dogged by bad luck; he realized how surely everything they loved was being destroyed day by day and he jumped up and cried out, "We'll have to get a doctor." And as if he realized to the full what was inevitably impending, he cried out, "You're right, Marthe, he'll die. That child will die. It's the luck that's following us. Then it's over. Everything's over. I tell you I'll curse the day I ever saw the light of the world. I'll curse the day we ever met and ever married. I'll smash everything I can put my hands on in this world."

"George, don't go on like that. You'll bring something dreadful down on us," she whispered in terror.

"What else can happen? What else can happen to us worse than this?"

"Nothing, nothing, but please don't go on saying it, George."

Then they both bent down over Walter and they took turns putting their hands on his head. "What doctor will come to us at this house when we have no money?" he kept muttering. "We'll have to take him to a hospital." They remained kneeling together, silent for a long time, almost afraid to speak.

Marthe said suddenly, "Feel, feel his head. Isn't it a little cooler?"

"What could that be?"

"It might be the aspirin working on him."

So they watched, breathing steadily together while the child's head gradually got cooler. Their breathing and their silence seemed to waken the child, for he opened his eyes and stared at them vaguely. "He must be feeling better," George said. "See the way he's looking at us."

"His head does feel a lot cooler."

"What could have been the matter with him, Marthe?"

"It must have been a chill. Oh, I hope it was only a chill."

"Look at him, if you please. Watch me make the rascal laugh."

With desperate eagerness George rushed over to the table, tore off a sheet of newspaper, folded it into a thin strip about eight inches long and twisted it like a cord. Then he knelt down in front of Walter and cried, "See, see," and thrust the twisted paper under his own nose and held it with his upper lip while he wiggled it up and down. He screwed up his eyes diabolically. He pressed his face close against the boy's.

Laughing, Walter put out his hand. "Let me," he said. So George tried to hold the paper moustache against Walter's lip. But that was no good. Walter pushed the paper away and said, "You, you."

"I think his head is cool now," Marthe said. "Maybe he'll be all right."

She got up and walked away from the bed, over to the window with her head down. Standing up, George went to follow her, but his son shouted tyrannically so he had to kneel down and hold the paper moustache under his nose and say, "Look here, look, Walter."

Marthe was trying to smile as she watched them. She took one deep breath after another, as though she would never succeed in filling her lungs with air. But even while she stood there, she grew troubled. She hesitated, she lowered her head and wanted to say, "One of us will find work of some kind, George," but she was afraid.

"I'll get dressed now," she said quietly, and she started to take off her kimono.

As she held it on her arm, her face grew full of deep concern. She held the kimono up so the light shone on the gay silken flowers. Sitting down in the chair, she spread the faded silk on her knee and looked across the room at her sewing basket, which was on the dresser by the mirror. She fumbled patiently with the lining, patting the places that were torn; and suddenly she was sure she could draw the torn parts together and make it look bright and new.

"I think I can fix it up so it'll look fine, George," she said.

"Eh?" he said. "What are you bothering with that for?" Then he ducked down to the floor again and wiggled his paper moustache fiercely at the child.

1935

# RIGMAROLE

After they had come in from the party, Jeff Hilton, the advertising man, looked up and saw his young wife, Mathilde, standing there beaming at him. She seemed to him to be glowing from the memory of many whispered conversations with young men who had been anxious to touch her hand or her arm; she smiled and went on dreaming and her wide dark eyes grew soft with tenderness. She began to hum as she walked over to the window and stood there looking down at the street in the early winter night; and as Jeff went on watching her he kept resenting that she should have had such a good time at a party that he had found so dull. She had left him alone a lot, but he had always remained aware of the admiration she aroused in the young men around her. And now she turned, all warm and glowing, and burst out, "Didn't you like the party, Jeff?"

"It was a lousy party," he said vindictively. "I'm fed up with that crowd. No one ever has anything new or bright to say. They've all gone a little stale."

Mathilde tried to stop smiling, but her dark, ardent face still glowed with warmth as she stood there with her hands clasped in front of her. Though Jeff went on talking with a kind of good-humored disgust his earnest face began to show such a desolate loneliness that she suddenly felt guilty; she longed to offer up to him all the tenderness, all the delight it had been so enchanting to have in her since the party. "I had an awfully good time," she said. "But I kept my eye on you. I know who you were with. Were you watching me, Jeff?" and she rushed over to him and threw herself on his lap and began to kiss him and rub her hand through his hair, laughing all the time like a little girl. "Did you think I was flirting? Did you think I laughed and whispered too much? Don't you love people to think I'm pretty?"

But Jeff who had had such a dull time felt only that she was trying to console him and make him feel good so he said irritably, "You don't need to feel you neglected me. Don't feel guilty. Nobody ever has to worry about me trailing you around. You can feel free."

"Jeff," she said, very softly. "I don't want to feel free. I don't feel free now."

"Sure you do. You'd be the first to complain if you didn't."

"Didn't you worry a little about me once tonight, Jeff?"

"Listen here, Mathilde," he said shortly, "jealous men are the greatest bores in the world."

"Jeff, put your arms around me."

"What's the matter with you? You don't need to mollify me or feel guilty because you had a good time. Surely we've got beyond that."

"I wasn't trying to mollify you," she said, looking quite lost, and she began to show in her face much of that curious discontent he had felt growing in her the last three months. She was pouting like a child and she had the shame of one whose innocent gift has been rejected curtly, and then she went away from him awkwardly and curled herself upon the couch, almost crouching, her eyes hardening as she stared at him.

After a while he said, "You're childish, Mathilde. Why are you sitting there as if you hate me?" But he began to feel helpless against her silent, unreasonable and secret anger. "These last few months you've become about as unreasonable as a sick woman. What on earth is the matter with you?" he said. And he got up and paced up and down and his voice rose as he went on questioning her, but every time he passed the couch where she was crouching he became more disturbed by the passionate restlessness he felt in her.

So he tried to laugh and he said, "This is a lot of nonsense, Mathilde," and he sat down beside her. In a rough, good-natured way he tried to pull her against him. When she pushed him away he stared at her for a long time till at last he began to desire her, and again he put his arm around her, and again she pushed him away. Then he lost his temper; he threw his arms around her and held her down while he tried to caress her. "Stop it, stop it Jeff," she cried. "Haven't you got any sense at all? Doesn't it mean anything to you that you didn't want me near you a few minutes ago? What do you think I am?" As she pulled away roughly she was really pleading with him to see that she was struggling to hold on to something he had been destroying carelessly month after month. "Doesn't it mean anything?" she asked.

"There you go," he said. "Why can't you be direct about things instead of sentimental."

"Because I don't want things that way," she said. And then she cried passionately, "You can't touch me whenever you like. You can't do that to me just when you feel like it," and her eyes were full of tears as if at last she had touched the true source of all her disappointment.

But he grabbed hold of her, held her a moment to show he could possess her, then pushed her away. "I'm not a little boy playing that old game," he shouted. "We've been married three years. Why all the rigmarole?" and he expressed the rage that was growing in him by banging her on the knee with his fist.

"Oh, you've hurt me," she said, holding the spot. "Why did you do that?" and she began to cry a little. "That ends it. You'll never hit me again," she said.

"Damn it all, I didn't hit you."

"You did. Oh, dear, you did. That settles it. I'll not stay around here. I'll not stay another night. I'm going now."

"Go ahead. Do what you want to."

"Don't worry. I'll soon be gone," she said, and with tears streaming from her eyes she ran into the bedroom. He stood gloomily at the door with his arms folded across his chest. He watched her pull out drawers, toss dresses into a suitcase, sweep silver at random from the top of the dresser. Sometimes she stopped to press her fists against her eyes. He began to feel so distressed, watching, that he shouted at last, "I won't stand for this stupid exhibition," and he jumped at her and flung his arms around her and squeezed her as though he would crush forever the unreasonable revolt in her soul. Then he grew ashamed and he said, "I won't stop you, and I won't stay and watch this stupid performance either. I'm going out." And when he left her she was still pulling out dresser drawers.

As soon as Jeff walked along the street from the apartment house on that early winter night he began to feel that he really had not left that room at all, that wherever he walked, wherever he went, he would still be pulled back there to the room to watch her, and when he went into the corner tavern to have a glass of beer he sat there mopping his forehead and thinking, "Not just what I want, not just when I feel like it! I can't go on with that stuff when we're so used to each other. I'd feel stupid."

In the crowded tavern men and women leaned close together and whispered and while he listened Jeff kept hearing her voice beneath the murmuring voices and the clink of glasses and seeing her face in the smoke of the tavern, and as he looked around a dreadful fear kept growing in him that whatever was warm and vital among people was being pushed out of his reach; and then he couldn't stop himself from getting up and hurrying back to the apartment house.

He saw her coming out wearing her brown coat, and her felt hat was pulled down over her eyes. She was carrying her bag. A taxi was waiting. In a foolish way, to hide his eagerness, he smiled and said, "May I take the bag for you, madam?" He even made a little bow.

"No thanks," she said, and she swayed the bag away from his outstretched hand, looking at him in that shy pleading way.

"Are you sure you wouldn't like me to take it?"

"Quite sure," she said.

"All right," he said politely, and he stood there trying to smile while she got into the cab, and when the cab actually moved off along the street, he stood there, worried and unbelieving, feeling there was no place to go.

But he went into the apartment and as he wandered aimlessly into the bedroom and looked at the empty dresser drawers his loneliness deepened, and he thought, "I tried to use some common sense anyway. She'll come back. If I went on struggling with her like that all the time I'd never be able to hold my job. I'll bet a million dollars she'll be back."

And he waited and was desolate remembering the shy pleading look in her eyes as she swayed the bag away from him on the sidewalk, and he listened for every small sound from the street, the stairs and the door; and when at last he heard the key turning in the lock he jumped up triumphantly and rushed to meet her.

She came in quietly with a timid, apologetic smile, and as she pulled off her hat she said in a bantering tone, "What were you doing, Jeff? What was keeping you up till this hour?"

"Waiting for you, of course."

"You mean you missed me?"

"Sure I missed you. You know I did, too," he said. He helped her off with her coat, begged her to sit down, rushed to the icebox to get a snack for them and his face kept showing all of his childish triumph. She was delighted to be waited on in this different way. Every time the broad smile came on his face she asked, "What are you laughing at, Jeff?"

"How does it feel to be free?" was all he said.

But when they were going to bed and she had buried her dark head in the pillow she began to cry brokenly, and no matter how he coaxed her, or how gently he spoke she would not be quiet. "Aren't we happy now, Mathilde? Isn't it all over now," he kept saying.

"No, I'm not happy. I can't bear it," she said.

"You can't bear what?"

"The way you let me go. No matter what happened I didn't think you'd ever let me go. You wouldn't have done it two years ago."

"But you wanted to go, Mathilde, and if I thought you wanted to . . ."

"Two years ago you would have made me come back. You would have been afraid of losing me."

"I knew you'd come back like a homing pigeon."

"Yes, you were so sure of it. You were so very sure," she said, and then she put her hands over her face and she turned her head away, mumbling, "I'm silly. I guess I sound silly. I guess I don't know what I want," and he could only see the back of her neck and her hand moving over her cheek.

As he walked around the bed, looking at her, he thought, "Why didn't I stop her? Why can't she see that knowing we love each other is better than worrying that we don't?" but he began to feel terribly afraid. "Nobody loves insecurity," he said, knowing his words sounded weak and apologetic. For a while he watched her, then went to speak, but he found himself shyly fumbling what seemed to be old words, so he stood there, silent, with his love becoming an ache, for it seemed a terrible thing that such words should sound strange just because they had grown used to each other. Then he knew that his fear had been that he would never be able to express all the feeling he had for her. And all he said was, "I had a glass of beer at the corner and I began to feel terrible."

"Did you?" she said without looking up.

"I think I know what you've been missing," he said.

"Yes," she said.

"I couldn't stay away from here," he said. "I felt you'd be pulled back too."

She looked up at him timidly for though the words he used were neither new, nor warm, nor strange, she began to feel his awkward shyness, she began almost to hear him thinking, "What happens that you can't keep showing your love when it's so strong in you?" She just waited there and grew shy too, and the feeling between them at that moment seemed so much deeper than any earlier time of impulse and sudden joy.

1935

# ALL THE YEARS OF HER LIFE

They were closing the drugstore, and Alfred Higgins, who had just taken off his white jacket, was putting on his coat getting ready to go home. The little grey-haired man, Sam Carr, who owned the drugstore, was bending down behind the cash register, and when Alfred Higgins passed him, he looked up and said softly, "Just a moment, Alfred. One moment before you go."

The soft, confident, quiet way in which Sam Carr spoke made Alfred start to button his coat nervously. He felt sure his face was white. Sam Carr usually said, "Good night," brusquely, without looking up. In the six months he had been working in the drugstore Alfred had never heard his employer speak softly like that. His heart began to beat so loud it was hard for him to get his breath. "What is it, Mr. Carr?" he asked.

"Maybe you'd be good enough to take a few things out of your pocket and leave them here before you go," Sam Carr said.

"What things? What are you talking about?"

"You've got a compact and a lipstick and at least two tubes of toothpaste in your pockets, Alfred."

"What do you mean? Do you think I'm crazy?" Alfred blustered. His face got red and he knew he looked fierce with indignation. But Sam Carr, standing by the door with his blue eyes shining brightly behind his glasses and his lips moving underneath his grey moustache, only nodded his head a few times, and then Alfred grew very frightened and he didn't know what to say. Slowly he raised his hand and dipped it into his pocket, and with his eyes never meeting Sam Carr's eyes, he took out a blue compact and two tubes of toothpaste and a lipstick, and he laid them one by one on the counter.

"Petty thieving, eh, Alfred?" Sam Carr said. "And maybe you'd be good enough to tell me how long this has been going on."

"This is the first time I ever took anything."

"So now you think you'll tell me a lie, eh? I don't know what goes on in my own store? You've been doing this pretty steady," Sam Carr said as he went over and stood behind the cash register.

Ever since Alfred had left school he had been getting into trouble wherever he worked. He lived at home with his mother and his father, who was a printer. His two older brothers were married and his sister had got married last year, and it would have been all right for his parents if Alfred had only been able to keep a job.

While Sam Carr smiled and stroked the side of his face very delicately with the tips of his fingers, Alfred began to feel a fright growing in him that had been in him every time he had got into such trouble.

"I liked you," Sam Carr was saying. "I liked you and would have trusted you." While Alfred watched, his pale eyes alert, Sam Carr drummed with his fingers on the counter. "I don't like to call a cop in point-blank," he was saying, very worried. "You're a fool, and maybe I should call your father and tell him you're a fool. Maybe I should let them know I'm going to have you locked up."

"My father's not at home. He's a printer. He works nights," Alfred said.

"Who's at home?"

"My mother, I guess."

"Then we'll see what she says." Sam Carr went to the phone and dialed the number.

Alfred was not ashamed, but there was that deep fright growing in him, and he blurted out arrogantly, like a strong, full-grown man, "Just a minute. You don't need to draw anybody else in. You don't need to tell her." Yet the old, child-ish hope was in him, too, the longing that someone at home would come and help him.

"Yeah, that's right, he's in trouble," Mr. Carr was saying. "Yeah, your boy works for me. You'd better come down in a hurry." And when he was finished Mr. Carr went over to the door and looked out at the street and watched the people passing in the late summer night. "I'll keep my eye out for a cop," was all he said.

Alfred knew how his mother would come rushing in with her eyes blazing, or maybe she would be crying, and she would push him away when he tried to talk to her, and make him feel her dreadful contempt; yet he longed that she might come before Mr. Carr saw the cop on the beat passing the door.

While they waited – and it seemed a long time – they did not speak, and when at last they heard someone tapping on the closed door, Mr. Carr, turning the latch, said crisply, "Come in, Mrs. Higgins." He looked hard-faced and stern.

Mrs. Higgins must have been going to bed when he telephoned, for her hair was tucked in loosely under her hat, and her hand at her throat held her light coat tight across her chest so her dress would not show. She came in, large and plump, with a little smile on her friendly face. Most of the store lights had been turned out and at first she did not see Alfred, who was standing in the shadow at the end of the counter. Yet as soon as she saw him she did not look as Alfred thought she would look: she smiled, her grey eyes never wavered, and with a calmness and dignity that made them forget that her clothes seemed to have been thrown on her, she put out her hand to Mr. Carr and said politely, "I'm Mrs. Higgins. I'm Alfred's mother."

Mr. Carr was a bit embarrassed by her lack of fear and her simplicity, and he hardly knew what to say to her, so she asked, "Is Alfred in trouble?"

"He is. He's been taking things from the store. I caught him red-handed. Little things like compacts and toothpaste and lipsticks. Stuff he can sell easily," the proprietor said.

As she listened Mrs. Higgins looked at Alfred and nodded her head sadly, and when Sam Carr had finished she said gravely, "Is it so, Alfred?"

"Yes."

"Why have you been doing it?"

"I've been spending money, I guess."

"On what?"

"Going around with the guys, I guess," Alfred said.

Mrs. Higgins put out her hand and touched Sam Carr's arm with an understanding gentleness, and speaking as though afraid of disturbing him, she said, "If you would only listen to me before doing anything." Her simple earnestness made her shy; her humility made her falter and look away, but in a moment she was smiling gravely again, and she said with a patient dignity, "What did you intend to do, Mr. Carr?"

"I was going to get a cop. That's what I ought to do."

"Yes, I suppose so. It's not for me to say, because he's my son. Yet I sometimes think a little good advice is the best thing for a boy when he's at a certain period in his life," she said.

Alfred couldn't understand his mother's quiet composure, for if they had been at home and someone had suggested that he was going to be arrested, he knew she would be in a rage and would cry out against him. Yet now she was standing there with that gentle, pleading smile on her face, saying, "I wonder if you don't think it would be better just to let him come home with me. He looks a big fellow, doesn't he? It takes some of them a long time to get any sense," and they both stared at Alfred, who shifted away, a cosmetic showcase light shining for a moment on his thin face and the tiny pimples over his cheekbone.

But even while turning away uneasily Alfred realized that Mr. Carr had become aware that his mother was really a fine woman; he knew that Sam Carr was puzzled by his mother, as if he had expected her to come in and plead with him tearfully, and instead he was being made to feel a bit ashamed by her vast tolerance. While there was only the sound of the mother's soft, assured voice in the store, Mr. Carr began to nod his head encouragingly at her. Without being alarmed, while being just large and still and simple and hopeful, she was becoming dominant there in the dimly lit store. "Of course, I don't want to be harsh," Mr. Carr was saying. "I'll tell you what I'll do. I'll just fire him and let it go at that. How's that?" and he got up and shook hands with Mrs. Higgins, bowing low to her in deep respect.

There was such warmth and gratitude in the way she said, "I'll never forget your kindness," that Mr. Carr began to feel warm and genial himself.

"Sorry we had to meet this way," he said. "But I'm glad I got in touch with you. Just wanted to do the right thing, that's all," he said.

"It's better to meet like this than never, isn't it?" she said. Suddenly they clasped hands as if they liked each other, as if they had known each other a long time. "Good night, sir," she said.

"Good night, Mrs. Higgins. I'm truly sorry," he said.

The mother and son walked along the street together, and the mother was taking a long, firm stride as she looked ahead with her stern face full of worry. Alfred was afraid to speak to her. He was afraid of the silence that was between them, so he only looked ahead too, for the excitement and relief was still strong in him; but in a little while, going along like that in silence made him terribly aware of the strength and the sternness in her; he began to wonder what she was thinking of as she stared ahead so grimly; she seemed to have forgotten that he walked beside her; so when they were passing under the Sixth Avenue elevated and the rumble of the train seemed to break the silence, he said in his old, blustering way, "Thank God it turned out like that. I certainly won't get in a jam like that again."

"Be quiet. Don't speak to me. You've disgraced me again and again," she said bitterly.

"That's the last time. That's all I'm saying."

"Have the decency to be quiet," she snapped.

They kept on their way, looking straight ahead.

When they were at home and his mother took off her coat, Alfred saw that she was really only half-dressed, and she made him feel afraid again when she said, without even looking at him, "You're a bad lot. God forgive you. It's one thing after another and always has been. Why do you stand there stupidly? Go to bed, why don't you?" When he was going, she said, "I'll make myself a cup of tea. Mind, now, not a word about tonight to your father."

While Alfred was undressing in his bedroom, he heard his mother moving around the kitchen. She filled the kettle and put it on the stove. She moved a chair. And as he listened there was no shame in him, just wonder and a kind of admiration of her strength and repose. He could still see Sam Carr nodding his head encouragingly to her; he could hear her talking simply and earnestly, and as he sat on his bed he felt a pride in her strength. "She certainly was smooth," he thought.

At last he got up and went along to the kitchen, and when he was at the door he saw his mother pouring herself a cup of tea. He watched and he didn't move. Her face, as she sat there, was a frightened, broken face utterly unlike the face of the woman who had been so assured a little while ago in the drugstore. When she reached out and lifted the kettle to pour hot water in her cup, her hand trembled and the water splashed on the stove. Leaning back in the chair, she sighed and lifted the cup to her lips, and her lips were groping loosely as if they would never reach the cup. She swallowed the hot tea and then she straightened up in relief, though her hand holding the cup still trembled. She looked very old.

It seemed to Alfred that this was the way it had been every time he had been in trouble before, that this trembling had really been in her as she hurried out half-dressed to the drugstore. He understood why she had sat alone in the kitchen the night his young sister had kept repeating doggedly that she was getting married. Now he felt all that his mother had been thinking of as they walked along the street together a little while ago. He watched his mother, and he never spoke, but at that moment his youth seemed to be over; he knew all the years of her life by the way her hand trembled as she raised the cup to her lips.

1935

# THE VOYAGE OUT

J eff found himself sitting next to her one night in a movie, and when he discovered that she was neat and pretty, he began to watch her furtively. Though she didn't even turn her head, he felt sure she was aware of him beside her. When she got up to go, he followed her out, and as she hesitated at the theater entrance, drawing on her gloves, he began a polite, timid conversation. Then they walked along the street together.

He soon found out that her name was Jessie, and that she worked in a millinery store and lived with her father and mother. Until that night a month later when they were standing in the hall of her apartment house, saying good night in the way they had so often done in the last weeks, he hadn't thought he had much chance of making love to her. They were standing close together, laughing and whispering. Then she stopped laughing and was quiet, as though the shyness which was hidden underneath her warm, affectionate ways was troubling her. She suddenly put her arms tight around him, lifted up her face, held him as if she would never let him go, and let him know she was offering all her love.

"I don't want to go home. Let me go in with you and stay a while," he pleaded.

"All right – if they're asleep," she whispered.

As they opened the door and tiptoed into her place, the boldness he felt in her made his heart beat loud. Then they heard her father cough. They stood still, frightened, her hand tightening on his arm.

"We'd better not tonight," she whispered. "They're awake. You'd better go quick."

"Tomorrow night then?"

"Maybe – we'll see," she said.

Brushing her face nervously against his, she almost shoved him out into the street.

As he loafed over to Eighth Avenue, his nervousness left him. He was full of elation, and he thought, "Gee whizz, she'll do anything I want now. It came so easy, just like I wanted it to," and a longing for her began to grow in him. He still could feel her warmth and hear her urgent whispering. He grinned as he loafed along, for he had thought it would take a long time and he'd have to go slow and easy. Lights in the stores, the underground rumble, and the noise of the cross-town buses on Twenty-Third Street seemed to be touched and made important by the marvelous tenderness within him. He wanted suddenly to lean against a bar or sit at a counter, hear men's laughter, and feel his own triumphant importance among them, and he hurried into the restaurant where he had a cup of coffee every night after leaving her.

At this time men from a bakery in the block came in for a lunch, and a smoke, and Jeff, who had got to know some of them, sat at the counter and ordered a cup of coffee and looked around to see who else was in the restaurant. There were two decently dressed girls, sitting at a table talking quietly. When

Jeff smiled at the girls without any shyness, because a warm feeling for everyone and everything was in him, they shrugged their shoulders in surprise and laughed at each other.

Then the men from the bakery, with the strong, sweet smell of freshly baked bread on them, and their pants white with flour, came in and sat in a row at the counter and began to order plates of hot food.

Sitting next to Jeff was a big, powerful, fair-haired fellow wearing a little flour-marked cap. The others called him Mike, and Jeff had often seen him in the restaurant. Having finished his plate and wiped his mouth, he winked at Jeff and said, "Hello, kid. You around here again tonight? What's new?"

"Nothing," Jeff said. "I've just been feeling pretty good." But he looked so happy as he grinned that Mike puckered up his eyes and appraised him thoughtfully, and the two girls at the table were watching him, too. To seem nonchalant, Jeff whispered to Mike, as he indicated the girls with a nod of his head, "How do you like the look of the blonde doll in the green hat?"

"That one?" Mike said as he turned on his stool and looked at the girls, who were whispering with their heads close together. "That one, son? She's a cinch. Didn't you see the glad eye she was giving you? She's a soft touch. She'd give you no trouble at all."

"She don't look like that to me," Jeff said.

"I guess I can put my finger on them by this time. If you couldn't go to town with her in two weeks, you ought to quit," Mike said. Then, as if ashamed to be arguing about women with a kid who was so much younger, he added, "Anyway, she's too old for you. Lay off her."

But Jeff kept shifting around on the stool, trying to catch a sudden glimpse of the girl in the green hat, so he could see her as Mike had seen her, yet knowing that to him she still looked quiet and respectable and good-natured. When she smiled suddenly, she seemed like any other friendly girl – a little like Jessie, even. "Maybe Mike could have looked at Jessie and known from the start it would only take a month with her," he thought. Feeling miserable, he kept staring at the girl, yearning to possess Mike's wisdom, and with a fierce longing growing in him to know about every intimate moment Jessie had had with the men who had tried to make love to her. "If I had been sure of myself, I guess I could have knocked Jessie over the first night I took her out," he went on thinking. The elation he had felt after leaving Jessie seemed childish, and he ached with disappointment.

The girls, who had become embarrassed by Jeff's sullen stare, got up and left the restaurant, and when they had gone Jeff said to Mike, "I get what you mean about the doll in the green hat."

"What did she do?" Mike asked.

"Nothing, nothing. It was just the way she swung her hips going out of the door," Jeff lied, and he lit a cigarette and paid his check and went out.

Jeff and his brother, who was a salesman out of work, had a small apartment on West Twenty-Second Street. As soon as Jeff got home, he realized that the sight of the food in the restaurant had made him hungry, and he went to the icebox and got a tomato, intending to cut some bread and make himself a sandwich. He was holding the tomato in his hand when there was the sound of someone rapping on the door.

It was his brother's girl, Eva, a tall, slim girl with fine brown eyes, who was only about two years older than Jeff. She often came to the apartment to see Jeff's brother. She was at home with Jeff, and laughed a lot with him, and never minded him having a cup of coffee with them. But tonight she looked dreadfully frightened. Her eyes were red-rimmed and moist, as though she had been crying.

"Hello, Jeff. Is Bill home?" she asked.

"He ought to be home any minute, Eva. I thought he was with you."

"He was, but he left me, and I thought he'd be here."

"Why don't you sit down and wait for him?" Jeff said.

When she had been sitting down a little while and they were talking, Jeff found himself trying to look at her as Mike had looked at the girl in the green hat in the restaurant, looking at the way she held her head, at her legs, at her eyes – with such a strange, shrewd glance that she became uneasy and began to smooth her skirt down over her legs.

"She knew what I was thinking," Jeff thought, smiling and cynical, and he tried to say with his eyes, "I know a lot more about you tonight than I used to know. I'll bet if I put my arms around you, you'd snuggle up against me."

"What's the matter with you tonight?" Eva said uneasily.

Startled, Jeff said, "Nothing. There's nothing the matter with me."

"I guess I'm restless. I can't sit still. I think I'll be going," she said, and with her face flushed, she got up and went out before he could think of anything to say that might keep her there.

When she had gone, Jeff, remembering the look of terror that had been in her eyes when she first came in, grew ashamed of the stupid, leering way he had looked at her. "I've driven her away. Thinking of Mike made me act like a fool." He hurried to the open window and looked down at the street, and he could see her pacing up and down, waiting.

He stayed at the window, watching, till he saw his brother coming along the street. Eva ran up to him, and they stopped under the light and began to talk earnestly. Then Bill took her by the arm very firmly and they started to walk toward the corner, but then they turned and came back and stood talking beneath the window.

In the murmur of their voices the words were indistinguishable, but Jeff knew, from the tone, that his brother was apologetic and fumbling. Then the voices rose a little and seemed to be lifted up to him, and there was a desperate pleading in the snatch of words, an eloquent sound Jeff had never heard in a girl's voice before. "It's all right. I wish you'd understand I'm not worrying and I'll never, never hold it against you." She stopped suddenly and grabbed at Bill's arm. Then she let him go and hurried along the street, while Bill stood still, looking after her.

When Bill came in, Jeff said, "Eva was in here waiting for you."

Throwing his hat on a chair, Bill walked aimlessly toward the bedroom. "I know she was here. I ran into her outside," he said.

"What did she want?"

"Nothing important."

"She was worked up about something, all right."

"Why are you staring at me? What's the matter with me? What's the matter with you? Do I look funny?" Bill said.

In Bill's eyes there was the same scared expression that Jeff had seen on the face of Eva. He was accustomed to having his older brother dominate him, even bully him a little. Bill seemed years older than Jeff, because his hair had got so thin. And now the worry, the wonder, and fright showing in Bill's eyes made Jeff feel helpless.

"Eva thinks she's going away, but I'm not going to let her," Bill said. "I'm going to marry her even if we have to all live here together."

"Doesn't she want to marry you?"

"She keeps saying it's her fault, and I didn't intend to marry her, and now she's put me in a hole at a time when we can't do anything about it. She wants to go away for a while till everything's all right." Then Bill, looking straight ahead, said quietly, "I don't know what I'd do if anything happened to Eva."

Jeff could still see Eva clutching at his brother's arm on the street – but not in the way Jessie had clutched at his own arm – and he said hesitantly, "I've got a girl of my own. I wouldn't want to get in the jam you're in."

"Nobody does. There's no use talking about it," Bill said, and he went into the bedroom and lay down on the bed.

Jeff knew that he was lying there quietly, fearing for Eva, loving her, and longing to protect her.

As Jeff watched his brother lying inert on the bed, he began to feel all his wretchedness and terror, and he himself grew timid. If he went back to Jessie, it might get for them like it was for Bill and Eva now. Who wouldn't want to duck that?

He sat and pondered and worried about his brother for a long time. Then he knew suddenly that he was no longer even thinking of his brother; without noticing it, he had begun to dream of the way Jessie had held him against her, and he was thinking of them being together and whispering tomorrow night in her place when it was very late. He could see her lifting her ardent face up to him.

He got up restlessly, realizing that neither Mike's wisdom nor his brother's anguish could teach him anything tonight. Standing at the open window, he looked out over the lighted streets where he walked a little while ago, looking over toward Jessie's place, stirred with a longing for more and more of whatever she would be able to give him. It had started now for them and it would keep going on. And then he was filled with awe, for it seemed like the beginning of a voyage out, with not much he had learned on that night to guide him.

1936

# AN ENEMY OF THE PEOPLE

I t is true that Luella Stevens at sixty-eight was a little too old to be singing in the choir of our church, but no one in the parish remembered when she had not sung her solo at the eleven o'clock mass. Anyone who glanced up at the delicate face and the detached expression of this plainly dressed, frail little woman realized that if the parish had ever had large attendances at mass, then she, with the possible exception of old Catherine Hogan who played the organ, was the only one who could remember them. For a long time everybody was glad to have Luella Stevens up in the choir.

The new, poorer people in town, or the farmers who drove in to church on Sundays, were uneasy when talking to Luella Stevens because she would never let them forget that she came from an old and once influential family. She had been the only daughter of a doctor. She lived alone now in an unpretentious brick cottage. People used to make up stories about how pretty she had been once, and how she had been in love years ago with a man who had gone to Chicago and become a wealthy merchant and the father of a large family. For a great many years afterwards, they said, she had cherished her secret of unfulfilled love until it was too late to bother with anyone else. Then her father had died; the people she had grown up with had gone away or were dead, too. The town had begun to decline and the only place that remained for Luella through the years, as it had been in her youth, as it had been for her family and the man who had been her lover and gone to Chicago, was the parish church and the choir with Catherine Hogan at the organ.

Yet there was no longer any use pretending that Luella had the beautiful voice of her youth. After mass on Sundays old parishioners like Mrs. Todd, the stout, stubborn-faced wife of the town flour-and-feed merchant, began to say, "My goodness, did you hear Luella Stevens today? I declare upon my soul she was positively shouting. Her voice is gone completely. Someone ought to tell the poor woman."

When this was said, prominent ladies of the parish, standing on the sidewalk under the trees in front of the church, nodded their heads gravely as if at last a scandal of tremendous importance had crept into the stagnant life of the town. Those who hardly ever listened to the choir made up their minds to listen eagerly the next Sunday.

Not knowing that her neighbors were now listening to her with a new rapt attention, Luella stood up on Sunday and, with as much confidence as she had ever had during the last thirty-five years, shouted at the top of her voice. Luella was aware, of course, that her voice was no longer a girl's voice, but by attacking the high notes with an extra enthusiasm she imagined she got over them very nicely. On this Sunday, those who had come to pass judgment on frail Luella Stevens turned in their pews and gawked up at her aristocratic old face and soon their own faces were full of indignation at the way she was shouting. The fidgeting young ladies of the choir were aware that at last, judging by the way heads kept turning round, people were noticing Luella: they were so embarrassed that they dropped their own voices in shame and sang so listlessly that the young priest. Father Malone, who had been in the parish only a year, looked up, wondering what was the matter.

After that mass, Mrs. Todd went around to the priest's house to speak to Father Malone. The priest confessed frankly that he thought Luella Steven's voice disrupted the whole choir. The wife of the flour-and-feed-merchant and the priest shook their heads sadly, talked in a low grave tone, and wondered who ought to speak to Luella. "Catherine Hogan is the one, she's been there as long as Luella," Mrs. Todd said in triumph. "A splendid suggestion," said the priest. He thanked Mrs. Todd warmly for her exemplary interest in the matter and then accepted an invitation to play cards next Tuesday night with her husband and their family.

So, one Sunday when the two old women, Catherine Hogan and Luella Stevens, were on their way home from church, they got into the discussion about church music and their own choir in particular. Catherine Hogan, the organist, was stooped and withered compared with Luella, who walked proudly upright. "Did you ever think, Luella, of letting some of the younger girls take some of the solos you've had so long?" Catherine asked. "Just so there'll be some chance for their advancement."

"It never entered my head," Luella said.

"There are those, and mind now, I'm not saying who they are, who think your voice isn't what it was, Luella, and that you shouldn't be singing so much at your age?"

"At my age, Catherine Hogan? And doesn't anyone seem to remember that you, at seventy-two, are four years older than

I am? Where's your own memory, Catherine? Why, when I was a child I always thought you were too old for me to play with. You know you were always far ahead of me in school like one of the older girls. I've always thought of you like that and will to my dying day. Isn't your eyesight failing you, Catherine?"

Catherine Hogan was full of rage, knowing Luella was deliberately making her out to be an old woman when everybody in town knew she could play the organ blindfolded, that it didn't matter if she had to be carried into the choir on a bed with her eyesight gone, she would still know the music. She was so offended she made up her mind never to mention the subject to Luella again.

When she was alone in her cottage, cooking her dinner, Luella, muttering to herself, said, "Old Catherine's mind must be wandering, the poor thing." She simply couldn't bear to think of leaving the choir. Instead of eating the food she had cooked she sat at the end of the table remembering all the tiffs she had had with Catherine in the last forty years; she thought of jealous women, of newer ones in the parish scheming to have their daughters take her place in the choir, and she grew frightened, wondering what there would be left in her life if her enemies were successful. She stood rigid, her lips began to move and soon she was giving everyone in the parish who had ever displeased her a thorough tongue-lashing.

On Sunday, as if to threaten those who would deprive her of her rightful place, she gave full throat to her favorite hymn, singing more bravely than ever. Yet never was it so apparent as on that morning that the woman was simply shouting, that the last bit of sweetness had gone forever from her voice. Young people, who by this time had taken an interest in the matter, began to snicker. Mrs. Todd and Mr. J.T. Higgins, the undertaker, turned and looked up at Luella with a withering severity, and then, glancing at each other and screwing up their lips in disgust, they felt they positively despised the arrogant woman. The whole congregation, looking up at Luella when she had finished singing, began to feel that somehow she was making a shameful mockery of them all by refusing to retire. When they bent their heads piously to pray they felt she really had become their enemy.

After the mass the priest, a tall man with powerful shoulders and a blunt nervous way of speaking, was white-faced, and when he left the altar he fumbled with his vestment, calling sharply to the altar boys who were beside him, "Quick, go up to the choir and tell Miss Stevens I want to speak to her."

When Miss Stevens came in, smiling benevolently at the young priest because she was always anxious to help, he stopped pacing up and down and dropped his hands to his sides. He wanted to blurt out, "You've become a perfect nuisance, I tell you. You distract me. I can't offer up the mass. I can't pray and listen to your terrible shouting," but controlling himself and taking a deep breath, he said, "Miss Stevens. I noticed for the first time today that your voice was failing. I noticed your voice distinctly. Perhaps you feel you've served the choir long enough."

"For over thirty years," she said coldly.

"Yes, indeed, I believe you're sixty-eight."

"Catherine Hogan was seventy-two last July," Luella said triumphantly.

"I don't care how old Catherine Hogan is," the priest, who was exasperated, said. "I don't want to be harsh. I'd like to have you pick up the suggestion yourself. However, I'll say frankly I think you ought to leave the choir."

"I understand," Luella said tartly. Bowing coldly, she went out. She meant she understood that those who were scheming for her position were now successful, and with her head tossing, she walked past the little crowd of people standing in the sunlight in front of the church, not noticing how outraged they were as they stared at her.

It was only when she was going down the old gray dust road, the road she had taken every Sunday of her life, that she began to feel frightened. By the time she got to the bridge over Swinnerton's Creek, she was dazed. Leaning against the rail, she trembled and looked back over the road she had come. It had gotten so that now there was only one main road in her life, the road from her cottage to the church. She wondered what had happened to her life, for though she had stood on this bridge often when she was a little girl, and often, too, when she was in love, and many times afterwards when she was alone, she had never had such a helpless feeling as she had now.

Luella Stevens went a little late to mass the next Sunday. She went in timidly like a stranger entering a great cathedral in a foreign city and she stood in the last pew at the back of the church. Those around her, who noticed her, could hardly stop smiling and nudging each other, and if they had not been praying they would have burst into loud, hearty laughter. But Luella felt lost down at the back of the church: she couldn't remember the last time she had been there, it was so long ago.

Everything went peacefully except that when it was time for her solo Luella began to hum, and then, mechanically, she began to sing, though she kept her voice as low as possible.

A week later she moved up a little closer to the altar where she could feel more at home, and she hummed and hummed and even sang a little louder. Mr. J.T. Higgins, the undertaker, nudged her sternly, but she simply moved away politely as if she understood that he wanted more room. The priest turned uneasily on the altar. Luella, noticing none of these things, was not aware of the rage and contempt they were all feeling for her. The undertaker went on turning page after page of his prayer book, and then finally he leaned over and whispered, "Would you please stop humming and singing? It's impossible for me to concentrate on spiritual things."

"My goodness," Luella whispered. "Has it got so that a poor body can't hum to herself the songs she's been singing for forty years?"

But the priest could stand it no longer and turning on the altar and looking over the heads of everybody, he said firmly, "There must be no noise in the church during mass."

Glaring angrily at the undertaker, Luella tried to say to him with her eyes, "You see, by talking away and making a fuss like a small boy you humiliate both of us in this way. God forgive you," but she really thought the priest was probably referring to small boys at the back of the church whose parents had raised them to be little savages.

Soon no one would sit in the pew with Luella. By herself, she felt free. She sang quite loudly. It was impossible for those around her to pray. It was impossible for anyone, including the priest, to think of God when she shouted a high note, so they thought, instead, of Luella and what a stupid, arrogant, shameless woman she was, denying them all. They began to hate her. They wanted to hurt her so she would leave the parish forever. The priest, stalking down from the altar with long strides, looked as if he wanted to keep going right down the aisle, out of the church, and out of the town.

While every man and woman in the parish who had self-respect and a love of the church was standing out on the sidewalk muttering and whispering of her scandalous conduct, Luella Stevens went home meekly. In the priest's house, Father Malone was sending a message to Hector Haines and Henry

Barton, two sober, middle-aged, prominent laymen, to come and see him on urgent business.

When the laymen were alone with him in his library, the priest, shrugging his shoulders and throwing up his hands helplessly, said, "I can't go on saying mass if these things keep on. I'm going to rely on you two men. Lord in heaven, it's a perfect scandal." Henry Barton and Hector Haines, two big, substantial men, cleared their throats and expressed a devout indignation. They were flattered to think the priest had come to them for assistance. The three of them talked gravely and bitterly, planning a way to handle Luella Stevens.

In her pew up at the front of the church next Sunday, Luella Stevens, almost cheerful now to be there, found herself singing with the choir as she had done for thirty years. As soon as Catherine Hogan sounded the organ note for Luella's old hymn, Luella began to shout as though she had never left the choir.

Up on the altar the priest, kneeling with his hands clasped, lowered his dark head deeper into his shoulders and then at last he stood up and said clearly. "Will someone please take that woman out of the church."

Hector Haines and Henry Barton, who were ready in the pew across the aisle waiting for his signal, stepped over quickly and grabbed Luella by the shoulders, one on each side of her. The priest had said to them, "Be quick, so there will be no confusion." Luella looked around, speechless and frightened. The faces of the two huge, prominent laymen were red and severe as they clutched her in their big hands and hustled her down the aisle. They towered over the small woman, grabbing her as though they were burly policemen throwing a thug out of a dance hall, rushing her down the center aisle.

It was odd the way those who stared at her frightened face, as she passed, felt that they were seeing the end of something. Mrs. Todd, the flour-and-feed merchant's wife, ducked her head and suddenly began to weep, and she only looked up to whisper, with her face bursting with indignation, "Oh, dear, this is so shameful." All the others stirred and shifted miserably in their pews: some wanted to jump up and cry out angrily, "This is an outrage. Who is responsible for this?" and they glared their bitter silent protests at each other. "If she were one of mine there'd be trouble about this, I tell you," Mr. Higgins, the undertaker, muttered, his face red with resentment. But the quieter ones were so humiliated that they could not bear to raise their heads. The priest, who had not counted on the great zeal of his two prominent laymen, thought, "God help us. What have we done?" and he was so distracted he could hardly go on with the prayers.

1936

# RENDEZVOUS

Have you ever known a man you couldn't insult, humiliate, or drive away? When I was working in an advertising agency in charge of layouts, Lawson Wilks, a freelance commercial artist, came in to see me with all the assurance of a man who expects a warm, fraternal handshake. As soon as I saw him bowing and showing his teeth in a tittering smile, as if he were waiting to burst out laughing, I disliked him. Without saying a word I looked at his work spread out on my desk and, though it was obvious he had some talent, I wasn't really interested in his work. I was wondering what was so soft and unresisting, yet so audacious about him that made me want to throw him out of the office.

"I'll get in touch with you if I ever need you," I said coldly, handing him his folder.

"All right. Thanks a lot," he said, and stood there grinning at me.

"Is there anything else I can do for you?" I asked.

"Oh, no, nothing. But I've wanted to meet you, that's all."

"You honor me."

"I've heard about you."

"What have you heard about me?"

"I know people who know you, and besides, I've admired your work a lot. I can open a newspaper and spot a layout that you've had a hand in at once."

"Thanks. Now you flatter me."

"Are you going out to lunch?"

"I've a very important date. I'm meeting my wife."

"I've often talked to my own wife about you. She'd like to meet you sometime," he said.

"Please thank her for me," I said. "And now if you'll excuse me . . ."

"Listen . . . let's have a drink together sometime. That's one of the two things we have in common," he said, shaking with soft laughter.

I was so enraged I couldn't answer for a moment. All my friends knew I had been drinking hard and couldn't stop and in the late afternoons my nerves used to go to pieces in the office. Sometimes it was terrible waiting for five o'clock so I could run out and get a whiskey and soda. Every day it got harder for me to go to work and, besides, I was doing crazy things with friends at night I couldn't remember the next morning that used to humiliate me when they were mentioned to me. I thought he was mocking me, but I waited a moment and said, "Drinking, yes! And you might be good enough to tell me what the other thing is we are lucky enough to have in common."

"Why, I thought you'd notice it," he said. He was so truly, yet good-naturedly embarrassed, that I was astonished. I stared at him. There he was about my size, plump, dark, overweight, wider across the middle than across the shoulders, and with a little black mustache.

"What is it?" I insisted.

"People have always said I looked like you," he said with a deprecating, yet easy swing of his arm.

"I see, I see what you mean," I said, and got up and was walking him toward the door.

"I'll phone you sometime," he said, and he wrung my hand very warmly.

As soon as he had gone, I looked in the mirror on the wall and rubbed my hand softly over my face. It was not a flabby face. I was fat, but my shoulders were strong and heavy. I began to make loud, clucking, contemptuous noises with my tongue.

One night a week later my legs went on me and I thought I was losing my mind. My wife begged me to take some kind of a treatment. It was about half past eleven at night and I was lying on the bed in my pajamas trembling, and with strange vivid pictures floating through my thoughts and terrifying me because I kept thinking I would see them next day at the office and I would not be able to do my work. My legs were twitching. I couldn't keep them still. My wife, who is very gentle and has never failed me at any time since we've been married, was kneeling down, rubbing my bare legs and making the blood flow warm and alive in them, till they began to seem as if they belonged to me.

Then the phone rang and my wife answered it and came back and said, "A man says he is a friend of yours, a business associate."

I didn't want any business associate to know I couldn't go to the phone so I put on my slippers and groped my way to it and said with great dignity, "Hello. Who is it?"

"It's Lawson Wilks," the voice said, and I heard his easy intimate self-possessed laughter.

"What do you want?" I yelled.

"I thought you might want to have a drink with me. I'm not far away. I'm in a tavern just two blocks from your place."

I suddenly had a craving for a drink and felt like going out to meet him, and then loathed myself and shouted, "No, no, no. I don't want a drink. I'm not going out. I'm terribly busy. Do you understand?"

"Okay," he said. "I'll call you again. I was just thinking about you."

I saw him in October, about a week after I had taken three months' leave of absence from the office, trying to get myself in hand so I wouldn't have to go away to a nursing home. I really wasn't making much of a fight and sometimes I was ashamed. I looked shabby, twitching a lot. I sat for hours smiling to myself. I couldn't bear to have anyone see me.

On a dark windy day I was sitting in the Golden Bowl Tavern with a whiskey and soda, promising myself I would not have another drink, not until I had read the Sunday paper at least. Then I looked up and saw that Wilks had come in and was grinning at me with warm delight, as much as I've ever seen on a man's face. While I turned away sullenly, he sat down, ordered a whiskey, and nodding at my glass, said, "The same thing, you see. Didn't I tell you?"

"Didn't you tell me what?" I said. He looked pretty terrible to me. His dull eyes were pouchy, and he seemed heavier and softer. As he raised his glass his hand trembled. When he noticed me staring at him, his face lit up with fraternal goodwill. I wanted to insult him. "You better watch out," I whispered. "The heeby-jeebies'll get you. They'll have to take you outa here soon."

In a tone that maddened me, because he meant no offence, he said, "We're taking the same trip, my friend."

"How so?"

"You don't mind me sitting here, do you?"

"Sit here if you want," I said. "I'm reading the paper."

It was a pleasure to see him looking such a wreck. I was delighted sitting there turning the pages of the paper slowly, never looking up at him while his voice droned on, patient, friendly, dead. Surely anyone else in the world would have found it too humiliating, sitting there like that, yet he said, "Do you mind letting me have the comics?"

"Take them," I said, letting him pull the paper from me.

"I thought I might as well be doing something while I waited for you," he said.

I folded my paper. "Sorry," I said, "I have got to go."

"Let's walk together to the corner," he said.

He was so contented on that dark and windy October afternoon that I decided to mock him. I began by asking questions and he told me he really hadn't been happy for some years. He didn't make much more than enough to live on and, besides, his wife wasn't very sympathetic to his work. On the nights when he wanted to drink and be surrounded by jovial companions and talk about his work and about art, literature and drama, his wife, a matter-of-fact woman, wanted to go out with the ladies and play bridge, and it was a game he couldn't stand.

"How about you? Does your wife play bridge?" he asked.

"She can't stand the game," I jeered at him.

"Maybe my wife and I got married too young. Sometimes I feel that she doesn't really love me at all. How about your wife?"

Full of gratitude to my wife for giving me another chance to widen the gulf between this man and me, I said crisply, "It's entirely different with us, thank you." Then I started to laugh openly, knowing I had been mocking him with my pretended interest in his wretched affairs. Chuckling, I left him standing on the corner, with that puzzled yet overwhelming smile of goodwill still on his weak and puffy face.

I didn't see him for a month. There were nights when I had some terrible experiences and I grew afraid for my wife and myself. I let them put me in the nursing home.

The first weeks were hard, terrifying, yet fascinating. I had a little room to myself and when I was normal and quiet I had the freedom of the house and the grounds, and I had some good conversations with the male nurses. Sometimes they locked me in. The door leading to the corridor had bars on it.

In the morning I often felt that I had floated out of my body at night and had remarkably interesting encounters in space with friends who were dear to me, interesting because they seemed to enlarge the borders of reality for me.

Then one morning one of the nurses said, "We have a patient just across the corridor who knows you."

"Who?"

"A Mr. Lawson Wilks."

"How is he?"

"Very bad for the most part."

"Look here," I begged. "I don't want to see him at all, you understand?"

It seemed terrible that he should be there making me hate him when I was better and looking forward to getting out of the place. I refused to go to the door to look across the corridor. I knew he was standing there looking across at my room and I had a truly savage pleasure in never letting him see me.

During one very bad night, the last bad night I had, I felt that part of myself that was truly me hovering around overhead, right overhead from where I was, except, of course, that I wasn't confined at all. I was smiling at Lawson Wilks, who had joined me, and we were having a very friendly and easy conversation about many simple things. We laughed a lot and liked each other and I was happier than I had been in years.

In the morning when I woke up, I lay in the bed a long time remembering the night and growing, bit by bit, more puzzled. Then I couldn't help getting up and sneaking over to the door and peering at Lawson Wilks' room.

When I got to the door I saw Lawson Wilks standing there looking over at me, and when he saw that I'd come at last to the door, he nodded his head in encouragement. His warm smile seemed even kindlier now. "You and me, we had a good time, didn't we?"

"We did?" I said, with a little cracked smile.

Pointing high over his head, he grinned and said, "It was wonderful last night, wasn't it?"

1937

# THE WHITE PONY

I t was a very beautiful white pony, and as it went round and round the stage of the village theater the two clowns would leap over its back or whistle and make it flap its ears and shake its long white mane. Tony Jarvis, like every other kid in the audience that summer afternoon, wondered if there wasn't some way he could get close to the pony after the show and slip his arm around its neck.

If he could persuade the owners to let him ride the pony down the street, or if he could just touch it or feed it a little sugar, that would be enough. After the show he went up the alley to the back of the theater to wait for the clowns and the pony. But the alley was jammed with kids – all the summer crowd from the city as well as the village boys – and Tony couldn't get close to the back door of the theater. The two clowns came out, their faces still colored with bright paint; then a big red-headed man, apparently the trainer, led the pony out. It shook its head and neighed, and all the kids laughed and rushed at it.

The big redhead, in blue overalls and an old felt hat that had the brim cut off, yelled, "Out of the way, you kids! Go on, or I'll pull the pants off you!" He began to laugh. It was the wildest, craziest, rolling laugh Tony had ever heard. The man was huge. His red hair stuck out at all angles under the lopped-off hat. He had a scar on his left cheek and his nose looked broken. Whenever the kids came close he swung his arm and they ducked, but they weren't frightened – only a little more excited. As he walked along, leading the white pony, a wide grin on his face, he seemed to be just the kind of giant for the job. If the pony started to prance or was frightened by the traffic, the big man would make a clucking noise and the pony would swing its head over to him and lick his hand with its rough tongue.

Tony followed the troupe along the street to the old garage they were using as a stable. Then the redhead yelled, "All right, beat it, kids!" and led the pony inside and closed the door. The kids stood around the closed door, wondering if accidentally it mightn't swing open. It was then that Tony left the gang and sneaked to the back of the garage. When he saw an old porch there, his heart pounded. He climbed up to the roof and crawled across the rotting shingles to the edge of a big window. At first he could see nothing. Then, with his eyes accustomed to the inner darkness, he saw the two clowns. Squatting in front of mirrors propped up on old boxes, they were scraping the paint off their faces. With a pail in his hand and singing at the top of his voice, the redhead walked over to a corner of the garage. Tony could see the pony's tail swishing back and forth.

He couldn't see the pony, but he knew it was rubbing its nose in the redhead's hand. The clowns finished cleaning their faces. One of them took a bottle out of a coat that was hanging on the wall and the redhead joined them and they all had a drink. Then the redhead began to talk. Tony couldn't make out the words, but he heard the rich rumble of the voice and saw the wide and eloquent gestures. The clowns were listening intently and grinning. Day after day he must have talked to them like that and it must have been just as wonderful every time. The white pony's tail kept swishing, and Tony could hear the pawing of the pony's hoofs on the floor.

But it was getting dark and Tony had to get home. When he tried to move, he found his legs were asleep. Pins and needles seemed to shoot through his arms. Afraid of falling, he grabbed at the window ledge and his head bumped against the pane. Before he could dodge away, the red-headed giant came over and stared up at him. "Get down out of there!" he yelled. "Get down or I'll cut your gizzard out!"

They were looking right at each other, and then Tony slid slowly off the roof. As he limped homeward, he felt an intimation of perfect happiness. He kept seeing the swishing white tail.

The next afternoon he went to the theater with two lumps of sugar in his pocket. At the end of the show, he pushed his way through the crowd of kids and got right up by the door. When the clowns came out, most of the kids started to yell and there was pushing and shoving, but Tony hung back, keeping well over to one side of the door, ready to thrust the sugar at the pony's mouth before the redhead could stop him.

The big man appeared at the door, the pony clopping behind. In his hands the redhead was carrying two water pails, and the rein that held the pony was in his right hand also. This time, instead of going on down the alley and forcing a path through the kids, he stood still and looked around. Then he grinned at Tony. "Come here, kid," he said.

"What is it, Mister?"

"What's your name?"

"Tony Jarvis."

Maybe the big man remembered seeing his face at the window, Tony thought. Anyway, the big man's grin was wide and friendly. "How would you like to carry these pails for me?" he asked.

Tony grabbed the pails before any other kid could touch them. The big, freckled, crazy, blue-eyed face of the giant opened into a smile.

Tony walked down the alley, carrying the pails. The big redhead walked beside him, leading the pony and grinning in such a friendly fashion Tony felt sure he understood why the pony swung his head eagerly to the giant whenever he made the soft, clucking noise with his tongue. While Tony was going down the street, his mind was filled with how it would be in the garage, making friends with the pony. Even now he might have reached out and touched the pony if he hadn't had a pail in each hand. The pails were heavy because they were filled with water-soaked sponges, but Tony kept up with the big man all right, and he held the pail handles tight.

"I guess the pony's worth a lot of money," he said timidly.

"Uh?"

"I guess a lot of people want to ride him."

"Sure."

"I guess a lot of kids have wanted a little ride on him, too." Tony said. When the man nodded and looked straight ahead, Tony was so stirred up he dared not say anything more. It was understood between them now, he was sure. They would let him hang around the garage and maybe even have a ride on the pony.

When they got to the garage he waited while the redhead opened the door and gave the pony a gentle slap on the rump and sent it on ahead. Tony was so full of pride he thought he would choke as he started to follow the pony in.

"All right, son, I'll take the pails," the redhead said.

"It's all right. I can carry them."

"Give 'em to me."

"Can't I go in?" Tony asked, unbelieving.

"No kids in here," the redhead said brusquely, taking the pails.

"Gee, Mister," Tony cried. But the door had closed. Tony stood with his mouth open, sick at his stomach, still seeing the redhead's warm, magnificent smile. He couldn't understand. If the redhead was like that, why would the pony swing its head to him? Then he realized that that was the kind of thing men like him took for granted in the world he had wanted to grow into when he had glimpsed it from the garage window.

"You big red-headed bum!" he screamed at the closed door. "You dirty, double-crossing, red-headed cheat!"

1938

## GETTING ON IN THE WORLD

That night in the tavern of the Clairmont Hotel, Henry Forbes was working away at his piano and there was the usual good crowd of brokers and politicians and sporting men sitting around drinking with their well-dressed women. A tall, good-natured boy in the bond business, and his girl, had just come up to the little green piano, and Henry had let them amuse themselves playing a few tunes, and then he had sat down himself again and had run his hand the length of the keyboard. When he looked up there was this girl leaning on the piano and beaming at him.

She was about eighteen and tall and wearing one of those sheer black dresses and a little black hat with a veil, and when she moved around to speak to him he saw that she had the swellest legs and an eager, straightforward manner.

"I'm Tommy Gorman's sister," she said.

"Why, say . . . you're . . ."

"Sure. I'm Jean," she said.

"Where did you come from?"

"Back home in Buffalo," she said. "Tommy told me to be sure and look you up first thing."

Tommy Gorman had been his chum; he used to come into the tavern almost every night to see him before he got consumption and had to go home. So it did not seem so surprising to see his sister standing there instead. He got her a chair and let her sit beside him. And in no time he saw that Tommy must have made him out to be a pretty glamorous figure. She understood that he knew everybody in town, that big sporting men like Jake Solloway often gave him tips on the horses, and that a man like Eddie Convey, who just about ran the city hall and was one of the hotel owners, too, called him by his first name. In fact, Tommy had even told her that the job playing the piano wasn't much, but that bumping into so many big people every night he was apt to make a connection at any time and get a political job, or something in a stockbroker's office.

The funny part of it was she seemed to have joined herself to him at once; her eyes were glowing, and as he watched her swinging her head around looking at the important clients, he simply couldn't bear to tell her that the management had decided that the piano wouldn't be necessary any more and that he mightn't be there more than two weeks.

So he sat there pointing out people she might have read about in the newspapers. It all came out glibly, as if each one of them was an old friend, yet he actually felt lonely each time he named somebody. "That's Thompson over there with the horn-rimmed glasses. He's the mayor's secretary," he said. "That's Bill. Bill Henry over there. You know, the producer. Swell guy, Bill." And then he rose up in his chair. "Say, look, there's Eddie Convey," he said. As he pointed he got excited, for the big, fresh-faced, hawk-nosed Irishman with the protruding blue eyes and the big belly had seen him pointing. He was grinning. And then he raised his right hand a little.

"Is he a friend of yours?" Jean asked.

"Sure he is. Didn't you see for yourself?" he said. But his heart was leaping. It was the first time Eddie Convey had ever gone out of his way to notice him. Then the world his job might lead to seemed to open up and he started chattering breathlessly about Convey, thinking all the time, beneath his chatter, that if he could go to Convey and get one little word from him, and if something bigger couldn't be found for him he at least could keep his job.

He became so voluble and excited that he didn't notice how delighted she was with him till it was time to take her home. She was living uptown in a rooming-house where there were a lot of theatrical people. When they were sitting on the stone step a minute before she went in she told him that she had enough money saved up to last her about a month. She wanted to get a job modelling in a department store. Then he put his arm around her and there was a soft glowing wonder in her face.

"It seems like I've known you for years," she said.

"I guess that's because we both know Tommy."

"Oh, no," she said. Then she let him kiss her hard. And as she ran into the house she called that she'd be around to the tavern again.

It was as if she had been dreaming about him without even having seen him. She had come running to him with her arms wide open. "I guess she's about the softest touch that's come my way," he thought, going down the street. But it looked too easy. It didn't require any ambition, and he was a little ashamed of the sudden, weakening tenderness he felt for her.

She kept coming around every night after that and sat there while he played the piano and sometimes sang a song. When he was through for the night, it didn't matter to her whether they went any place in particular, so he would take her home. Then they got into the habit of going to his room for a while. As he watched her fussing around, straightening the room up or maybe making a cup of coffee, he often felt like asking her what made her think she could come bouncing into town and fit into his life. But when she was listening eagerly, and kept sucking in her lower lip and smiling slowly, he felt indulgent with her. He felt she wanted to hang around because she was impressed with him.

It was the same when she was sitting around with him in the tavern. She used to show such enthusiasm that it became embarrassing. You like a girl with you to look like some of the smart blondes who came into the place and have that lazy, half-mocking aloofness that you have to try desperately to break through. With Jean laughing and talking a lot and showing all her straightforward warm eagerness people used to turn and look at her as if they'd like to reach out their hands and touch her. It made Henry feel that the pair of them looked like a couple of kids on a merry-go-round. Anyway, all that excitement of hers seemed to be only something that went with the job, so in the last couple of nights, with the job fading, he hardly spoke to her and got a little savage pleasure out of seeing how disappointed she was.

She didn't know what was bothering him till Thursday night. A crowd from the theater had come in, and Henry was feeling blue. Then he saw Eddie Convey and two middle-aged men who looked like brokers sitting at a table in the corner. When Convey seemed to smile at him, he thought bitterly that when he lost his job people like Convey wouldn't even know him on the street. Convey was still smiling, and then he actually beckoned.

"Gees, is he calling me?" he whispered.

"Who?" Jean asked.

"The big guy, Convey," he whispered. So he wouldn't make a fool of himself he waited till Convey called a second time. Then he got up nervously and went over to him. "Yes, Mr. Convey," he said.

"Sit down, son," Convey said. His arrogant face was full of expansive indulgence as he looked at Henry and asked, "How are you doing around here?"

"Things don't exactly look good," he said. "Maybe I won't be around here much longer."

"Oh, stop worrying, son. Maybe we'll be able to fix you up."

"Gee, thanks, Mr. Convey." It was all so sudden and exciting that Henry kept on bobbing his head, "Yes, Mr. Convey."

"How about the kid over there," Convey said, nodding toward Jean. "Isn't it a little lonely for her sitting around?"

"Well, she seems to like it, Mr. Convey."

"She's a nice-looking kid. Sort of fresh and – well . . . uh, fresh, that's it." They both turned and looked over at Jean, who was watching them, her face excited and wondering.

"Maybe she'd like to go to a party at my place," Convey said.

"I'll ask her, Mr. Convey."

"Why don't you tell her to come along, see. You know, the Plaza, in about an hour. I'll be looking for her."

"Sure, Mr. Convey," he said. He was astonished that Convey wanted him to do something for him. "It's a pleasure," he wanted to say. But for some reason it didn't come out.

"Okay," Convey said, and turned away, and Henry went back to his chair at the piano.

"What are you so excited about?" Jean asked him.

His eyes were shining as he looked at her little black hat and the way she held her head to one side as if she had just heard something exhilarating. He was trying to see what it was in her that had suddenly joined him to Convey. "Can you beat it!" he blurted out. "He wants you to go up to a party at his place."

"Me?"

"Yeah, you."

"What about you?"

"He knows I've got to stick around here, and, besides, there may be a lot of important people around there, and there's always room at Convey's parties for a couple of more girls."

"I'd rather stay here with you," she said.

Then they stopped whispering because Convey was going out, the light catching his bald spot.

"You got to do things like that," Henry coaxed her. "Why, there isn't a girl around here who wouldn't give her front teeth to be asked up to his place."

She let him go on telling her how important Convey was and when he had finished, she asked, "Why do I have to? Why can't we just go over to your place?"

"I didn't tell you. I didn't want you to know, but it looks like I'm through around here. Unless Convey or somebody like that steps in I'm washed up," he said. He took another ten minutes telling her all the things Convey could do for people.

"All right," she said. "If you think we have to." But she seemed to be deeply troubled. She waited while he went over to the head waiter and told him he'd be gone for an hour, and then they went out and got a cab. On the way up to Convey's place she kept quiet, with the same troubled look on her face. When they got to the apartment house, and they were

ANCIENT LINEAGE AND OTHER STORIES

standing on the pavement, she turned to him. "Oh, Henry, I don't want to go up there."

"It's just a little thing. It's just a party," he said.

"All right. If you say so, okay," she said. Then she suddenly threw her arms around him. It was a little crazy because he found himself hugging her tight too. "I love you," she said. "I knew I was going to love you when I came." Her cheek, brushing against his, felt wet. Then she broke away.

As he watched her running in past the doorman that embarrassing tenderness he had felt on other nights touched him again, only it didn't flow softly by him this time. It came like a swift stab.

In the tavern he sat looking at the piano, and his heart began to ache, and he turned around and looked at all the well-fed men and their women and he heard their deep-toned voices and their lazy laughter and he suddenly felt corrupt. Never in his life had he had such a feeling. He kept listening and looking into these familiar faces and he began to hate them as if they were to blame for blinding him to what was so beautiful and willing in Jean. He couldn't sit there. He got his hat and went out and started to walk up to Convey's.

Over and over he told himself he would go right up to Convey's door and ask for her. But when he got to the apartment house and was looking up at the patches of light, he felt timid. It made it worse that he didn't even know which window, which room was Convey's. She seemed lost to him. So he walked up and down past the doorman, telling himself she would soon come running out and throw her arms around him when she found him waiting.

It got very late. Hardly anyone came from the entrance. The doorman quit for the night. Henry ran out of cigarettes, but he was scared to leave the entrance. Then the two broker friends of Convey's came out, with two loud-talking girls, and they called a cab and all got in and went away. "She's staying. She's letting him keep her up there. I'd like to beat her. What does she think she is?" he thought. He was so sore at her that he exhausted himself, and then felt weak and wanted to sit down.

When he saw her coming out, it was nearly four o'clock in the morning. He had walked about ten paces away, and turned, and there she was on the pavement, looking back at the building.

"Jean," he called, and he rushed at her. When she turned, and he saw that she didn't look a bit worried, but blooming, lazy, and proud, he wanted to grab her and shake her.

"I've been here for hours," he said. "What were you doing up there? Everybody else has gone home."

"Have they?" she said.

"So you stayed up there with him!" he shouted. "Just like a tramp."

She swung her hand and smacked him on the face. Then she took a step back, appraising him contemptuously. She suddenly laughed. "On your way. Get back to your piano," she said.

"All right, all right, you wait, I'll show you," he muttered. "I'll show everybody." He stood watching her go down the street with a slow, self-satisfied sway of her body.

1939

# VERY SPECIAL SHOES

All winter eleven-year-old Mary Johnson had been dreaming of a pair of red leather shoes she had seen in a shoe-store window on the avenue one afternoon when she was out with her mother doing the shopping. Every Saturday she had been given twenty-five cents for doing the housework all by herself and the day had come at last when it added up to six dollars, the price of the shoes. Moving around the house very quietly so she would not wake her mother who seemed to need a lot of sleep these days, Mary finished up the last of the dusting and hurried to the window and looked out: on such a day she had been afraid it might rain but the street was bright in the afternoon sunlight. Then she went quickly into the bedroom where her mother slept, with one light cover thrown half over her. "Mother, wake up," she whispered excitedly.

Mrs. Johnson, a handsome woman of fifty with a plump figure and a high color in her cheeks, was lying on her left side with her right arm hanging loosely over the side of the bed: her mouth was open a little, but she was breathing so softly Mary could hardly hear her. Every day now she seemed to need more sleep, a fact which worried Mary's older sisters, Barbara and Helen, and was the subject of their long whispering conversations in their bedroom at night. It seemed to trouble Mr. Johnson too, for he started taking long walks by himself and he came home with his breath smelling of whiskey. But to Mary her mother looked as lovely and as healthy as ever. "Mother," she called again. She reached over and gave her shoulder a little shake, and then watched her mother's face eagerly when she opened her eyes to see if she had remembered about the shoes.

When her mother, still half asleep, only murmured, "Bring me my purse, Mary, and we'll have our little treat," Mary was not disappointed. She gleefully kept her secret. She took the dime her mother gave her and went up to the store to get the two ice-cream cones, just as she did on other days, only it seemed that she could already see herself coming down the street in the red leather shoes: she seemed to pass herself on the street, wearing the outfit she had planned to wear with the shoes, a red hat and a blue dress. By the time she got back to the house she had eaten most of her own cone. It was always like that. But then she sat down at the end of the kitchen table to enjoy herself watching her mother eat her share of the ice-cream. It was like watching a big eager girl. Mrs. Johnson sat down, spread her legs, and sighed with pleasure and licked the ice-cream softly and smiled with satisfaction and her mouth looked beautiful. And then when she was finished and was wiping her fingers with her apron Mary blurted out, "Are we going to get my shoes now, Mother?"

"Shoes. What shoes?" Mrs. Johnson asked.

"The red leather shoes I've been saving for," Mary said, looking puzzled. "The ones we saw in the window that we talked about."

"Oh. Oh, I see," Mrs. Johnson said slowly as if she hadn't thought of those particular shoes since that day months ago. "Why, Mary, have you been thinking of those shoes all this time?" And then as Mary only kept looking up at her she went on fretfully, "Why, I told you at the time, child, that your father was in debt and we couldn't afford such shoes."

"I've got the six dollars saved, haven't I? Today."

"Well, your father . . ."

"It's my six dollars, isn't it?"

"Mary, darling, listen. Those shoes are far too old for a little girl like you."

"I'm twelve next month. You know I am."

"Shoes like that are no good for running around, Mary. A pair of good serviceable shoes is what you need, Mary."

"I can wear them on Sunday, can't I?"

"Look, Mary," her mother tried to reason with her, "I know I said I'd get you a pair of shoes. But a good pair of shoes. Proper shoes. Your father is going to have a lot more expense soon. Why, he'd drop dead if he found I'd paid six dollars for a pair of red leather shoes for you."

"You promised I could save the money," Mary whispered. And then when she saw that worried, unyielding expression on her mother's face she knew she was not going to get the shoes; she turned away and ran into the bedroom and threw herself on the bed and pulled the pillow over her face and started to cry. Never in her life had she wanted anything as much as she wanted the red shoes. When she heard the sound of her mother moving pots and pans in the kitchen she felt that she had been cheated deliberately.

It began to get dark and she was still crying, and then she heard her mother's slow step coming toward the bedroom.

"Mary, listen to me," she said, her voice almost rough as she reached down and shook Mary. "Get up and wipe your face, do you hear?" She had her own hat and coat on. "We're going to get those shoes right now," she said.

"You said I couldn't get them," Mary said.

"Don't argue with me," her mother said. She sounded blunt and grim and somehow far away from Mary. "I want you to get them. I say you're going to. Come on."

Mary got up and wiped her face, and on the way up to the store her mother's grim, silent determination made her feel lonely and guilty. They bought a pair of red leather shoes. As Mary walked up and down in them on the store carpet her mother watched her, unsmiling and resolute. Coming back home Mary longed for her mother to speak to her, but Mrs. Johnson, holding Mary's hand tight, walked along, looking straight ahead.

"Now if only your father doesn't make a fuss," Mrs. Johnson said when they were standing together in the hall, listening. From the living room came the sound of a rustled newspaper. Mr. Johnson, who worked in a publishing house, was home. In the last few months Mary had grown afraid of her father: she did not understand why he had become so moody and short-tempered. As her mother, standing there, hesitated nervously, Mary began to get scared. "Go on into the bedroom," Mrs. Johnson whispered to her. She followed Mary and had her sit down on the bed and she knelt down and put the red shoes on Mary's feet. It was a strangely solemn, secret little ceremony. Mrs. Johnson's breathing was heavy and labored as she straightened up. "Now don't you come in until I call you," she warned Mary.

But Mary tiptoed into the kitchen and her heart was pounding as she tried to listen. For a while she heard only the sound of her mother's quiet voice, and then suddenly her father cried angrily, "Are you serious? Money for luxuries at a time like this!" His voice became explosive. "Are we going crazy? You'll take them back, do you hear?" But her mother's voice flowed on, the one quiet voice, slow and even. Then there was a long and strange silence. "Mary, come here," her father suddenly called.

"Come on and show your father your shoes, Mary," her mother urged her.

The new shoes squeaked as Mary went into the living room and they felt like heavy weights that might prevent her from fleeing from her father's wrath. Her father was sitting at the little table by the light and Mary watched his face desperately to see if the big vein at the side of his head had started to swell. As he turned slowly to her and fumbled with his glasses a wild hope shone in Mary's scared brown eyes.

Her father did not seem to be looking at her shoes. With a kind of pain in his eyes he was looking steadily at her as if he had never really been aware of her before. "They're fine shoes, aren't they?" he asked.

"Can I keep them? Can I really?" Mary asked breathlessly.

"Why, sure you can," he said quietly.

Shouting with joy Mary skipped out of the room and along the hall, for she had heard her sisters come in. "Look, Barbara, look, Helen," she cried. Her two older sisters, who were stenographers, and a bit prim, were slightly scandalized. "Why, they're far too old for you," Barbara said. "Get out, get out," Mary laughed. "Mother knows better than you do." Then she went out to the kitchen to help her mother with the dinner and watch her face steadily with a kind of rapt wonder, as if she was trying to understand the strange power her mother possessed that could make an angry man like her father suddenly gentle and quiet.

Mary intended to wear the shoes to church that Sunday, but it rained, so she put them back in the box and decided to wait a week. But in the middle of the week her father told her that her mother was going to the hospital for an operation.

"Is it for the pains in her legs?" Mary asked.

"Well, you see, Mary, if everything comes off all right," her father answered, "she may not have any pains at all."

It was to be an operation for cancer, and the doctor said the operation was successful. But Mrs. Johnson died under the anaesthetic. The two older sisters and Mr. Johnson kept repeating dumbly to the doctor, "But she looked all right. She looked fine." Then they all went home. They seemed to huddle first in one room then in another. They took turns trying to comfort Mary, but no one could console her.

In the preparations for the funeral they were all busy for a while because the older sisters were arranging for everyone to have the proper clothes for mourning. The new blue dress that Helen, the fair-haired one, had bought only a few weeks ago, was sent to the cleaners to be dyed black, and of course Mary had to have a black dress and black stockings too. On the night when they were arranging these things Mary suddenly blurted out, "I'm going to wear my red shoes."

"Have some sense, Mary. That would be terrible," Helen said.

"You can't wear red shoes," Barbara said crossly.

"Yes, I can," Mary said stubbornly. "Mother wanted me to wear them. I know she did. I know why she bought them." She was confronting them all with her fists clenched desperately.

"For heaven's sake, tell her she can't do a thing like that," Helen said irritably to Mr. Johnson. Yet he only shook his head, looking at Mary with that same gentle, puzzled expression he had had on his face the night his wife had talked to him about the shoes. "I kind of think Mary's right," he began, rubbing his hand slowly over his face.

"Red shoes. Good Lord, it would be terrible," said Helen, now outraged.

"You'd think we'd all want to be proper," Barbara agreed.

"Proper. It would be simply terrible, I tell you. It would look as if we had no respect."

"Well, I guess that's right. All the relatives will be here," Mr. Johnson agreed reluctantly. Then he turned hopefully to Mary. "Look, Mary," he began. "If you get the shoes dyed you can wear them to the funeral and then you'll be able to wear them to school every day too. How about it?"

But it had frightened Mary to think that anyone might say she hadn't shown the proper respect for her mother. She got the red shoes and handed them to her father that he might take them up to the shoemaker. As her father took the box from her, he fumbled with a few apologetic words. "It's just what people might say. Do you see, Mary?" he asked.

When the shoes, now dyed black, were returned to Mary the next day she put them on slowly, and then she put her feet together and looked at the shoes a long time. They were no longer the beautiful red shoes, and yet as she stared at them, solemn-faced, she suddenly felt a strange kind of secret joy, a feeling of certainty that her mother had got the shoes so that she might understand at this time that she still had her special blessing and protection.

At the funeral the shoes hurt Mary's feet for they were new and hadn't been worn. Yet she was fiercely glad that she had them on. After that she wore them every day. Of course now that they were black they were not noticed by other children. But she was very careful with them. Every night she polished them up and looked at them and was touched again by that secret joy. She wanted them to last a long time.

1943

# A CAP FOR STEVE

Dave Diamond, a poor man, a carpenter's assistant, was a small, wiry, quick-tempered individual who had learned how to make every dollar count in his home. His wife, Anna, had been sick a lot, and his twelve-year-old son, Steve, had to be kept in school. Steve, a big-eyed, shy kid, ought to have known the value of money as well as Dave did. It had been ground into him.

But the boy was crazy about baseball, and after school, when he could have been working as a delivery boy or selling papers, he played ball with the kids. His failure to appreciate that the family needed a few extra dollars disgusted Dave. Around the house he wouldn't let Steve talk about baseball, and he scowled when he saw him hurrying off with his glove after dinner.

When the Phillies came to town to play an exhibition game with the home team and Steve pleaded to be taken to the ball park, Dave, of course, was outraged. Steve knew they couldn't afford it. But he had got his mother on his side. Finally Dave made a bargain with them. He said that if Steve came home after school and worked hard helping to make some kitchen shelves he would take him that night to the ball park.

Steve worked hard, but Dave was still resentful. They had to coax him to put on his good suit. When they started out Steve held aloof, feeling guilty, and they walked down the street like strangers; then Dave glanced at Steve's face and, half-ashamed, took his arm more cheerfully.

As the game went on, Dave had to listen to Steve's recitation of the batting average of every Philly that stepped up to the plate; the time the boy must have wasted learning these averages began to appal him. He showed it so plainly that Steve felt guilty again and was silent.

After the game Dave let Steve drag him onto the field to keep him company while he tried to get some autographs from the Philly players, who were being hemmed in by gangs of kids blocking the way to the club-house. But Steve, who was shy, let the other kids block him off from the players. Steve would push his way in, get blocked out, and come back to stand mournfully beside Dave. And Dave grew impatient. He was wasting valuable time. He wanted to get home; Steve knew it and was worried.

Then the big, blond Philly outfielder, Eddie Condon, who had been held up by a gang of kids tugging at his arm and thrusting their score cards at him, broke loose and made a run for the club-house. He was jostled, and his blue cap with the red peak, tilted far back on his head, fell off. It fell at Steve's feet, and Steve stooped quickly and grabbed it. "Okay, son," the outfielder called, turning back. But Steve, holding the hat in both hands, only stared at him.

"Give him his cap, Steve," Dave said, smiling apologetically at the big outfielder who towered over them. But Steve drew the hat closer to his chest. In an awed trance he looked up at big Eddie Condon. It was an embarrassing moment. All the other kids were watching. Some shouted. "Give him his cap."

"My cap, son," Eddie Condon said, his hand out.

"Hey, Steve," Dave said, and he gave him a shake. But he had to jerk the cap out of Steve's hands.

"Here you are," he said.

The outfielder, noticing Steve's white, worshipping face and pleading eyes, grinned and then shrugged. "Aw, let him keep it," he said.

"No, Mister Condon, you don't need to do that," Steve protested.

"It's happened before. Forget it," Eddie Condon said, and he trotted away to the club-house.

Dave handed the cap to Steve; envious kids circled around them and Steve said, "He said I could keep it, Dad. You heard him, didn't you?"

"Yeah, I heard him," Dave admitted. The wonder in Steve's face made him smile. He took the boy by the arm and they hurried off the field.

On the way home Dave couldn't get him to talk about the game; he couldn't get him to take his eyes off the cap. Steve could hardly believe in his own happiness. "See," he said suddenly, and he showed Dave that Eddie Condon's name was printed on the sweatband. Then he went on dreaming. Finally he put the cap on his head and turned to Dave with a slow, proud smile. The cap was away too big for him; it fell down over his ears. "Never mind," Dave said. "You can get your mother to take a tuck in the back."

When they got home Dave was tired and his wife didn't understand the cap's importance, and they couldn't get Steve to go to bed. He swaggered around wearing the cap and looking in the mirror every ten minutes. He took the cap to bed with him.

Dave and his wife had a cup of coffee in the kitchen, and Dave told her again how they had got the cap. They agreed that their boy must have an attractive quality that showed in his face, and that Eddie Condon must have been drawn to him – why else would he have singled Steve out from all the kids?

But Dave got tired of the fuss Steve made over that cap and of the way he wore it from the time he got up in the morning until the time he went to bed. Some kid was always coming in, wanting to try on the cap. It was childish, Dave said, for Steve to go around assuming that the cap made him important in the neighborhood, and to keep telling them how he had become a leader in the park a few blocks away where he played ball in the evenings. And Dave wouldn't stand for Steve's keeping the cap on while he was eating. He was always scolding his wife for accepting Steve's explanation that he'd forgotten he had it on. Just the same, it was remarkable what a little thing like a ball cap could do for a kid, Dave admitted to his wife as he smiled to himself.

One night Steve was late coming home from the park. Dave didn't realize how late it was until he put down his newspaper and watched his wife at the window. Her restlessness got on his nerves. "See what comes from encouraging the boy to hang around with those park loafers," he said. "I don't encourage him," she protested. "You do," he insisted irritably, for he was really worried now. A gang hung around the park until midnight. It was a bad park. It was true that on one side there was a good district with fine, expensive apartment houses, but the kids from that neighborhood left the park to the kids from the poorer homes. When his wife went out and walked down to the corner it was his turn to wait and worry and watch at the open window. Each waiting moment tortured him. At last he heard his wife's voice and Steve's voice, and he relaxed and sighed; then he remembered his duty and rushed angrily to meet them.

"I'll fix you, Steve, once and for all," he said. "I'll show you you can't start coming into the house at midnight."

"Hold your horses, Dave," his wife said. "Can't you see the state he's in?" Steve looked utterly exhausted and beaten.

"What's the matter?" Dave asked quickly.

"I lost my cap," Steve whispered; he walked past his father and threw himself on the couch in the living room and lay with his face hidden.

"Now, don't scold him, Dave," his wife said.

"Scold him. Who's scolding him?" Dave asked, indignantly. "It's his cap, not mine. If it's not worth his while to hang on to it, why should I scold him?" But he was implying resentfully that he alone recognized the cap's value.

"So you are scolding him," his wife said. "It's his cap. Not yours. What happened, Steve?"

Steve told them he had been playing ball and he found that when he ran the bases the cap fell off; it was still too big despite the tuck his mother had taken in the band. So the next time he came to bat he tucked the cap in his hip pocket. Someone had lifted it, he was sure.

"And he didn't even know whether it was still in his pocket," Dave said sarcastically.

"I wasn't careless, Dad," Steve said. For the last three hours he had been wandering around to the homes of the kids who had been in the park at the time; he wanted to go on, but he was too tired. Dave knew the boy was apologizing to him, but he didn't know why it made him angry.

"If he didn't hang on to it, it's not worth worrying about now," he said, and he sounded offended.

After that night they knew that Steve didn't go to the park to play ball; he went to look for the cap. It irritated Dave to see him sit around listlessly, or walk in circles, trying to force his memory to find a particular incident which would suddenly recall to him the moment when the cap had been taken. It was no attitude for a growing, healthy boy to take, Dave complained. He told Steve firmly once and for all he didn't want to hear any more about the cap.

One night, two weeks later, Dave was walking home with Steve from the shoemaker's. It was a hot night. When they passed an ice-cream parlor Steve slowed down. "I guess I couldn't have a soda, could I?" Steve said. "Nothing doing," Dave said firmly. "Come on now," he added as Steve hung back, looking in the window.

"Dad, look!" Steve cried suddenly, pointing at the window. "My cap! There's my cap! He's coming out!"

A well-dressed boy was leaving the ice-cream parlor; he had on a blue ball cap with a red peak, just like Steve's cap. "Hey, you!" Steve cried, and he rushed at the boy, his small face fierce and his eyes wild. Before the boy could back away Steve had snatched the cap from his head. "That's my cap!" he shouted.

"What's this?" the bigger boy said. "Hey, give me my cap or I'll give you a poke on the nose."

Dave was surprised that his own shy boy did not back away. He watched him clutch the cap in his left hand, half crying with excitement as he put his head down and drew back his right fist: he was willing to fight. And Dave was proud of him.

"Wait, now," Dave said. "Take it easy, son," he said to the other boy, who refused to back away.

"My boy says it's his cap," Dave said.

"Well, he's crazy. It's my cap."

"I was with him when he got this cap. When the Phillies played here. It's a Philly cap."

"Eddie Condon gave it to me," Steve said. "And you stole it from me, you jerk."

"Don't call me a jerk, you little squirt. I never saw you before in my life."

"Look," Steve said, pointing to the printing on the cap's sweatband. "It's Eddie Condon's cap. See? See, Dad?"

"Yeah. You're right, Son. Ever see this boy before, Steve?"

"No," Steve said reluctantly.

The other boy realized he might lose the cap. "I bought it from a guy," he said. "I paid him. My father knows I paid him." He said he got the cap at the ball park. He groped for some magically impressive words and suddenly found them. "You'll have to speak to my father," he said.

"Sure, I'll speak to your father," Dave said. "What's your name? Where do you live?"

"My name's Hudson. I live about ten minutes away on the other side of the park." The boy appraised Dave, who wasn't any bigger than he was and who wore a faded blue windbreaker and no tie. "My father is a lawyer," he said boldly. "He wouldn't let me keep the cap if he didn't think I should."

"Is that a fact?" Dave asked belligerently. "Well, we'll see. Come on. Let's go." And he got between the two boys and they walked along the street. They didn't talk to each other. Dave knew the Hudson boy was waiting to get to the protection of his home, and Steve knew it, too, and he looked up apprehensively at Dave. And Dave, reaching for his hand, squeezed it encouragingly and strode along, cocky and belligerent, knowing that Steve relied on him.

The Hudson boy lived in that row of fine apartment houses on the other side of the park. At the entrance to one of these houses Dave tried not to hang back and show he was impressed, because he could feel Steve hanging back. When they got into the small elevator Dave didn't know why he took off his hat. In the carpeted hall on the fourth floor the Hudson boy said, "Just a minute," and entered his own apartment. Dave and Steve were left alone in the corridor, knowing that the other boy was preparing his father for the encounter. Steve looked anxiously at his father, and Dave said, "Don't worry, Son," and he added resolutely, "No one's putting anything over on us."

A tall, balding man in a brown velvet smoking-jacket suddenly opened the door. Dave had never seen a man wearing one of these jackets, although he had seen them in department-store windows. "Good evening," he said, making a deprecatory gesture at the cap Steve still clutched tightly in his left hand. "My boy didn't get your name. My name is Hudson."

"Mine's Diamond."

"Come on in," Mr. Hudson said, putting out his hand and laughing good-naturedly. He led Dave and Steve into his living room. "What's this about that cap?" he asked. "The way kids can get excited about a cap. Well, it's understandable, isn't it?"

"So it is," Dave said, moving closer to Steve, who was awed by the broadloom rug and the fine furniture. He wanted to show Steve he was at ease himself, and he wished Mr. Hudson wouldn't be so polite. That meant Dave had to be polite and affable, too, and it was hard to manage when he was standing in the middle of the floor in his old windbreaker.

"Sit down, Mr. Diamond," Mr. Hudson said. Dave took Steve's arm and sat him down beside him on the chesterfield.

The Hudson boy watched his father. And Dave looked at Steve and saw that he wouldn't face Mr. Hudson or the other boy; he kept looking up at Dave, putting all his faith in him.

"Well, Mr. Diamond, from what I gathered from my boy, you're able to prove this cap belonged to your boy."

"That's a fact," Dave said.

"Mr. Diamond, you'll have to believe my boy bought that cap from some kid in good faith."

"I don't doubt it," Dave said. "But no kid can sell something that doesn't belong to him. You know that's a fact, Mr. Hudson."

"Yes, that's a fact," Mr. Hudson agreed. "But that cap means a lot to my boy, Mr. Diamond."

"It means a lot to my boy, too, Mr. Hudson."

"Sure it does. But supposing we called in a policeman. You know what he'd say? He'd ask you if you were willing to pay my boy what he paid for the cap. That's usually the way it works out," Mr. Hudson said, friendly and smiling, as he eyed Dave shrewdly.

"But that's not right. It's not justice," Dave protested. "Not when it's my boy's cap."

"I know it isn't right. But that's what they do."

"All right. What did you say your boy paid for the cap?" Dave said reluctantly.

"Two dollars."

"Two dollars!" Dave repeated. Mr. Hudson's smile was still kindly, but his eyes were shrewd, and Dave knew that the lawyer was counting on his not having the two dollars; Mr. Hudson thought he had Dave sized up; he had looked at him and decided he was broke. Dave's pride was hurt, and he turned to Steve. What he saw in Steve's face was more powerful than the hurt to his pride; it was the memory of how difficult it had been to get an extra nickel, the talk he heard about the cost of food, the worry in his mother's face as she tried to make ends meet, and the bewildered embarrassment that he was here in a rich man's home, forcing his father to confess that he couldn't afford to spend two dollars. Then Dave grew angry and reckless. "I'll give you the two dollars," he said.

Steve looked at the Hudson boy and grinned brightly. The Hudson boy watched his father.

"I suppose that's fair enough," Mr. Hudson said. "A cap like this can be worth a lot to a kid. You know how it is. Your boy might want to sell – I mean be satisfied. Would he take five dollars for it?"

"Five dollars?" Dave repeated, "Is it worth five dollars, Steve?" he asked uncertainly.

Steve shook his head and looked frightened.

"No, thanks, Mr. Hudson," Dave said firmly.

"I'll tell you what I'll do," Mr. Hudson said. "I'll give you ten dollars. The cap has a sentimental value for my boy, a Philly cap, a big-leaguer's cap. It's only worth about a buck and a half really," he added. But Dave shook his head again. Mr. Hudson frowned. He looked at his own boy with indulgent concern, but now he was embarrassed. "I'll tell you what I'll do," he said. "This cap – well, it's worth as much as a day at the circus to my boy. Your boy should be recompensed. I want to be fair. Here's twenty dollars," and he held out two ten-dollar bills to Dave.

That much money for a cap, Dave thought, and his eyes brightened. But he knew what the cap had meant to Steve; to deprive him of it now that it was within his reach would be unbearable. All the things he needed in his life gathered around him; his wife was there, saying he couldn't afford to reject the offer, he had no right to do it; and he turned to Steve to see if Steve thought it wonderful that the cap could bring them twenty dollars.

"What do you say, Steve?" he asked uneasily.

"I don't know," Steve said. He was in a trance. When Dave smiled, Steve smiled too, and Dave believed that Steve was as impressed as he was, only more bewildered, and maybe even more aware that they could not possibly turn away that much money for a ball cap.

"Well, here you are," Mr. Hudson said, and he put the two bills in Steve's hand. "It's a lot of money. But I guess you had a right to expect as much."

With a dazed, fixed smile Steve handed the money slowly to his father, and his face was white.

Laughing jovially, Mr. Hudson led them to the door. His own boy followed a few paces behind.

In the elevator Dave took the bills out of his pocket. "See, Stevie," he whispered eagerly. "That windbreaker you wanted! And ten dollars for your bank! Won't Mother be surprised?"

"Yeah," Steve whispered, the little smile still on his face. But Dave had to turn away quickly so their eyes wouldn't meet, for he saw that it was a scared smile.

Outside, Dave said, "Here, you carry the money home, Steve. You show it to your mother."

"No, you keep it," Steve said, and then there was nothing to say. They walked in silence.

"It's a lot of money," Dave said finally. When Steve didn't answer him, he added angrily, "I turned to you, Steve. I asked you, didn't I?"

"That man knew how much his boy wanted that cap," Steve said.

"Sure. But he recognized how much it was worth to us."

"No, you let him take it away from us," Steve blurted.

"That's unfair," Dave said. "Don't dare say that to me."

"I don't want to be like you," Steve muttered, and he darted across the road and walked along on the other side of the street.

"It's unfair," Dave said angrily, only now he didn't mean that Steve was unfair, he meant that what had happened in the prosperous Hudson home was unfair, and he didn't know quite why. He had been trapped, not just by Mr. Hudson, but by his own life. Across the road Steve was hurrying along with his head down, wanting to be alone. They walked most of the way home on opposite sides of the street, until Dave could stand it no longer. "Steve," he called, crossing the street. "It was very unfair. I mean, for you to say . . ." but Steve started to run. Dave walked as fast as he could and Steve was getting beyond him, and he felt enraged and suddenly he yelled, "Steve!" and he started to chase his son. He wanted to get hold of Steve and pound him, and he didn't know why. He gained on him, he gasped for breath and he almost got him by the shoulder. Turning, Steve saw his father's face in the street light and was terrified; he circled away, got to the house, and rushed in, yelling, "Mother!"

"Son, Son!" she cried, rushing from the kitchen. As soon as she threw her arms around Steve, shielding him, Dave's anger left him and he felt stupid. He walked past them into the kitchen.

"What happened?" she asked anxiously. "Have you both gone crazy? What did you do, Steve?"

"Nothing," he said sullenly.

"What did your father do?"

"We found the boy with my ball cap, and he let the boy's father take it from us."

"No, no," Dave protested. "Nobody pushed us around. The man didn't put anything over us." He felt tired and his face was burning. He told what had happened; then he slowly took the two ten-dollar bills out of his wallet and tossed them on the table and looked up guiltily at his wife.

It hurt him that she didn't pick up the money, and that she didn't rebuke him. "It is a lot of money, Son," she said slowly. "Your father was only trying to do what he knew was right, and it'll work out, and you'll understand." She was soothing Steve, but Dave knew she felt that she needed to be gentle with him, too, and he was ashamed.

When she went with Steve to his bedroom, Dave sat by himself. His son had contempt for him, he thought. His son, for the first time, had seen how easy it was for another man to handle him, and he had judged him and had wanted to walk alone on the other side of the street. He looked at the money and he hated the sight of it.

His wife returned to the kitchen, made a cup of tea, talked soothingly, and said it was incredible that he had forced the Hudson man to pay him twenty dollars for the cap, but all Dave could think of was Steve was scared of me.

Finally, he got up and went into Steve's room. The room was in darkness, but he could see the outline of Steve's body on the bed, and he sat down beside him and whispered, "Look, Son, it was a mistake. I know why. People like us – in circumstances where money can scare us. No, no," he said, feeling ashamed and shaking his head apologetically; he was taking the wrong way of showing the boy they were together; he was covering up his own failure. For the failure had been his, and it had come out of being so separated from his son that he had been blind to what was beyond the price in a boy's life. He longed now to show Steve he could be with him from day to day. His hand went out hesitantly to Steve's shoulder. "Steve, look," he said eagerly. "The trouble was I didn't realize how much I enjoyed it that night at the ball park. If I had watched you playing for your own team – the kids around here say you could be a great pitcher. We could take that money and buy a new pitcher's glove for you, and a catcher's mitt. Steve, Steve, are you listening? I could catch you, work with you in the lane. Maybe I could be your coach . . . watch you become a great pitcher." In the half-darkness he could see the boy's pale face turn to him.

Steve, who had never heard his father talk like this, was shy and wondering. All he knew was that his father, for the first time, wanted to be with him in his hopes and adventures. He said, "I guess you do know how important that cap was." His hand went out to his father's arm. "With that man the cap was – well it was just something he could buy, eh Dad?" Dave gripped his son's hand hard. The wonderful generosity of childhood – the price a boy was willing to pay to be able to count on his father's admiration and approval – made him feel humble, then strangely exalted.

1952

# AFTERWORD

BY WILLIAM KENNEDY

The first time I met Morley Callaghan was at his son Barry's dining room table in Toronto and I offered him effusive praise for his memoir, *That Summer In Paris,* which I had read and reread. The book had given me a world of literary exuberance, inhabited by writers I was obsessed with – James Joyce, Scott Fitzgerald, Ernest Hemingway – and included the spectacular tale of Morley knocking down Hemingway in the second round of a boxing match, after which Fitzgerald, the timekeeper, confessed he'd let the round run four minutes instead of three. Hemingway reacted: "All right, Scott, if you want to see me getting the shit knocked out of me, just say so. Only don't say you made a mistake."

Preposterous consequences continued for years thereafter: a permanent wedge driven between Hemingway and Fitzgerald, the press distorting it into comeuppance for Hemingway the bully, Hemingway repeating the story without the knockdown, also writing Fitzgerald biographer Arthur Mizener that the second round had lasted thirteen minutes. The whole comic opera served over time to isolate Morley from his very good friends – Fitzgerald, who had introduced

Morley's writing to his own editor at Scribner's, Max Perkins, who became Morley's editor; and especially from Hemingway, who had befriended Morley in Toronto and helped him publish short stories in Ezra Pound's *Exile*, and Ernest Walsh's *This Quarter*, both literary magazines in Paris.

In 1925 Morley sent Hemingway three stories. He liked them but singled out one, "A Wedding Dress," which is in this collection, and called it "a hell of a good story, a complete finished story, well written, damned good." He added, "Let me tell you right now and you can cut this out and paste it in the front of your prayerbook, that you have the stuff and will be a hell of a fine writer and probably the first writer that's ever come out of Canada . . . Write a lot but see a lot more. Keep your ears and eyes going and try all the time to get your conversations right. Often your conversation is perfect. That's what's really a creative ear. About the most valuable asset you could have."

But Hemingway went farther than heavy praise for Morley. He sent a letter and the manuscript of a long Morley story to his own publisher, Robert McAlmon, and offered to pay half the cost of publishing it. (This hitherto unknown letter was found in April 2012 in a Toronto library by *Toronto Star* reporter Bill Schiller.) McAlmon had just published, in Paris, Hemingway's first book, *Three Stories and Ten Poems*, and Hemingway wrote him:

"I read it four months ago and find I still remember it and that parts of it seem very actual. It seems as though the kid were working along the real line and naturally, in Canada, with anything but encouragement . . . He seems to me like a kid that is worth doing something about. If you like it I'd be glad to go 50-50 with you on the cost of publishing it because I think once he gets published it will clear things up and he can go on and not worry about this stuff. I know that's the way it made me feel."

In those days Hemingway was hardly flush; his career was just beginning. So that 50-50 offer escalates his generosity to a new high in my estimation.

McAlmon never published the story, which Barry Callaghan thinks was "An Autumn Penitent," first published in an anthology of fiction and poetry called *1928: The Second American Caravan: A Yearbook of American Literature.*

In my dinner conversation with Morley many years later I was well aware of Hemingway's vexation over the knock-down and his recurring rancor toward Morley, who recalled it all at length, with vivid memories of the small detail of the famous fight but, amazingly, no rancor whatever toward Hemingway. I'd bought a new copy of *That Summer* so he could inscribe it, and he wrote this: "To Bill after a rather wonderful evening when I felt so close to him I talked away like a fish wife – because I enjoyed myself so much." And I remember it, too, as a great conversation that revealed Morley's capacity for friendship, and his very early judicious valuing of the complexity of other people (including Hemingway), which I now see as an enduring virtue that has kept his work continuously surprising, his characters serially leaping off the page, flaunting their singularity and imperishability.

All that good feeling for the Ernest Hemingway Morley had known in Toronto and Paris had never been seriously damaged by the mercurial hostility of Hemingway-the-boxer's exfoliating ego. The two men did have a shared history, both with a jaundiced view of higher education's effect on a fiction writer, both coming to serious fiction through journalism, Hemingway actually mentoring the seven-years-younger Morley in their talks about writing when they worked together on the *Toronto Star*. Their fiction exhibits simplicity of language; both place a heavy emphasis on dialogue – those "conversations" Hemingway urged Morley to get right. Both writers came under the early influence of Sherwood Anderson and his pared-down style. Anderson suggested Hemingway move to Paris (not Italy, which had been his destination), and he there introduced him to the expatriate literati – Joyce, Gertrude Stein, Ezra Pound *et al*. And for Morley, reading Anderson's work touched a chord that made him write "feverishly and with confidence . . . All around me seemed to be people who were stories, or as Anderson himself called them, unlighted lamps."

In 1926 Morley wrote a brief essay on Hemingway, focusing on his first short-story collection, *In Our Time*: "He is a fine naturalist, who instead of piling up material and convincing by sheer weight of evidence, in the manner of Dreiser or Zola, cuts down the material to essentials and leaves it starkly authentic . . . Nothing stands between the reader and (the character's) movements. So accurate is Hemingway's reporting that this movement has an exhilarating reality in these days of the psychological novel. One moves with his people, knows what they are thinking."

In this piece Morley was echoing what he had already done in his own short stories and would continue doing: being a master of concision, of direct statement, of the arrow of action, a writer who avoided baroque language and detailed dissection of motivations. But the two writers differed in subject matter: Hemingway was writing an extended version of himself in almost all his novels and many of his stories, whereas Morley's focus was, from early on and forever after, outward toward others. Morley condensed psychological fiction's analytical sprawl into brief illuminations in dialogue or thought that defined characters so swiftly and deftly that on first reading it's possible to miss their full meaning in the compelling rush of his narrative.

When you read "Amuck in the Bush," a story he wrote at twenty-four, the impulse is to ask, why did he write this? – a savage episode of vengeance by a brutish, stupid lout. But the lout, fired from his job after trying to seriously injure his boss, is something beyond a vengeful savage – he's a creature driven by a self-destructive sexual compulsion that he himself doesn't understand. He sets out to revenge his firing by kidnapping the boss's six-year-old daughter, but is distracted repeatedly by the big hips and full red lips of his boss's wife, and, when he does attack the wife and child, he tells the wife, "You got to let me have the kid." Yet when he makes his crucial lunge, it's not at the child but at her, and he wonders why. He's out for love, savage style: he wrestles her to the ground and tells her, three times, "You got to lie there" – a rapist's ardent foreplay. He rips her sweater off, she bites him, he feels crazy and doesn't know why he's attacking her, then shoots to kill her and misses, and she and the child run off. His attention to the wife doesn't affect his predictable fate, but it does reveal an unconscious complexity well beyond the primitive.

Edmund Wilson, the great American critic who put Morley's short stories on a level with Chekhov's and de Maupassant's, said, "his triumph, and his deepest irony, is his perception of the inextricable tangle of motives that makes man a creature of beauty and deformity, aspiration and destruction . . . [and he presents] a moral point of view without making judgments of any conventional kind ... we are never certain what the characters are up to (they're often not certain themselves)."

In the very quiet story, "A Sick Call," an elderly and beloved Catholic priest is summoned to the bedside of a dying

woman who two years ago left the church and became
estranged from her family when she married a man who hated
all church people. She had a happy marriage, but now, fearing
eternity, she wants absolution for her sins. Her husband says no
– no confession, no priest, we were always alone together and
nothing will separate us now. The priest cajoles, bluffs, prays
and argues but the husband won't yield. The priest asks for a
glass of water and during the one minute the husband is gone
the priest hears, very speedily, the woman's confession and
absolves her. The husband comes back, sees a change in his
wife, knows what happened, and tells the priest: she's turned
away from me, you weren't quite fair. The priest admits to
himself he indeed was not, but rejoices at bringing "one who
had strayed" back into the fold. But he wonders, did I come
between them? He admires the beauty in the husband's staunch
love for his wife, but concludes it is "just a pagan beauty, of
course." Yet this conclusion overrides his joy and makes him
"inexpressibly sad" – presumably over separating a loving
couple in their last moments and sending the wife off to heav-
enly bliss, the husband to outer darkness – the pagan's lot. So
Morley leaves the priest with a hovering counterclaim against
the morality of his act, his calling and the beliefs of his faith.

Morley published the stories in this volume from the
mid-1920s through the end of the 1930s, only two from sub-
sequent decades; and so we constantly encounter a bygone
world – boarding houses, gaslight, the Depression, the terror
of pregnancy, women as second-class, deferential creatures;
but there is nothing bygone in the themes of the stories – fear,
shame, weakness, the sense of always being wrong, the inabil-
ity to act, innocence, longing, bewilderment, initiation, awak-
ening – and the attendant mysteries these conditions present
to the characters whom they torture.

In "One Spring Night" a young girl is out walking with her date after a movie, they're feeling close, they walk on, her heel is killing her, it gets to be four in the morning, her father will be angry, maybe she should stay with a girlfriend . . . or someplace. Her words are a subtle offer and they excite her and, seeing this, the young man feels a "slow unfolding." But his guilt over the lateness prompts him to argue that her father trusts him, there'll be no trouble, they'll get a cab. They do and she turns sullen. He smoothes it out with her father but she grows furious, all you do is talk talk talk, why don't you leave? He stands alone on the street, wondering what happened, longing for the joy he felt with her on their walk, feeling more of that slow unfolding, which he will soon recognize as his astounding romantic stupidity.

Morley had a long life – he died at 88 in August 1990. I was at his eighty-eighth birthday party at Barry's house and, as he was coming down the stairs from the second floor, the gathered crowd broke into song – "For He's a Jolly Good Fellow." Morley paused at mid-stairs, heard them out, accepted the applause, then said in reply: "I am not now, nor have I ever been, a jolly good fellow."

Jolly, maybe not. But he was a good fellow, original and humane, with a singular set of convictions that pervade all that he wrote. In *A Literary Life*, the lively and sagacious collection of his reviews, meditations and casual essays published in 2008 by Barry, Morley wrote (he was seventy) that he felt that life had outrun the convictions he had always lived by.

"Sometimes I feel my belief in man's essential humanity isn't right for the time," he wrote, using the work of, and an encounter with, Jerzy Kosinski as a way into discussing the kind of modern writing Kosinski's novel, *The Painted Bird*, represented: that life is a snakepit of violence and that men, at heart, are pigs and apes, when they are not clowns and frauds. Morley didn't buy it.

"So, I go on believing," he wrote, "that a few people, just a few people, at a given moment will stand up and demonstrate that man has buried within him a sense of inherent dignity, or some sense of conscience. Maybe I've wasted many years as a writer trying to hold to this conviction about man, though I always knew that even at the Crucifixion the disciples had failed."

Morley didn't shun violence, he often used it in his novels and stories; but he was seeing it here as a fashionable development in literature, "bestial violence for its own sake." It was not a fashion he could adapt to, but it was something new to be understood. And then he gave us the key to the creative drive that had been forming in him since his youthful short-story days of so long ago.

"What the great storyteller does," he wrote, "whether he be a Maupassant, Proust, Joyce or Chekhov, is give you a new effect, a new sensation in literature. Even if he is telling only about a man and a woman in a room, he is making you feel he sees something going on between them that was never quite seen in this way before. A Robbe-Grillet tries to do this with a technique. Simple technique! Fine. An experiment! But what is really new in seeing and feeling comes out of the storyteller's own temperament, his own eyes, his own heart, his own sensibility. If he has great talent he'll make ordinary things seem remarkable. For him, there'll always be thousands of new stories because there are thousands of people around him, all begging to be seen as they were never seen before. The ancient hunger."

Morley Callaghan's hunger.

# BY MORLEY CALLAGHAN